Knuckledraggers

by
M.T. Baird

Knuckledraggers by M.T. Baird

Copyright © 2017 by M.T. Baird

Praise for Knuckledraggers:

KNUCKLEDRAGGER , KNUCKLE-DRAGGER

knuck·le \ 'nə-kəl - drag·ger \ 'dra-gər

Noun

Definition - This term generally refers to a person of little intelligence reminiscent of the hunched over cave man, with his arms to the ground. An individual, usually male, who lacks intelligence and/or culture.

Military slang referring to Marines, infantry or Special Forces personnel, or paramilitary components of the US Intelligence Community. Also used as a term of familiarity among mechanics or friendly reference in various circles.

Acknowledgements

My special thanks to Garrette Turcotte and Mark Brooks, two of my very good friends and fellow employees who lived on either side of my RV for years in the LAX employee parking lot. The primary instigators and culprits involved with the frequent pranks, air-soft gun battles, and various adventures prompted the whole idea. And whose questionable living standards, hygiene, morals, drinking habits and social status helped inspire two of the characters in this book.

757 pilot and friend Teresa Payton, who cheered me on and refrained from doing barrel roles so I could tap away quietly on my laptop while riding in the jump seat. But she couldn't read my material in public because it made her burst out laughing.

Beth Lynne at BZHercules.com, my wonderful editor, for holding my hand and answering all of my stupid questions throughout the process.

Laura LaRoche at LLPix.com for using her magic on the cover and having patience with my ideas.

Hunter S. Jones of RA Jones Productions for her assistance with publicity for this novel.

My brother Noah Baird, whose success as a published author gave me the nudge to start the project.

My kids, who, throughout their childhood, have unknowingly sculpted my personality into the warped and twisted wreck that it is. And I loved every minute of it.

To my wonderful wife Kristy, for keeping me alive and not killing me.

Table of Contents

Chapter 1: For the Love of Cooking Animals

I watched through the window as people chuckled at the pile of clothes that were still smoldering in the back of my truck. I was stewing in a bar, drinking and smoking while listening to Chris Cornell moaning out "Number One Zero," which seemed oddly appropriate. The bartender knew me as a regular and gave me a pitiful smile as she brought me another beer. It was a typical gray and drizzly winter day in Indiana, which went along with my mood perfectly.

My cell phone started to ring and I stared at it awhile as I contemplated whether or not to answer it. When I picked it up, I heard a familiar voice.

"What's goin' on, my brotha' from anotha' mutha'? How you been?" I heard from the other end of the phone.

"Better," I said, still looking at my truck.

He just chuckled and said, "I'm sure I don't want to know. What was her name?"

"Doesn't matter. What's up?" I replied.

"Where are you?" he asked.

"I'm in Indy. How 'bout you?"

"I'm in L.A. and you need to come here."

"Yeah? Whatcha got?"

"Tell you all about it when you get here."

That was all I needed to hear. I left the bar, gassed up the truck, and jumped on I70 headed west, all the happier to leave this town and get far away from a relationship that just went up in flames, literally.

* * *

I had been living with my hot-blooded Latino girlfriend in a trailer park and, other than the occasional Latin meltdown, things were good. I was trying to be a good boyfriend one day by doing some work on her car. I changed the brakes, plugs and wires, filters, belt—you know, all the usual stuff. I was just about to start the car when her cat jumped up on the fender, so I stopped to get the cat and shut the hood so he wouldn't get hurt. It's hard to chalk up good boyfriend points if the cat goes through the radiator fan.

I went back to working on the car when my girlfriend came storming out of the house a few minutes later, holding her cat. Evidently, I got grease on his white fur when I picked him up with my greasy paws. She got all pissy and accused me of purposely getting grease on the cat because she thought that I really didn't like him. This was only partly true, I like dogs, but I was never mean to her cat. I just never really paid much attention to it.

Now she was upset and wanted me to clean the grease off her cat, which I was not really sure how to do. My first attempt was a wet rag with a little dish detergent. Dish detergent cuts grease, right? So I figured it should work, but it didn't, so then I was walking around trying to find something more effective while holding the cat.

Keep in mind that this is a cat, and by nature, cats are not very cooperative, which is one reason why I don't care for them much. I found some turpentine in the shed and thought, *Ah, a solvent, that should work*, so I set out to wipe the grease off his fur while holding him down again. By this time, the cat was

3

getting hostile and kept trying to scratch me because the turpentine stunk and he wanted nothing to do with it.

Eventually, the cat broke free and ran under the trailer before I could finish cleaning him up. My arms and hands were scratched up and my patience was exhausted. So I gave up on the cat, finished up with the car, put everything away, and sat on the porch to smoke a cigarette. While I was sitting there, my girlfriend decided to have a little mercy on me and came out of the house with a nice cold beer for me. When the cat heard "Mama's" voice, he came out from under the trailer and ran straight toward her and right by me. Out of reflex, I reached out to grab him without remembering that the lit cigarette was still in my hand. Turpentine is flammable, in case you didn't know that. Apparently, the turpentine hadn't evaporated from his fur, and so when I grabbed him with a lit cigarette, he caught fire.

If you're ever looking for a little fun and excitement on a Saturday night, I don't recommend setting your girlfriend's cat on fire. I can only imagine how this scene might have looked to someone passing by; a hysterical woman running after and throwing things at a guy chasing a flaming cat!

For the record, I would like to point out that the cat was not burned; just some singed fur. My relationship, on the other hand, was toast. She accused me of doing it on purpose despite me trying to convince her otherwise. So when I got back from the vet with a clean bill of health for the cat, all of my clothes and various belongings were in a nice pile in the front yard, on fire. Being the astute individual that I am, I assumed that this was her subtle way of letting me know that the relationship was over.

Chapter 2: Living like a Rock Star

Everyone calls me "Del," which is short for my last name, DelRio. I have a history of ignoring gravity, flying small rugs, and a unique ability to irritate the hell out of women. I have a tattoo on my butt cheek of a dog urinating on a rose. Frogs creep me out because of the way they stare. I don't like that I smoke and I never take anything seriously. A girl once told me that dating me was like drinking a Singapore Sling out of a combat boot and I still have no idea what the hell that means.

When I was stationed in the Philippines for a bit while doing time in the Marines, I sat in on a poker game in the back room of a "massage" parlor. When a huge fight broke out, the military police came crashing through the front door and evidently, in the ensuing melee, several "massage" rooms were raided and Strap was found with a girl who was wearing a huge strap-on dildo. As word got out around the unit, he acquired the nickname Strap-on. He insists that it wasn't him, but it was actually some Navy guy in the room next to his. In all the confusion, his name was used. Over time, Strap-on was shortened to Strap and he just lived with it, but his real name is Harry.

We got out of the Marines and cruised around the U.S. on our Harleys for a few years and were basically just itinerant bums living in unstable places. It was fun for a while, but eventually, we decided to hire on with an airline as mechanics.

After 9/11, we got laid off and kind of drifted our separate ways for a couple of years until he called me that day.

Fast forward to L.A. I'm happy to be sans girlfriend and intend to stay that way. The only thing I want to hear from a woman these days is "what time are you leaving in the morning?"

Strap and I each live in cozy little travel trailers/RVs, now parked amongst dozens of other RVs in the middle of a huge parking lot at the LAX airport in Los Angeles, California. The airport authority allows pilots, flight attendants, and aircraft mechanics to park a personally owned recreational vehicle to use as a temporary place to crash while working away from home.

There aren't any campground hookups here; this is just several acres of black asphalt with a big fence around it; very scenic. For electricity, most use a combination of solar panels and a portable generator. Fortunately, there is no shortage of sunshine in southern California for the solar panels.

For water and waste, we have to rely on the storage tanks in the RVs and service them at a local campground from time to time. This parking lot is also located at the east end of one of the runways, so we get the pleasure of watching and hearing large planes land and take off just a couple hundred feet over our heads all day.

Everyone else here in the lot is an airline employee and has an actual home and family somewhere else in the country. Strap and I are the only two that do not work for an airline or have another home and family. This is our home and we live right here in the middle of Los Angeles, off the grid. We don't have legitimate jobs with an airline and we don't have addresses. We don't have electric bills, water bills, or sewage bills. We don't get paychecks and we don't use bank accounts. Our RVs and vehicles were paid for with cash and registered to a dummy corporation.

Strap and I are aircraft mechanics, but we work "under the table" for a guy that provides emergency aircraft maintenance services internationally. All aircraft are required to have a logbook for maintenance documentation to ensure that any maintenance, whether scheduled or unscheduled, is performed by a licensed mechanic and in accordance with the aircraft manufacturer's specifications and the country of registration's laws. For example; in the U.S., it's the FAA. But there are many individuals and organizations that do not wish to operate their aircraft in the legal sense in that they use them to transport things that are illegal but of high value. These people or organizations sometimes need maintenance performed but aren't concerned with the manufacturer's specifications or any governing authority. They're willing to pay handsomely to have their aircraft repaired quickly and quietly with the logbook and any documentation in apparent order so that they may get on with transporting whatever it is they like to transport without having to worry about the formalities.

This is where Strap and I come in; this type of work tends to get a little dangerous at times because it takes us to some very out-of-the-way places and forces us to deal with a few unsavory characters. This is also why our tools include handguns and such when we travel because we tend to end up in some unusual situations. Obviously, this job doesn't come with a pension plan or 401K, but we get paid with a lot of tax-free cash.

* * *

Our "boss," as we call him, got into the business back in the seventies when he started flying drugs into South Florida from South and Central America. In the early eighties, his connections provided him an opportunity to fly for a company called SETCO, which was contracted by the CIA to fly guns and equipment to the Contras that were fighting the Sandinistas down in Nicaragua. Unfortunately, the gunrunning pipeline provided a return pipeline for drugs that certain departments of our government were forced to turn a blind eye to until around 1986. That was when Senator John Kerry began an investigation into the allegations of the drug running and came out with what became known as the "Kerry Report." Kerry then took his findings to Senator Richard Lugar, who was at the time the Chairman of the Senate Foreign Relations Committee.

When he saw the "writing on the wall," our boss cut his losses and got out before the excrement hit the proverbial fan. And hit the fan it did, as we can all recall watching President Reagan and Marine Colonel Oliver North tap dancing on the news in what became known as the Iran/Contra Affair.

In the ensuing fallout, many of the people that were involved took the fall either by getting thrown in prison or assassinated by the cartels. Among those, a pilot named Barry Seal who had been flying drugs and also working for the CIA was shot to death in 1986 by the Medellin Cartel down in Baton Rouge. In 1991, a Marine Colonel stationed at Marine Corps Air Station El Toro was found dead right before he was about to blow the whistle over evidence he discovered involving the Marine Corps. And even an investigative reporter named Gary Webb was found dead years later after he dug up some embarrassing information. That was ruled a suicide by the coroner, even though he was found with two bullet holes in his head.

After disappearing for several years, our boss has since returned with a new identity and a new plan but maintains contact with many of his old connections. He now skirts the edge of the drug and gunrunning business by providing much needed maintenance support to many of those old connections.

* * *

Because this line of work has the potential to be short lived, my personal retirement strategy comes from watching those shows about former rock stars and where they are now. Too many of those guys just partied their millions away and have nothing to show for it, literally. The same with sports heroes who couldn't see far enough into the future to realize that their career could end during the next game.

My idea is to do a few years of this without winding up with any extra holes in me and save up enough cabbage to get out while the "gettin' is good." The problem is knowing when the gettin' isn't about to be good anymore.

I don't trust the stock market or anything that requires my social security number, like IRAs or any other type of retirement account. I don't want the government to ask any questions about my money, how I got it, or how much money in taxes that they might think that I owe them.

This is why I store cash, gold, and silver in a handful of extremely safe locations so I have a little something to disappear with when the time comes.

If, for some reason, I turn up missing or return dead from one of our little adventures, a preaddressed, postage-paid letter will be mailed to a P.O. Box. The letter has instructions to the owner of the P.O Box on where to find another envelope that is securely hidden and sealed. This envelope contains a letter that explains why they have received it, enough money for a plane ticket to LAX and other expenses, instructions, and a map with directions on where to find my little retirement stashes. No one other than me knows about any of this. The person who gets to go on the treasure hunt and win this little lottery is the one person who I owe everything to and is the only person that I can remotely call family, even though we aren't even related.

Chapter 3: Turd in the Punch Bowl

Obviously, our new careers lend to an odd work schedule, which is basically no schedule at all. We work when we're called and do whatever in between those times. Because of the lack of any sort of adult supervision, the "whatever" part tends to turn into something more suited for a "Three Stooges" show.

On an average day like today, I like to start things out quietly with some coffee and some quiet time. I think there are times when a person needs to have a moment to him or herself to have some quiet and peacefulness, whether to reflect or meditate or what have you. Some go to faraway places yearly, some may go periodically to a park or something. Some much more frequently, such as me. I do it almost every morning on the shitter.

 I think that taking a dump might actually be proof of creation. Out of the few basic functions that we do naturally as humans, I think this one is unique. Our bodies need to eat, drink, sleep, breathe, and defecate to keep functioning. But we could prevent ourselves from doing any of the above if we were willing. All but one; how do you prevent yourself from having to crap? Using something in the form of a cork only has the potential to create a low-flying projectile. I think that is the proof right there because as humans, we normally avoid doing anything that we don't like; it's human nature. I think that most people would avoid having to crap if they didn't have to because it's inconvenient. It's also messy, it stinks, you have to dispose of it properly, and you have to clean yourself really well or you'll get an itchy butt and skid marks in your underwear. I think we were designed so that we could not avoid crapping because we wouldn't if we didn't have to. That is why I think that out of all of our most basic functions, it is the only one that we could not actually prevent ourselves from doing if we wanted. That is why I think that having to crap is proof that we were created!

As I was sitting there, it slowly started to occur to me that I could be onto something big here. This could be a revelation! If this hit print, I was thinking interviews, talk shows, speaking tours, diaper ads, toilet paper endorsements—you name it! And let's not forget the Pope. The Pimpin' Pontiff and the funky bunch out there in the Vatican are God's biggest groupies; they'd be all over this like a mullet on a redneck!

While marveling at my self-proclaimed brilliance in odoriferous delusions of grandeur, I was quickly reminded of where I am. Through the thin walls of my twenty-seven-foot RV that I call home, I heard my portable generator suddenly stop working. This was immediately followed by a loud slap on the outside wall and a cheerful "How's the morning shit going, scumbag?" I just hung my head and sighed.

No generator means no electricity to power the water pump to flush the toilet in the RV. Which means that now I have to go outside to start it back up again before I can complete the whole process in the bathroom. And of course, the dirt bag that I sometimes refer to as my buddy, who parks his RV next to mine, knows this and will be waiting to ambush me with an air-soft rifle as soon as I come outside (air-soft rifles are toy guns that shoot plastic BBs). So now I have to retrieve my own air-soft rifle so that I can defend myself long enough to restart my generator. I think I'll set his RV on fire when I'm through wiping my ass.

Having known each other for as long as he and I have means he knows that when my generator is running in the morning, I'm on the toilette. This is why I don't feel bad about leaving the raw fish to rot in the air vents on his roof every so often.

Chapter 4: A Little Apple with Your Silicone?

Strap takes a slightly different approach to women and relationships than I do these days. Maybe it's because he has a better history with the perplexing beings than I do. Whatever the reason, it was obvious that his motivation for their constant pursuit has far outlasted my own as he pulled up between our RVs with a female on the back of his Harley.

"Del, Tonya. Tonya, Del." I tipped my beer in her direction and welcomed her to our little patch of asphalt.

"We met at Sully's," he said as he climbed off the bike. Sully's is a local biker bar that we tend to frequent from time to time because the beer is cold and the women are…well, let's just say friendly. They settled in to our picnic table that sits between our RVs and helped themselves to the beer cooler and the light conversation began.

After some time and several beers, I began to suspect that Tonya probably used to go by Tony. Tall, thin, very fake tits, no real curves or bumps where they should be, not really a feminine voice but more soft spoken and, last but not least, an Adam's apple! A smirk started to grow on my face as I sipped my beer and listened to the conversation and thought about how perfect this was. Knowing full well that Strap had a few beers already before they got here and had been ogling her with alcohol-enhanced vision, aka beer goggles, he obviously had no idea what I realized.

Now I was faced with a dilemma; should I pull him aside and apprise him of my suspicions or let him figure it out in due time? After watching him continuously slide his hand over her thigh while he gurgled down more beer, I was torn. Finally, I decided that I should make a responsible decision and do what was right because I am his friend and we watch out for each other. So, as his friend, I decided that friends definitely let friends try to screw transvestites! I had no doubt he would make the same decision for me.

Now that I'd worked through my moral dilemma, I helped myself to another beer, sat back, and let nature take its course. As the night progressed, she/he excused herself to use the restroom in Strap's RV and he commented to me on the shapeliness of her posterior when she walked away. Again, me being the good buddy that I am, I agreed wholeheartedly with his assessment. After she returned, he asked her if she noticed the extensive collection of beer bottle caps that he had so tastefully adorned the inside of his RV with and then went into his story about how he started his collection and where some of them had come from. Having heard this before, I knew that this was the precursor to getting a girl into the RV for a couple of rounds of "hide the salami."

Earlier in the day, I contemplated jumping on the Harley tonight for a ride down to Hermosa Beach to hook up with a few friends, but I decided that staying here for a while longer could turn out to be much more entertaining!

As the she/he feigned excitement at the prospect of seeing Strap's prized beer bottle cap collection, they moved away for an evening of alcohol-induced romance. I just smiled and reached into the beer cooler for a replacement and stoked up a nice cigar. In addition, I got my phone out and strategically placed it on the picnic table in video mode and aimed it at his door. This could be one of those cherished moments that I might want to share with friends for years to come!

As I was settling in with my cigar and some of Stone Brewery's finest Arrogant Bastard Ale, watching airplanes coming in for landing just a couple hundred feet over my head, Shaky Jake came sauntering over for a visit.

"Just in time, buddy. Grab a beer." Then I told him what I suspected was about to happen behind closed doors.

Shaky Jake is another lot-lizard, as we like to call ourselves, but his residency is a bit more permanent, or less so; I haven't decided. He's our resident homeless guy who's been around here for God only knows how long. He doesn't have an RV and so everyone here just sort of adopts him by giving him food or whatever he needs without him having to ask. His clothes are usually an interesting combination of old airline uniforms donated to him by other lot-lizards. Most everyone here gives him food, but Strap and I seem to be his primary source of alcohol and entertainment and it's not uncommon to find him stretched out sleeping in the bed of one of our pickup trucks.

We call him Shaky Jake because his eyes constantly twitch back and forth in a horizontal motion and we don't know his real name. He can be hard to look at when you're talking to him, which is why he usually wears sunglasses. He says it's called congenital peripheral nystagmus due to a pre-existing neurological disorder. He says it doesn't affect his ability to see or focus; it just affects other people because it freaks them out. He says it's the reason why he was always unable to keep jobs or relationships because people are uncomfortable around him; that and the fact that he has a fetish for groping cheese.

Oddly though, for a homeless guy, Jake is extremely intelligent and says his IQ is in the 160s, but he claims that the eye thing and poor social skills have made life difficult to the point where he just quit trying and gave up. He also has a weird calmness about him that immediately puts you at ease when he's around. He is very relaxed and his speech and movements are slow and deliberate. So here he lives and hangs out at the airport by the beach in southern California.

In all actuality, I think if you're going to go the homeless route, southern California is the place to do it. I mean, why battle freezing temperatures up north or God awful heat and humidity in the southeast when you can live outdoors in relative comfort year-round?

As Jake and I relaxed and enjoyed craft beer and cigars, suddenly there came a loud and profound string of expletives from Strap's RV. My brilliant deductive reasoning skills told me that Strap had discovered that Tonya had to be still be using Tony's sports equipment and probably wanted to hide his own salami!

I was leaning over to make sure my phone was still in video mode and recording when the door to Strap's RV came banging open and Tonya/Tony was launched through the opening like a discarded bag of trash! Strap, in a full rage, came bursting out next, swinging wildly and trying to kick Tonya without success. Tonya was impressive with the way she was dodging and weaving while getting up on her feet and started sprinting through the parking lot screaming like a raped ape! By this time, Jake and I were laughing so hard that I had beer coming out of my nose and tears running down my face! I think I might have even cracked a rib. Strap saw the phone propped up on the table and realized that I had been waiting for this moment.

"You son of a @#$%*! You knew?" Now I was the one sprinting through the parking lot as he was chasing me, but it didn't last long because he was too out of shape to last more than a hundred yards.

"I can't believe you didn't tell me!" he said while gasping for breath.

"Adam's apple, dumbass. Learn to look for it!" I said. "And as your friend, I am obligated to find or provide as many opportunities as possible to laugh at you." His only reply was a middle finger.

He sat down with a beer and let Jake and me harass him the rest of the night as we broke out some cards and slipped in a Led Zeppelin CD for another typical night in the lot.

* * *

Another plane coming in for landing directly over my head let me know another day had arrived in fine southern California fashion, with the sun producing sharp pains behind my eyes. I glanced around to find Strap in his RV where he had been sitting until he passed out half in and half out of the doorway. Shaky Jake was lying underneath my truck with his t-shirt still snagged on the corner of the tailgate where he had been sitting before rolling off after too many drinks. I was lying on my back on top of the picnic table with the doormat to my RV lying under me. Evidently, I had been grooving to Steppenwolf's "Magic Carpet Ride" again. I really needed to stay away from tequila. Fortunately, my sunglasses are always hanging around my neck and the painkillers were close by in my RV, so I could make use of some of those while I made some coffee.

Outside, beer cans littered the area, so I picked one up and hurled it at Strap and nailed him square in the knee. A foot twitched. Another beer can bounced off the back wall of his RV, just missing his head. No movement. I decided that this would be a great opportunity for some target practice, so I walked over and very carefully placed an empty beer can on his forehead and went back to my RV and got my air-soft rifle. Standing in my doorway, I had a straight shot into his and I shot it off his head.

That definitely did the trick because he jumped up and tried to hurl beer cans back at me while cussing and stumbling around.

All the commotion brought Jake back to life, but he just lay there looking straight up and blinking with his t-shirt that was stretched out two feet over his head.

"You gonna help him or what?" Strap said as he went in my RV to help himself to the coffee. I brought Jake a cup and helped him to his feet and over to the picnic table where we all sat in silence, soothing our hangovers.

We had been enjoying relative silence for a while until Dinger came around the corner with his tinfoil-lined hat.

"Hey, magic carpet man, how was the flight last night? Bahahahaha!"

I showed him the backside of my middle finger in response.

"Good thing there weren't any gumball machines around this time, huh? Bahahahaha!" Strap and Jake started to chuckle. I really hate this guy. Most people who know me also know that if you want to liven up the party, break out the Mezcal in front of Del. If I'm sober and clear-headed, I won't touch the stuff, but if I've already had a few beers, then tequila becomes a seductive bitch. So the gumball machine jokes are a result of one of those evenings that I'll have to talk about later now, I guess.

Chapter 5: Banzai Bunghole

Mike Dinger is a short, round, bespectacled guy that parks his RV on the next row over from us. He flies bug-beaters for some little podunk airline carrying the extremely thrifty vacationer types to Mexico, Vegas, and wherever else. Bug-beaters are what we call small, prop-driven airplanes because the props beat the bugs as it flies. Even though he can be annoying as hell, I kind of like the guy because he's somewhat entertaining and he keeps tabs on everything that goes on in the lot. Strap calls him the crowd disperser because when he walks up to a group of people, everyone suddenly has something else to do.

Dinger has sort of adopted us or maybe it's the other way around and so he visits with us frequently, probably because he doesn't really have any other friends. He and Shaky Jake like to quibble with each other a lot and so Strap and I refer to them as "the kids" sometimes. He's really not a bad guy, I think he just tries too hard to make friends and be accepted sometimes. This is why I think he volunteers to lead little projects and organizations and such so people are required to come to him. This is also how he has become the unofficial "Mayor" of the parking lot. He makes it a point to keep everyone informed about things he deems important, like when the propane guy is coming through if you need your tanks filled or when the port-a-potty guy is coming through if you need your other tanks emptied; stuff like that. He also started organizing monthly lot-lizard meetings so we can all talk about any issues or concerns we may have. Personally, I could care less about any of this because no one ever bothers us out here, but I go anyway just for the entertainment and because they're held in between my and Strap's RVs.

One time, he brought us all these little tin foil inserts that he made to put inside our hats because, apparently, living in RVs, we're more susceptible to the government's spy satellite mind reading energy beams or whatever the thinking is. Strap and I usually try to make sure we're good and sauced for these meetings so we can get a good chuckle out of them. It seems that most others usually have the same idea because many will arrive with small coolers in tow.

Over time, the monthly meetings have taken on a new and rather unintended focus, if you will. It started out as Dinger bringing chips and salsa to one of the meetings for everyone to share and then each meeting others would bring dips and snacks and such and, before long, it turned into a monthly potluck/meeting. At one point, someone requested that I start making Armadillo eggs for each meeting, so now that has become a regular thing. Armadillo eggs are Jalapeno peppers cored out and stuffed with flavored cream cheese and wrapped with bacon and cooked on the grill.

Well, one meeting, it seems someone brought food that may have been a little too far past its "freshness date" and it had a rather negative effect on a few people. The worst of which I think was Dinger because it hit him faster than he could react and maybe that was because he already had a lot to drink by that point. Nonetheless, when he realized what was happening, he jumped up out of his chair and, as he was trying to make a quick escape, his butt exploded in mid stride! It was disgusting too; he was wearing beige cargo shorts and flip-flops, and the force of the explosion instantly soaked through his whole backside and ran down his legs and the whole crowd of about thirty or so people cheered and gave him a standing ovation!

The poor guy just shuffled off in shame to go clean himself up, but to his credit, he was brave enough to return to the meeting, which really weren't meetings anymore as you've probably guessed. When he returned, everyone cheered and goaded him to produce the underwear of shame and so he left and returned with them, hanging from a broomstick like a flag. It was deemed the Flag of Shame and he, through peer pressure, was required to hang it from his RV!

About a month later at the next meeting, Dinger started off with talking about making sure that any food that was brought should be safe for human consumption blah, blah, blah, when he was immediately interrupted by Cooter Holland, one of the airline mechanics from Texas. "Hey poopy pants, let's have a Flag of Shame contest!" Dinger stood there dumbfounded as everyone clapped and cheered the idea while Strap and I just sat back and laughed! And to think, I used to think these meetings were bogus! So the rest of the meeting turned into planning how the contest should work: If you chose to participate, then you could bring one ingredient to add to a pot that would become a stew. The ingredients could not be foul or rotten, but something that you thought might give a person diarrhea and if you brought something for the stew, then you had to eat a bowl. It was also decided that the Flag of Shame contest should be held quarterly instead of monthly.

Afterwards, each person must produce their underwear to be voted on and then the winner gets to fly their Flag of Shame until properly dethroned. Although I have not won the right to fly the highly coveted flag, I am proud to say that I was runner up once!

Chapter 6: Gooney Bird

Just as Dinger and Shaky Jake were slowly gearing up for another verbal sparring match, my cell phone rang and I looked at Strap when I recognized the number.

"Strap with you?" was the greeting I got from the male voice at the other end. "You two ladies be at the bird in an hour. It's getting fueled right now."

"Got it," was my only response and we both got up and headed to our RVs.

"Time to earn a paycheck, kids. Catch ya later." Jake followed me in to top off his coffee before I left and Dinger started in with his usual line of questions when Strap and I have to exit the party suddenly.

"What kind of top secret government stuff you guys gonna do today? Assassinate somebody?" Nobody in the lot knows what Strap and I really do or who we work for, but it doesn't stop the rumors or speculation. It seems to bug Dinger the most because he's already a conspiracy theorist and this kind of thing sends his imagination into overdrive. But he knows his boundaries and doesn't pry too much because I think he's afraid he'll get "rubbed out" if he gets too inquisitive.

I keep a backpack already packed with clothes and essentials in the bedroom. The essentials being my trusty ole .45 that I've nicknamed "Persuasion" with a few clips and a toothbrush. My backpack is a rugged military issue style with a camelback water pouch. Usually when we're flying to wherever we're going, I will empty my clothes from the backpack and replace them with survival gear that we keep stored on the plane. We also keep four M4 rifles, four tactical shotguns, two sniper rifles in .308, food, water, two satellite phones, ammo, and a fun assortment of other party favors. The idea is that if we get into a bad situation in some of the out-of-way places that we tend to frequent, we can defend ourselves and survive on the ground while we try to escape and evade.

Strap and I jumped in his truck for the short ride to the corporate terminal area of LAX where the plane sits. The airport security guy there gets a nice Christmas bonus every year from our employer so we don't have to go through the usual security probe and grope when we walk through his checkpoint. "What's up, Huggy Bear? How's it hangin?" I have no idea why we started calling him that.

"Straight down, man," he replied.

"Sorry to hear that. Everything kosher in Huggyville?"

"Nah. man, it ain't, and you two jokers ain' helpin', always makin' me nervous packin' all dat hardware dat I ain't spoda see!"

"Don't sweat it, big sexy. You know we aren't terrorists!" I smiled and slapped him on the shoulder. "Maybe I'll bring you back something nice this time."

He just shook his head and said, "Yeah, das wut you always say, I'm surprised yous two still alive n' shit, da way y'all look when you gets back sometimes." He was referring to a few rather unfortunate, let's call them "cultural misunderstandings" we've had in the past. "Don't worry about us, Huggy. You'll still get your Christmas bonus from the boss."

The plane was sitting on the ramp between John Travolta's Qantas 707 that he sometimes uses and a Gulfstream G-5 that belongs to some NBA player. Our plane is a little unique in that it's an old Douglas DC-3 that's been retrofitted with PT-6 turboprops, a slightly longer fuselage, updated avionics, and a customized interior. The custom work was all done by us with bunks, comfy chairs, table, couch, a lavatory with shower, and a galley with plenty of supplies. In the back by the main entry door is a small shop area with tools, equipment, and some parts and sheet metal. We had it painted olive drab like they were during WWII and we named her *The Green Manalishi*, which is our little salute to Peter Green along with some cool nose art. These old planes were designed and built back in the thirties and forties for air transport. The military used them extensively during WWII and designated them the C-47 Skytrain, but many of the troops just called them Gooney Birds. Over the years, many variants were made as they were known to be very rugged and reliable aircraft.

Even with turboprops, this plane is slow by today's standards, but because we sometimes need to land this thing on rough terrain with short distances for take-off and landing, the design is perfect for what we need. The turbo-props give it a higher altitude ceiling, max gross take-off weight, and faster cruise speed than the original versions that came with radial engines. We've also added an additional fuel bladder in the belly and optional wing tanks for added fuel range.

This particular plane has a history similar to our boss's in that it was used extensively in the eighties to fly drugs and guns back and forth in Central America. Although he didn't own it during that period, he managed to use it to disappear to southeast Asia and lay low with it for a few years when things started to get ugly in our government. Now it's sporting a different tail number and paint job and owned by a dummy corporation.

The pilots, Tack and Sanchez, were doing their preflight walk-around and walked over when Strap and I came strolling up. "You guys look like hell as usual. Another long night?" one of them said.

"Just stay out of the thunderstorms and we won't have any messes to clean up," I replied.

"How've you guys been?" Strap asked. "Haven't seen you two since our last little escapade."

Tack and Sanchez were both Marine C-130 pilots stationed at Marine Corps Air Station El Toro, CA in the early eighties. They both became inadvertently involved in the same operation when, in addition to SETCO and the other companies, the CIA was also using our military to transport arms to the Contras down in Central America. They knew and even worked with the Marine Colonel that came across the incriminating information about the Marine Corps' involvement in the affair. When he suddenly ended up dead on his back porch on base, Tack and Sanchez knew exactly why he was killed and weren't surprised when it happened because they knew that several people had already met the same fate. When the Colonel started asking questions, they started making contingency plans to disappear off the grid by deserting the Marine Corps and leaving the country. Better to be a deserter than a corpse. When he was found dead, they split and used the connections that they had made before while flying the guns and disappeared. They holed up down in Nicaragua and made a living by flying various cargo around Central America for whoever was paying the right price. Years later, they ran into our current boss one day when the C-123 they were flying suffered severe damage while landing in a field. The cargo was supposedly toy "tea sets" destined for the U.S. In all actuality, the ceramic used for the cups and saucers was infused with cocaine that would be crushed up and extracted back out once they were safely screened through customs. The cargo, being worth millions in street value, was worth the price of getting the right people involved that could fix the plane and get it to its destination.

Our boss was looking for some extra help at the time and had met Tack and Sanchez years before when they were all flying for the CIA. After they told him their story and what happened to the Colonel, our boss made them a better employment offer, and so here they are. Because these two are now considered military deserters and are convinced that they're still being hunted by the CIA, their real names are long forgotten. They're still living off the grid, but they live in cabin sailboats anchored just off shore or cruise up and down the coast. Our boss, through his connections, helped them get fake identifications and such, but they still have to be careful. Strap and I both knew Tack and Sanchez because we each spent some time at El Toro before we went overseas, even though Strap and I wouldn't meet each other until a later time in the Philippines.

After Strap and I got laid off from the airlines, he came out to California looking for work. It was Tack that he ran into while walking into the corporate office facility at LAX in hopes of finding a job. Tack told the boss about Strap and mentioned that he would be perfect for the job as they were looking for a couple of mechanics. Not just any mechanics, but mechanics that were willing to live a unique lifestyle in exchange for a unique job. And then Strap called me and so here we are. It's a small world sometimes.

"So where will you two fine gentlemen be whisking us off to today?" I inquired.

"Isabela Island, Galapagos," Sanchez replied as he climbed up the stairs.

"Wha-huh? Where?" Strap and I both questioned simultaneously as we followed them up into the plane.

"A volcano island west of Ecuador. We're going over water most of the way, so I hope you two brought your water-wings," Sanchez said, smiling as he handed us a map. "Evidently, some poor cartel schlep broke his Citation in the dark this morning while taxiing it around some little dirt-water airport. And because his high-end toy was acquired through questionable means, he needs some questionable maintenance performed by some questionable mechanics," he said, chuckling.

I rolled my eyes over at Strap. "This is gonna be a long, boring trip."

Ever the enthusiast, Strap headed straight for the galley, where we keep an impressive selection of alcohol, and started mixing us a couple of drinks. "No problem, buddy. Get the cards going. As I remember, I'm into you for a couple hundred that I've been waiting to win back."

A couple hours into the trip, Strap and I took turns relieving Tack and Sanchez to let them eat and stretch for a while. We all thought it would be a good idea if Strap and I learned to fly and got type certified on this plane. It not only makes us a more effective team, but it also makes sense in case something happens and we're short a pilot. Tack and Sanchez usually lend a hand if we need it when we're on the ground repairing a plane and watching our backs while we work.

Tack was kicking back with a sandwich and a coke, venting about the Marine Corps with me while Strap and Sanchez were flying the plane. "You know one thing that used to piss me off about the Corps? Everyone would always judge you by your rank. It didn't matter if your opinion made any sense or not, if your rank wasn't within the upper half of those in the room, your opinion was crap!" he complained. I nodded my head in agreement.

"I can completely relate to this, but I'm fairly certain that goes for every branch of the service," I replied.

We tend to complain a lot about the Marines, but it's only because of our love for the Marine Corps. You hate it when you're in but miss it when you're out. The four of us always get together for the Marine Corps birthday if we aren't already out on a trip, but we will bring in the new birthday in fine Marine Corps fashion…which just means that we get drunk.

"Hey, man, the sailboat gig is starting to wear on me. Is there any room in the RV lot with you guys?" Tack asked.

"Oh yeah, no problem there, but you're gonna have to get used to trading in the peace and quiet of the ocean for the roar of airplanes coming in for landing over your head," I said.

"Yeah, I thought about that, but some days being isolated from people so much gets old, ya know?" he said. "And I think it's turning me into an alcoholic."

"Well, dude," I said, chuckling. "I don't think moving in by us is going to help with that. Besides, I think we'll have to run this by the Home Owners Association anyway. We can't just let any gunrunning riffraff with government hitmen on their tail in the lot. We have an image to keep, you know!"

He just shook his head, smiling. "I understand. Think you can put in a good word for me?"

"I can try. What about Sanchez? Is he thinking about coming over to the dark side too?" I asked.

"He's on the fence 'cause he feels we're safer out there. But I don't think anyone knows we're even back in the States now and we can still remain incognito out by you guys. I mean, look at you; you're pulling it off without even really trying and you don't have somebody out there that wants you dead." I nodded my head in agreement.

"Well, I may have an ex-girlfriend or two out there that may disagree with you," I said. "But you'll probably be all right."

"Let's all sit and throw this around later when we get a chance and then run it by the boss," he said.

"Sounds good." I said as I got up. "I think I'll get a shower and try to get a little nap."

I woke up when the wheels hit ground somewhere in Central America when we landed for a gas stop before we continued on to the Galapagos. Oftentimes when we make these runs, we will stop at little out-of-the-way airfields for fuel because they don't keep records of what planes fly in and out. Sometimes you'll be lucky if you can even find someone that works there. This way, we can keep our movements under the radar a little better.

When I looked out the window, all I could see was jungle on each side of the runway as we turned around and start taxiing back. I could feel the humidity already and smell the wetness mixed with plant decay typical of the jungle.

"I don't think we're in Kansas anymore," Strap quipped as he climbed out of the plane and headed off toward the only building around in the hopes of getting a fuel truck out to the plane. I had no idea where we were. A couple of Cessna 152s, an old Piper, and an Aero Commander were the only planes parked nearby. Other than some rusty old equipment, a few chickens, and a donkey wandering around, the place was empty. I tucked the .45 into a clip-on holster in the small of my back and jumped out of the plane to get a feel for the area. Better to have it and not need it than need it and not have it. Besides, some of these places can be a little shady and you never know who you might be dealing with down in these parts. Tack and Sanchez climbed out to stretch a bit as I wandered off to see if Strap needed any help.

One of the issues that we tend to run across down here is the quality of fuel that we get and sometimes these little strips don't have what we need exactly. One problem with jet fuel is that microorganisms can start growing in it if you don't keep it treated right. These microorganisms have the ability to clog fuel filters, stall an engine, and turn your plane into a lawn dart. Because of this, we always carry extra fuel filters and fuel additive to use in our tanks to prevent this from happening.

Strap came be-bopping from around the corner of the shed.

"We're in luck; the guy in there says he's got jet fuel. He's going bring it over to the plane," he said.

"How much did he say?" I asked.

"He doesn't know; nobody has needed any in quite a while," he replied.

Just then, we heard a puttering little engine gradually getting louder. As we turned toward the direction of the noise, we saw a guy driving an ancient-looking riding lawn mower pulling a wood wagon with eight 55-gallon drums and a hand pump on top.

"Perfect," I said, smiling and shaking my head.

Back in the air and headed to the island, the constant drone of the engines put me in a state of lull. There wasn't really any conversation going on at all, each man to his own thoughts. These are the times when I think about her and wonder what she's doing, knowing that she is wondering about me. It's about time for a visit again soon, I guess. We don't talk or write; I just show up at her door from time to time.

Chapter 7: Givin' the Dog a Bone

The calm, that short period of time between the drunks and bar fights rush hour and the morning commute accidents. A time reserved for taking a moment with a fresh cup of coffee and catching up on some paperwork. Just a few days after Christmas 1966, decorations and lights still adorning the waiting area, other nurses talked quietly about holiday time spent with family. Out of habit, Anna glanced over the counter that separated the walk-in patients from the nurses' station and noticed a small figure moving slowly and doubled over just outside the double glass doors.

"Jo-Ann, we got somebody out there!" she said, shouting to the head nurse as she jumped up and raced around out to the covered drive-thru area where the ambulances came. Outside was a very young and very pregnant woman gasping for air, whimpering and barely able to stand.

"Gurney!" Anna commanded as she and three other nurses came through the doors and quickly supported the woman before she dropped to the concrete. Inside, the nurses quickly got the woman to a room and a flurry of activity began as they started prepping her for delivery, as it was very obvious that she was about to give birth. The doctor on staff appeared and got a rundown from the nurses. No information on the woman was available yet; deep gasps and groans were their only responses to questions, not even a name yet. Not the first time, though. He figured they'd get all that figured out after everything calmed down.

A healthy nine-pound, four-ounce baby boy was delivered without incident except that the mother slipped off into a deep sleep from the exhaustion and Anna took the baby to the nursery. Even though her shift ended during the delivery, she wanted to see this one through because she loved holding the newborns and hoped that it wouldn't be long before she was holding one of her own one day. Softly cooing at the baby and holding his tiny hand and fingers, she got him to open his eyes just a fraction.

"Oh, there you are, little blues eyes. Welcome to the world. My name is Anna. What's yours going to be?" she said softly to him and rubbed the back of her finger to his cheek.

On her way to her apartment, she decided to stop by the grocery to get some milk and eggs, but she didn't really need much else because Mom had loaded her up with leftovers from Christmas dinner. She contemplated a couple of offers to New Year's Eve celebrations as she guided the grocery cart through the store. Mom and Dad were going to the annual Country Club dinner and celebration again and invited her along. Mom hoped she'd meet a nice young doctor or lawyer there, but all she would do was fend off the old married ones that hit on her, sometimes right in front of their wives! One couple that was old enough to be her parents even hinted at a threesome. She almost threw up in her mouth again remembering that one; definitely was not going to that again. Some of the nurses at work were getting together with their husbands and friends and invited a few doctors from the hospital. They made a point to tell her that they invited Dr. Reynolds. She smiled unconsciously at the thought of that. He was just too cute and too single. He always made a point to chat with her if they weren't too busy, but they'd never really been able to talk for more than a few minutes at a time.

Her mind drifted back to that young woman who came in alone earlier and gave birth, wondering where her husband was or the rest of her family, for that matter. Poor thing had to go through that alone and just four days after Christmas. Anna was going to make a point to go visit her when she went back in to work tomorrow. Maybe get her some flowers from the hospital gift shop or something.

Hours later, the young woman awakened to find herself alone in a warm and quiet hospital room, sun streaming in through the blinds, soft pastel flower wallpaper, her clothes neatly folded on a little night table. She could see that the bed next to her was empty because the curtain was pulled back. She sat up and took advantage of the water that was left for her on the hospital tray next to the bed. Slowly getting out of bed, she tested her balance and discovered that she was still very sore as she shuffled into the bathroom. Removing what appeared to be a big disposable diaper of sorts given to women after giving birth, she stepped into the open stall for a long overdue shower. Letting the hot water just run over her relaxed her tense shoulders for a moment while she gathered her thoughts. She was relieved that she had gotten to the hospital in time. Relieved knowing that the baby was safe and being cared for, but she cried softly because she could not be the one to care for him.

Dressed in the clothes that she came in, she slipped quietly down the hallway away from the nurses' station and walked out of the hospital, hoping that one day she might be able to find him and explain but knowing deep down she would probably never see her little boy again.

One of the nurses making her rounds stopped to check on the young mother to see if she was still sleeping but found the bed empty. Entering the room, she went into the bathroom and found that the woman had showered and figured she must have gone in search of the nursery, anxious to see her baby boy. After a cursory search of the hospital, though, realization began to settle over the staff on the baby ward that they might have an orphan on their hands.

Anna decided to come to the hospital a little early to give herself time to visit the new mom and bring her some flowers, but she wanted to stop by the nursery to see the baby first. When she arrived on the ward, she saw the head nurse on floor talking to a lady whom she knew was from child services in Savannah. Her stomach knotted instantly because she knew that this woman only came when a baby was to become a ward of the state and her eyes began to well up with tears as she automatically knew who she was there for.

The head nurse found Anna in the nursery holding the baby and told her that he was going to stay at the hospital for a few more days while the state processed the paperwork. Anna got an idea and handed the baby to her and ran out to catch the woman from the state before she left. She had a "spur of the moment" idea that maybe she could adopt him instead of letting him go to an orphanage; it was just breaking her heart to think of him having to grow up without a mom.

The woman told her how to apply for adoption and wished her luck, but what she didn't tell her was that young, single women were rarely approved for adoption in those days, especially in the Deep South. The thinking in those days was that a child should be adopted by a married couple in order to provide the proper environment for a child to grow up in. Single mothers just weren't viewed as socially acceptable; it was not the norm.

When Anna told her parents what she had planned, surprisingly, it was her mom who was the less compassionate one. She completely rejected the idea by telling her that adopting a baby would completely ruin her chances of getting married and having a "normal" family. Her dad, on the other hand, was much more supportive and offered to help her, which infuriated Mom, who ended the conversation by stomping out of the room. Anna went through with the adoption process anyway and jumped through all the hoops required by the state, only to be rejected weeks later.

During the process, Anna visited the little boy whenever time permitted at the hospital and then at the orphanage when he was taken there. She became close with the people involved while she was going through adoption process and they agreed to let her name him, even though it hadn't been approved by the state yet. Anna named him after her father; William Truman DelRio, and even when her adoption application was denied, the baby was able to keep the name.

Although I don't remember any of this, I know the story well of how my life started in this world. She visited me often at the orphanage and always brought me things and the staff let her take me places even though there were restrictions in place that limited that sort of thing to protect the kids. But by then, the Headmaster and staff knew her and the story well and could see that letting her help was the right thing to do. When I was little, I asked her if she was my mom, which just drew a waterfall of tears and she hugged me so hard I had to ask her to let go so I could breathe. She explained to me why she was not my mom, but that she tried to be at one time. Then I asked her if I could call her Mom anyway and again with the waterworks and squeezing the life out of me. I was always surprised at how much water this woman stored in her face.

We would do things for holidays and she would bring me to her home or her parents' for Thanksgiving and Christmas and stuff like that. I could not bring many of my gifts back to the orphanage/boys' home because we didn't have a lot of personal space to keep things. Besides, there was a good chance that anything nice that you had would just end up stolen or broken anyway.

When I was around six or seven, the guy she had been dating proposed to her and she said yes, but evidently, the idea of adopting me as a couple didn't sit well with him, as he wanted to start his own family. Soon after they were married, she got pregnant and then again a couple years later, and she visited me less and less. She would still pick me up and take me to a movie or get a hamburger and she would still bring me to her home to spend time with her family, but she just couldn't do it as much. Her husband was always nice to me, but as much as she tried to not make it seem like it, I was never part of the family, and I always knew it would be that way.

The attention that I got from Anna always caused me problems with some of the other kids at the boys' home. They were jealous of me and I understood that completely, but it didn't stop the fights every week or me being targeted for a gang style beat-down. Anna became concerned by the fact that every time she came to see me, I had a new collection of facial accoutrements. She cried when my nose got broken…all three times…and when I got a tooth knocked out. She would hold my face in her hands and kiss my wounds and tell me she didn't want this for me. I always thought to myself, *Well, no shit; I don't want it for me either.*

She would bring her concerns to the staff, but there was only so much they could do as they could not watch all of us all of the time. The regularity of these incidents turned me into a fairly scrappy fighter and I got to the point where I could hold my own pretty well. Whoever my real dad was must have been a good-sized guy because I was gradually outgrowing many of the boys my own age; that and the fact that I started making full use of the very limited weight set and bench someone had donated to the orphanage. Taking a punch became easy and eventually I got to the point where I was the one breaking bones and inflicting serious injury, and I became feared and respected by the other boys, even by many older than I. I became good at acting tough when I needed to, but with Anna, I could still be a kid.

Anna would always tease me that my blue eyes and good looks would make me a heartbreaker and that my slightly crooked nose and the little scar under my right eye made me look rugged. When I was a teenager, Anna taught me how to drive and talked to me about sex and how to respect girls and how not to become a chauvinist. I think she was concerned that growing up in the boys' home and the lack of exposure to girls or women would turn me into some sort of sex-crazed womanizer. Well, at least she tried.

When I turned eighteen, I saw the Marine Corps as my ticket to freedom and a different life and asked her to take me to see a recruiter; again with the bear hug and sprinkler system. There was never any doubt in my mind as to how much this woman loved me, this woman that let me call her Mom. From a very young age, I knew that she and I were just victims of circumstance and if she could have changed it, she would have. And for that I will always owe everything to her and because she is the one person that I will call family.

Chapter 8: Kumquats and Quaaludes

Finally, we reached Isabela Island and flew over the airport to assess the area before we landed. We could see the Citation sitting on the side of the runway where it looked like he tried to make his own taxiway. "Ouch, that looks expensive," I said, chuckling at the crippled plane as we were flying low and slow over the airfield. Strap was peering out of the window next to me and noted that the Citation looked very out of place with not one plane even remotely close to its price range on the airfield. A Cessna Citation is a small twin-engine business style jet that can cost a few million, depending on which variant you get. We could see one very old-looking Piper Cub that didn't even really look airworthy and an old AG parked in the grass.

"What's this guy doing landing out here? Never mind; I don't want to know," I said.

We landed the plane and taxied over next to the Citation and shut down the engines. Strap and I climbed down and surveyed the area—not a soul in sight, not even a car parked anywhere that we could see. The problem with this kind of work is that communication can be almost nonexistent for the most part. It kind of goes like this: our boss will receive a phone call from whoever—I'm not really sure how he has things set up on his end and how he works that. They give him a location and whatever information they might have about the plane that needs repairs. A payment arrangement is made and then we get a call. Rarely is there any contact information as far as a number to call, who owns the plane, who to look for when we arrive; nothing. We just have to wing it when we arrive, which is why we always come armed.

We were on the eastern side of the island among a few others that looked like a bunch of big volcanoes. There wasn't a lot of vegetation; clumps of small trees here and there, mostly tall grasses and shrubs amongst a rocky terrain. We could see a small coastal town a few miles away below us and to the south. Even though it was fairly humid, there was a constant breeze coming over the island from the west, which made it tolerable.

Walking around the Citation, it was obvious to me that his right main landing gear was damaged on landing or while he was taxiing or something. As I was peering under the wing getting a closer look at the gear, Strap came around from behind the tail.

"Hey, you're not going to believe what he hit with the plane! A giant turtle!" he said excitedly.

"A what? I gotta see this." Sure enough, a huge tortoise lay destroyed off the side of the runway. It must have been three to four feet high when walking around.

"Wow, that thing looks like a tank! No wonder the gear looks like it does. I bet it would total your car if you hit one of those things on the freeway!"

Tack and Sanchez came walking over. "Holy train wreck, Batman. Look at the size of that thing!" Sanchez likes to use Robin quips from the old *Batman and Robin* TV series. "That guy was probably over a hundred years old!" he said.

"How old?" Strap asked while staring at him. "I didn't know they could live that long."

"Oh yeah, supposedly they can outlive us by several decades and get up to several hundred pounds," Sanchez replied. "These suckers are all over these islands around here."

"I've seen where planes have hit birds, deer, and coyotes on landing, but I've never seen one hit a giant turtle before," Strap said while standing there with his hands shoved down in his pockets.

"Tortoise; there's a difference," Sanchez corrected.

"Are they any good to eat?" I asked while envisioning a campfire with a spit full of turtle meat. "I think we have some BBQ sauce in the plane," I added. The three of them just stared at me for a moment and then turned and walked away.

"I ain't eatin' that thing," Tack said.

"What? It might be good," I said as I started following them.

"It's all yours, buddy; go for it," Strap replied.

Just then, we heard a car engine and turned to see a guy driving up in an old jeep.

"Are you here to repair the aircraft?" asked a very nicely dressed olive-skinned gentleman with short dark hair and a South American accent.

"Yep, is it yours?"

"No, it is my employers'; he is currently conducting business down in that little town right now. I am Armando. I am here to provide you with any assistance that you might need. He would like to know how long this might take in case he chooses to arrange for other transportation home."

"Should be less than twelve hours, I'm guessing. We can probably get y'all up and running enough to fly and get it somewhere to get it permanently repaired," I said. "He may have to fly with his gear down, though. Looks like the retract actuator is shot. It's pissing hydraulic fluid everywhere."

"Thank you, gentlemen. I will inform him of this and will be back soon. Do you require anything of me?" he asked.

"Nope, I think we're good for now," I said as I turned to the other guys. "Polite little dude; you could probably learn a few things from him so you don't have to walk around acting like a grumpy old bastard all the time," I said, poking at Strap.

"Whatever, jackass. Why don't you go play with your turtle?" he said.

"Tortoise!" Sanchez corrected.

"Whatever!"

Tack and Sanchez were going to try to get some sleep while Strap and I worked on the plane as it was getting dark. We hauled out a small jack for the gear and got the cutting torch ready so we could cut away any broken and twisted metal. The gear door was mangled, so we just cut it off and then we discovered that the drag brace was bent. The only thing we could really do was manufacture some bracing so the gear could support the aircraft. The retract actuator was useless as I suspected, so we disconnected the hydraulic lines to it and capped them. Fortunately, the wheel, tire, and brake were okay, but we had to replace some of the brake lines with some stock tubing and swage kit that we keep on the plane.

I cut lengths of metal extrusion while Strap welded brackets to the frame and then we bolted them to the strut to support it. After about seven and a half hours, we had it ready. Armando dropped in on us a couple of times to see how things were going, but then he left again and Tack and Sanchez were still crashed in the Gooney Bird.

"It's Miller time!" Strap announced as he climbed out of the plane with four beers for the two of us. We decided that it would be a good time to kick back next to the plane and fire up a couple of cigars.

I looked over at Strap and said, "Hey, when it gets light, let's go on a little hike. I want to explore this area a little bit."

"Awright," he replied.

The runway ran east and west, so you had to kind of fly west into the mountain to land and then you would take off to the east. So basically, if you weren't airborne by the end of the runway, you were going for a pucker ride down the mountain. Strap and I decided to go uphill toward the west for our little adventure because we could see what looked like an interesting-looking rock outcropping. Looking out over the ocean, we could see more islands in the distance. I could barely make out what looked like a cruise ship way off to the north. Being up there gave me a sense of how small we are compared to how big the ocean is. Our hike sort of ended there because we both just sat on those rocks just looking way out over the Pacific, lost in our own thoughts.

Strap isn't much of a talker when it comes to relaying things on his mind. Not when it comes to thoughts that are deep down anyway. I'm not saying that little worms of introspection don't ever wiggle their way out of the dirt clod that he uses for a head; it's just that it's a rarity when they do. And I usually get the honor of being the one who gets to witness them. And this was going to be one of those times, evidently, because he started out with:

"Ya know what I think is jacked up?" That's usually how these conversations start.

"God only knows," I quipped.

"Why is it that people can't be happy with who they are?" Immediately, I knew what this was about.

"I mean, when we were kids, we didn't say, 'Hey, this is bullshit. Why do I gotta be a boy? I wanted to be a girl!' We didn't think like that. What the hell is with that? Who questions that kinda thing? You are what you are and you just roll with it. It ain't like we're a friggin' vending machine selection or something, right? Ya know, like; hey looky here, we gots twinkies, zingers, potato chips, ah shoot, I pushed the wrong button. Looks like I got ding dongs instead of the cherry pie!"

His analogies are so blunt at times, the only thing I can do is shake my head and laugh.

"I agree, man. I don't get it either," I said. "Actually, I really don't care if people want to change their gender; just don't tromp around being pissed at the world about it like it's everyone else's fault."

Nodding his head, he chimed in, "Yeah, and they should be required to wear a sign or something givin' everyone a warning. Like a shirt that says *Caution: Log in the road!*" Now that really had me laughing!

"And yer a jerk for not telling me, you ball-bag! Are you really gonna put that on the internet?" he asked. This was his way of asking me not to.

"Are you kidding? I just wish I had a video of your face when you reached in her pants and latched on to her cock!" I said. At that, I was rolling off the rock, laughing with tears streaming down my face.

Now he was laughing too and shaking his head.

"I gotta put that memory outta my head," he said finally.

"Oh, I don't think I can let you do that, buddy. I'm gonna remind you every chance I get!" I said.

"Oh, I'm sure. Remind me why I hang around with you," he said, looking at me.

"'Cause you don't have any other friends, jackass, and farm animals don't count!" I replied.

"I have friends," he said.

I could see Armando's jeep working its way up the mountain road in the distance, so we decided to head back to the plane to meet him. Tack and Sanchez were up and about checking out our handiwork when we arrived. Tack was watching us as we approached with a smirk on his face.

"You two lovers go roll around in a flowery field together or something?" he asked.

Expecting a comment along those lines, I was ready.

"Maybe. Why? Are you jealous?" I answered.

Armando and another gentleman were walking around the plane and surveying the landing gear. This other guy looked pretty rough, like he had seen a hard life, and looked a little disheveled as if he'd been up for a few days straight. Armando, on the other hand, looked very neat and refreshed.

"Gentlemen, I would like you to meet my employer, Mr. Smith," Armando said as an introduction.

Smith? Sure, he looks like a Smith. I wonder just how many "Mr. Smiths" there are in the drug business, I thought to myself.

"You chure dis ting fly?" he asked. I was a little surprised by his demeanor and broken English after dealing with Armando. For some reason, I sort of expected a debonair type like Mr. Roarke from the *Fantasy Island* TV series back in the seventies. This guy was anything but that and he was acting like he was high on something as well.

"Yep, it'll fly, but taking off and landing, I think, was more your concern. That repair will get you outta here, but you can't retract the gear, which will slow you down. You'll just have to fly it somewhere where they can replace the whole gear assembly," I said.

"Das okay, das okay, we fine, no prolem. Where hue guys fly here from? You li' kamkats?" Mr. Smith asked.

"Wyoming. Did you say kumquats?" I asked with a bewildered expression.

"Wyahmeeng? Dey haf kamkats in wyahmeeng?" he asked.

"Not that I know of. Sure, we like kumquats, I guess," I said, turning to look at the other guys to find a mixture of cocked eyebrows and shrugging shoulders.

"Come, come, I cho you." We followed him around to the plane's entry door where he climbed in and grabbed a crate full of kumquats and then almost fell out of the door while trying to hand them to Armando. He opened the crate and started handing out kumquats to everyone.

"Eat, very goot, I luf dees tings!" he said as he bit into one.

This whole exchange was just getting more and more weird and I was really beginning to wonder what this guy was high on. Armando seemed to act like this was normal behavior for this guy and maybe it was. I guess if you're a cartel drug lord or wherever this guy landed in the cartel rank structure, you can act however you want, and wrecking a multimillion-dollar plane full of kumquats was just a normal day for this clown.

What I was really wondering was, who is supposed to fly this thing? We hadn't seen any pilot types hovering around yet and this guy couldn't fly a Frisbee, much less a jet right now. Just then, Sanchez piped up.

"Ya know, these things are pretty good." And everyone nodded in agreement as we snacked away on the little fruits.

Mr. Smith disappeared into the plane again and we heard noises and banging around while he was rummaging around for something. "Armando!" he yelled from somewhere in the plane.

"Si?" Armando answered as he poked his head in the door. There was a muffled conversation in Spanish inside the cabin that ended with Mr. Smith snapping at Armando. Armando reached in his pocket, extracted something, and handed it to his boss.

"What was that?" was Strap's question and Armando ignored him.

"Quaaludes," Sanchez said as we all turned to look at him.

"He was trying to find a Quaalude and Armando didn't want to give him one," he continued.

"I thought they quit making those things years ago," Strap said while trying to search his memory.

"I thought so too. I think they just call them something else now," Tack noted.

"I don't know about you guys, but I'm ready to roll before things get really weird," I said as I walked off.

The four of us started picking up our gear and putting it in our plane and then Strap and I cracked open the engine cowls to give them a onceover for our flight back. Tack and Sanchez walked around the rest of the plane to look over the gear and flight controls.

Armando came over to us after a few minutes.

"Will you be leaving shortly?" he asked.

"We'll leave after we make sure that you guys get off the ground okay," I answered.

"Watch out fer them giant turtles!" Strap said while chuckling.

"Yes, thank you. I think I will do most of the flying for a while this time. Thank you for your services, gentlemen. Payment was secured with your employer when we initially contacted him," he said, shaking hands with us.

"Anytime, Armando. Feel free to give us a call again sometime," I said.

"Thank you, but I am hoping that won't be necessary," he replied.

As he walked off, I turned to Strap. "It all makes sense now. Mr. Quaalude was driving the plane when he rammed the turtle."

"That's brilliant detective work, Sherlock," Strap quipped.

"Thank you, I do my best," I said.

"The good thing is that he's about to go fly again while he's all drugged up!" he replied. "That's good fer us, as long as we have idiots out there that keep wreckin' their airplanes, we'll still have a job."

"Amen to that," I said. "I have a feeling we'll be seeing that guy again one day."

We watched them take off without incident and got the Gooney Bird fired up and ready to roll. I was looking forward to this trip home because I was fairly sure I would sleep the whole way. Strap plugged in an old Iron Butterfly CD in the cabin audio system and was already in the galley mixing us both a Bloody Mary. Jammin' to "In a Gadda Da Vida," he came out and handed me one.

"Woohoo, breakfast of champions, buddy!" *So much for getting some sleep,* I thought. Tack looked back over his shoulder at us through the open door of the cockpit and smiled, giving us a thumbs-up.

Chapter 9: The Family Hood Ornaments

At some point in the flight, I finally succumbed to the combination of alcohol, weariness, and the drone of the engines. And I was sleeping well, right up until the wheels chirped on the runway, letting me know that we just landed somewhere. Poking my head up to get an idea of where we were, I immediately recognized the surroundings.

"Cabo! Sweet! Sleep later; it's time for some real fun!" I said as I kicked Strap to wake him up.

Smiling, I poked my head into the cockpit as we were taxiing and clapped Tack and Sanchez each on the shoulder.

"Looks like we need gas and this just happens to be along the way!" Tack said with a large grin on his face.

"Anyone talk to the boss yet?" I asked.

"Nope, gonna call him now and give him an update," Sanchez replied.

We usually try to incorporate some fun time at the end of our little excursions if we can. Cabo San Lucas is one of our more favorite locations because we're usually flying up from the Central or South American region and it's a good place to stop for fuel before the last stretch up the coast to LA. Oh yeah, and we always have fun here…always.

Stepping out of the cockpit, I noticed that Strap had a less than enthusiastic expression on his face.

"Oh yeah, I forgot that you had someone get a little mad at you the last time we were here," I said, chuckling.

"Yeah, just a little," he replied.

"I'm sure she's over it by now, buddy. She probably even forgot," I said without trying to sound convincing.

"Yeah right!" he shot back. "I'm sure she already knows we're here. People know our plane around here and I'm sure she got a call by now and she's probably headed over here with a shotgun right now!"

"Gee, that's a shame. Can I have your Harley when you die? I need a good parts bike," I replied. It's so much fun to harass him.

"What! You ain't using my bike for a parts bike. It should be the other way around, considerin' that rag you've been ridin!" he said as he got defensive.

I just laughed because I know he gets touchy about his bike, which is why I tease him when I can.

"What am I gonna do about Myha?" he asked.

I was already switching out the contents of my backpack.

"I dunno. That's your problem," I replied. "But I do know that there's a sail fish out there just swimmin' around waiting for me to catch him. You should go too; you'll be safe from her out in a boat."

"I get seasick on those boats. Besides, I wanna do some diving," he said.

Tack and Sanchez joined us in the cabin while we were talking.

"The boss gave us two days until he wants us back, but we'll need to keep the phone handy and the plane ready to go on short notice," Tack said as they both started throwing things in duffle bags.

"Perfect!" I said. "But ole Strap here has an issue."

Tack was smiling and shaking his head. "You can hang back here and guard the plane. We gotta have somebody watch it anyway," he said.

"I'm not staying in this plane while we're in Cabo. We can get Francisco to guard it again. I'll take my chances out in town!" Strap replied.

"Ah-ha, looks like somebody had this little stop already planned out!" I said as I noticed Sanchez pulling out his golf clubs from a storage closet.

He feigned innocence but couldn't contain his smile.

"What, I'm just always prepared. That's all," he said.

After going through customs, we contacted Francisco (we call him Franko) and made arrangements with him before we climbed in a cab and headed to our usual hotel on the beach. Using the company credit card, we each checked in under our famous deceased musician names. In order to maintain anonymity, we have fake IDs for use outside the U.S. Even Tack and Sanchez, who are already using false names in the States, have different IDs for when we're out of the country. We don't even bring our real identification when we leave to go on a trip in case somebody gets on the plane and finds them.

"Hola, Senior Moon." The desk receptionist recognized us as we strolled through the lobby. They know me as Keith Moon.

"Hola, would you guys happen to have four rooms available?" I replied.

"Si, Senior Moon. Ocean views again, I presume?"

"Absolutely!" After I, John Bonham, Bon Scott, and Jerry Garcia all checked in, we went our separate ways, but we always seemed to find each other later in one of the popular beach bars.

After changing, I decided I would grab a beer at the hotel bar before heading out, but before I could, Strap came banging on my door in a panic.

"She's here, man!" he said, squeezing through the door as soon as I opened it.

"How do you know?" I asked, stepping aside and closing the door.

"I saw her in the lobby as I was coming back down the stairs. We should've stayed at a different hotel. She knows we always stay here!" he said in a panic.

"Probably, but it's too late now. What do you want to do?" I asked while trying to appear concerned.

"Let's go out the back and I'm hangin' with you the rest of the day so you can help me watch out for her!" he said while walking to the back door.

"That's all you got, genius? Sneak out the back? Why don't you quit being a wimp and just confront her and get it over with?" I asked.

"Hell no! You've seen how those Spanish chicks get when they're pissed. It's all teeth and nails! Trust me, this is…" He stopped in mid-sentence because of the loud banging and shouting at the door.

"Gee, I wonder who it could be," I said, grinning and looking at him. He was already looking over the balcony wall, considering his escape.

"Go for it; it's only three stories up. What's the worst that could happen, broken ankle?" I said while shaking my head.

"Don't let her in, man. She's out of control! You can't reason with her when she's like that!" he said, staring at me.

"Relax, buddy, I'll talk to her first and see if I can get her to calm down a little, okay?" I said.

I opened the door to find Myha standing there looking very beautiful and intense. I could definitely see why he was attracted to her: tall, thin, long dark hair, dark skin, and very angry brown eyes.

"Hello, Keith, I know he is hiding in there like a coward!" she said with her nostrils flaring.

"Hi, Myha, how've you been?" I said, smiling and trying to be pleasant. "He's willing to explain things to you, but we were hoping we could keep the violence to a minimum today," I said soothingly.

"Sure, right after I cut off his balls and hang them on the front of my car!" she said, smiling right back me.

"I see. Does it have to be both of his balls? Maybe you could let him keep one, just for old times' sake?" I was hoping to lighten the mood a little.

"How about I hang both yours and his from my car, *pendejo*?" she shot back. So much for that idea.

"Look, I know he's sorry for whatever it is that he did and he didn't mean to do it," I said. "Just let him explain before we discuss losing any body parts, okay?"

"Oh, I'm sure he didn't mean to sleep with both of my sisters while he was seeing me!" She was yelling this at door behind me.

"They took advantage of me while I was drunk!" This was Strap defending himself from the other side of the door behind me.

Now I was looking down and just shaking my head.

"You slept with both of her sisters? I thought you said you slept with her best friend!" I said loudly so he could hear me.

"What?" His voice went up an octave or two. "I never said that! Myah, he's kidding. That never happened!" he yelled back.

Now she was beside herself and screaming through the door while trying to get in. She was so loud that the other guests were coming out of their rooms to see what the commotion was all about. I couldn't understand what she was saying in Spanish, but I could hear him yelling at me as I was laughing and extracting myself down the hall.

"Del, you're a jerk! Tell her you were kidding! Del!" he was yelling.

I really should try to be a better friend. I don't know what it is, but sometimes, I just can't help myself. It's like a situation presents itself and instead of trying to be the Good Samaritan, I have to stir the pot just a little. And I only do it for my own entertainment. Some people are born with different talents or gifts; I think my gift is being an instigator. It must be. It comes so easy. So based on that, who am I to deny a gift that I was obviously born with?

As I was heading down to the hotel bar to have that beer, the manager and a security guard passed me by on the way up. *I'm sure they'll get everything straightened out*, I thought while chuckling to myself.

I sat down and ordered a beer and chatted with the bartender for a bit. I turned to the sound of some commotion and saw them escorting a very irate Myha through the lobby and out of the front door of the hotel. Then I ordered two beers and waited for Strap to join me. After about five minutes, he slid onto the stool next to me, took a long sip of beer, and let out a big sigh.

I glanced over at him with a sly grin.

"Glad to see you could make it, buddy. By the way, you didn't mention that it was both of her sisters," I said.

He just shrugged. "Yeah, well…"

"And her best friend! You scoundrel!" I said, giving him a berating look and trying to sound admonishing.

He started laughing.

"I should've known you were gonna pull something. I can always count on you make things harder on me!" he said.

"You're welcome. You shouldn't make it so easy. I just can't help myself," I replied while taking another sip.

The rest of our stay was fairly uneventful as far as Myha was concerned. I fished, and Strap and I did some diving while the other guys golfed and surfed. We stayed up into the wee hours of the mornings having fun drinking and frolicking with the local ladies. Strap, intent on preventing the family jewels from becoming a hood ornament, kept looking over his shoulder for his crazed, knife-wielding ex-lover.

Back on the plane, all gassed up and ready for the last run up the coast to LA, we taxied out and took off down the runway. While watching the blue water and white sand beaches shrink away, Strap turned to me.

"Maybe it wouldn't hurt to find another place to stop and fuel in the future," he said.

I ran my fingers through my hair and sighed.

"Why? Whose reputation did you tarnish this time?"

Chapter 10: Mongo Baby and the Lonesome Sluggards Band

Back in the lot, it was life as usual. Shaky Jake camped out in the back of my truck while we were gone and mentioned that he was glad we were back because the beer cooler was empty.

"Glad we're missed for somethin'. I'll make a beer run. Any y'all need anything?" Strap asked.

"I shall require a steak and a cold beer right now, boy! And make it snappy. I'm hungry!" I said, snapping my fingers at him. This drew a derogatory response, of course, as I think he suggested something that I'm pretty sure is physically impossible. I grabbed my airsoft gun and shot him in the butt real quick while he was facing the other way.

"Jackass!" He came running over and slammed me onto the picnic table and we started wrestling.

"Get off me, ya big homo. I'm not one of your transvestite friends!" I said as I fended him off. This only provoked him even more, of course.

"Is this going to take long?" Jake asked as he sat down and watched us.

"Nope," I said. "Just as soon as Sluggo here realizes that I'm not a farm animal, he'll leave me alone!" This last crack got Strap laughing and he let me go.

"Are you two still in junior high school?" Jake asked while shaking his head.

"Nah, this idiot never made it past the third grade!" I said as I shoved Strap away from me.

"I did too," Strap replied.

After the grocery run, we grilled some steaks and kicked back with beer and cigars. As the sun began to settle, a loose gathering of fellow lot lizards began growing, and before long, we were having a nice little get-together. One of the female flight attendants in the lot seemed to have developed some sort of instinctive need to "mother" over Shaky Jake whenever she saw him. For a while, he would resist her and try to escape when he saw her coming, which was a little comical to watch, but over time, he just gave in. Now he willingly talks to her and we joke with him about her being his girlfriend. Now she was with him and making him try on some sweaters that she picked up from somewhere, which we all knew he wouldn't wear.

A friendly little card game broke out on the picnic table and, after a while, I felt a large presence standing behind me. Others at the table smiled at me and I looked up to see a big figure smiling down at me. "Hey, Wes," I said.

"What's up, losers?" This was his typical greeting.

"What prompts you to venture out of your RV tonight? Pop a hole in your blow-up doll again?" I asked him. I save my favorite greetings just for him.

"Ha ha, funny. You guys just get back?" he asked.

"Yep, as a matter of fact, we were down in your favorite part of the woods. There's a donkey asking about you down in Mexico," I replied. This drew a few chuckles from those familiar with the story.

"I'm sure. I still owe you a little payback for that, Del," Wes said.

"That was just a small misunderstanding for which I am deeply sorry for and sincerely regret." I almost said this with a straight face. "Have a beer and cigar on me as a symbol of my sincerity for such an unfortunate incident."

This is typical of the usual banter that goes on between Westley and me, mainly because we don't like each other. Don't get me wrong; we aren't enemies and we don't mind hanging out together. It's just that we pick on each other quite a bit, kind of like siblings, if you will. He's not really a bad guy; it's just the way he comes off sometimes because he's dumb but tries too hard to act like he is more intelligent than everyone else. I think he does this because he knows he's dumb.

He doesn't like me because I gave him the nickname Mongo-Baby, which seems to have caught on quite well and the fact that I harass him quite a lot. This guy is about six feet, four inches tall and works out regularly. He was born with an unfortunately large low brow and sloping forehead, so he looks like a Neanderthal. That and the fact that he's big, has an awkward gait when he walks, and he's a mouth breather, which is why I came up with the nickname. He kind of reminds me of a big goofy dog that bumps into everyone, slobbers on you, and knocks things over with his tail whenever he's around.

So the unfortunate incident I was referring to and why he is now somewhat leery of me started out like this:

Once upon a time, a few of us were expanding our cultural diversity, if you will, down in Tijuana, Mexico. What turned out to be an evening of overindulgence and debauchery started out as a peaceful charity mission for our friend Mongo-Baby, who just wanted to see a donkey show. He had become obsessed with wanting to see one after hearing so many stories about them. Personally, I had yet to see one either, but I was fairly sure that I could get through the rest of my life without feeling that I had not fulfilled all of my dreams if I didn't.

58

Inevitably, our little escapade led us through and around a few areas not usually frequented by tourists. Go figure, right? So we ended up at a bar slash whorehouse that advertised a donkey show but turned out to be just a poor donkey painted up to look like a zebra tied up in the corner of the bar! I was never really sure if there was supposed to be a regular "show" with the donkey or what the deal was, but the place had all the right ingredients for a good time and so we planted ourselves there nonetheless.

The five of us managed to garner the attention of several of the young female employees as it was clear we were there to have a good time and were willing to spend the money for it. The tequila flowed and I was in prime condition for my usual antics and the comedy was in full swing. At one point, Strap decided that the donkey looked lonely and bored all by himself in the corner and invited him over by untying him and bringing him to our table. We bought a pitcher of beer for the donkey to drink and he actually seemed to like it and didn't mind the attention.

We were having fun watching the donkey try to slurp the beer out of the pitcher when Mongo-Baby decided he wanted to go for a ride on him. This turned into a fiasco because he was too intoxicated to climb on and started stumbling around while he made the attempt. The donkey wasn't cooperating and kept trying to get away from him by running around the table while vocalizing his own objections to the idea. This commotion was accompanied by the usual hoots and hollers at Mongo-Baby along with various challenges to his manhood.

He gave up after the donkey ran off and he sat down next to me, where of course I couldn't resist making cracks about him being lonely and his apparent attraction to farm animals. This drew an additional barrage of wisecracks from everyone seated and so the drunken bantering was elevated to yet another level.

At one point, some of the girls around the bar were dancing to salsa music and Strap, being moved by the music, I guess, got up and decided to dance with them. Oddly enough, I'm the one that you can usually count on to get up and start the weird gyrations when the tequila comes out. But not this night; ole Strap was looking to get his groove on and wanted to give everybody a show, but his dancing turned out to be what looked like a combination of bull riding, air humping, and an epileptic seizure. I laughed so hard that I almost threw up under the table while watching the disaster.

As the night wore on and the weirdness continued, I couldn't resist harassing Mongo-Baby a little more while he was seated next to me. By now, he had a young lady sitting on his lap and so I got an idea and leaned over and quietly told him that the girl on his lap was actually a guy. Initially, he wouldn't believe me, but knowing how gullible he can be, I continued to try to convince him. Finally, I told him that one of the other girls told this to me because she was afraid that he didn't know. At that, he immediately launched this poor lady off of his lap (who probably didn't weigh more than 115 lbs. soaking wet) and onto the floor about five feet away! I really wasn't expecting him to do that. Everyone at the table jumped up as Mongo-Baby started screaming obscenities her and wiping his mouth with his hand and spitting, presumably because he had been kissing her. Now the girl was up and yelling back at him in Spanish and several of the other ladies that worked there joined the fray. The next thing I knew, the girl had taken off one of her high heels and was on him like a cat as she launched herself at him and started beating him in the head with it. Mongo-Baby was still yelling as he was trying to pry her off of his head and ended up falling over a chair and crashing to the floor. Now the rest of the women were screaming and started throwing bottles and glasses at the rest of us as well and it was all we could do to get away.

The whole place was in uproar because no one else knew what had happened and everyone was already drunk and so the drama level went through the roof. Thanks to me.

Naturally, we were all thrown out and now Mongo-Baby was all scratched up and bleeding from the forehead and we were wandering around lost in the middle of the night. For some reason, I decided that this would be a good time to fess up and tell Mongo-Baby that I had made all that up and that she really wasn't a guy. Everyone else thought that this was funny except him oddly enough, because he tackled me right there in the street. So here we were, the drunk and stupid Americans, rolling around in the middle of the street and waking up the whole neighborhood. Both of us were too drunk to really hurt each other and I figured out that he really wasn't that mad.

At some point, and I don't know how, but we found our way back to a familiar part of town and back across the border to our vehicles without further incident.

I do feel a little bad about the incident, although it always makes for a good laugh when someone retells the story.

Mongo-Baby settled in at the picnic table and the conversation shifted to airline talk as usual—what company is merging with who, who's changing their routes—that kind of stuff. The pilots and flight attendants are always good for some funny passenger stories. Mechanics are usually complaining about the unions or just life in general. Strap and I can both relate, having worked for an airline in a previous life and happy that we aren't anymore.

Chapter 11: Doin' the Funky Chicken

Eventually, our fellow lot-lizards drifted off to their respective RVs and I climbed into mine, thankful for a chance at a decent night's sleep. The next morning, I could see that I was up before my neighbor and decided it was time for a little payback for shutting off my generator the other morning. After I got some coffee going, I went outside and started tossing bread on top of Strap's roof. There are always plenty of black crows around looking for an easy meal, and their claws make a heck of a racket on the roof of an RV because it's made of thin aluminum.

When the coffee was ready, I went outside to sit at the table and waited for show to begin. Sure enough, one, then another, and then several crows landed on top of his RV and started fighting and squawking over the bread. Before long, his roof was covered with crows and I saw his RV move from side to side, telling me he was up and moving around. Suddenly the door burst open with Strap standing there in shorts, hair all askew, blinking at me with a bewildered look on his face.

"Morning," I said as politely as I could while I tried to act like nothing was wrong, of course.

He stepped out of the RV and stared at the birds in bewilderment. Then he looked back at me, then back at the birds.

"What the hell?" he said when he looked at me. I just shrugged my shoulders and feigned innocence. He climbed back in his RV and came back out with his airsoft rifle and started blazing away at the crows until they flew away! Cursing, he went back into his RV and slammed the door, presumably to get some more sleep. Within a few minutes, more bread appeared on his roof and the crows returned. Of course, out comes Strap with the airsoft rifle, yelling obscenities while firing wildly at them until they flew away again. This was great early morning entertainment! It went on several times before he gave up and came over to get a cup of coffee and sat down.

"I know you had something to do with that," he said, glaring at me.

"Hmm? Me? Nooo. Thought that was kinda weird myself." I couldn't keep a straight face to save my life.

"Whatever, jackass. Let's go get some breakfast at Joe's," he replied.

"I'm up for that!" I replied. Eat at Joe's is a popular little restaurant down in Redondo Beach where you can get a great breakfast, or any meal, for that matter.

Over breakfast, we decided it would be a great day to take a ride on our bikes down the coast to San Diego. Besides, it was time to hit our favorite brewery anyway, Stone Brewery, home of the Arrogant Bastard Ale! Ah yes, I could see this was going to be a good day!

After breakfast, we left Joe's and started winding our way up the hill through Palos Verdes. Traffic was light and then I figured out that it must be the weekend because I noticed a few yard sale signs. I never know what day of the week it is anymore. I was enjoying the scenery as we rode and was getting relaxed when Strap suddenly pulled over in front of a house that was hosting a yard sale. Confused, I pulled up behind him but kept the bike idling in neutral. Now I'm the one wondering "what the hell"? When you live in an RV and ride a motorcycle, yard sales are not something that you'll find yourself frequenting for obvious reasons. As Strap climbed off his bike, he turned, gave me a big grin as he waggled his eyebrows, and started up the walkway. Sitting on the bike, I'm still wondering what he has seen that he evidently can't live without. As he's walking, I'm surveying the various items displayed for sale, trying to see what has caught his interrrressst...

Ah-ha! Behold, o ye of little faith, and look down not on thy brother for he hath cast his gaze upon a damsel's pair!

He was not interested in the yard sale; he was interested in the two ladies in bikinis that were apparently hosting the yard sale! How the hell he spotted them from up the road where we were is beyond me, though; the guy is like a hound!

Okay, I'm up to speed now. I hopped off the bike and followed him up the walkway, feigning mild interest in their wares. Ole Strap didn't feign anything though; he just walked straight up to those girls and started talking immediately. Both of them were cute enough and the one he was talking to seemed friendly enough and fairly talkative herself, but the other seemed a little quiet. I just took this for a little shyness and maybe a little hesitance because of our appearances, but I was sure that we could get past that. They asked what we were doing today and blah, blah, blah, you know, the usual chit-chat get-to-know-you talk. I kept trying to talk to the other girl, whom I found out was named Jennifer. She would only mumble simple, one-word replies to my conversation and after a while, I was beginning to wonder if something was up.

Okay, maybe it was just me; maybe I was creeping her out a little. I guess both Strap and I could give someone the wrong impression with our scruffiness or the lack of attention to detail when it comes to personal appearances. Her buddy seemed to warm up to us fairly easily so you would think that maybe she would see that and be more comfortable. Maybe? I don't know, so I tried a different tack by getting her to talk about herself for a bit. She's a woman, so this should work, right? Anna would pop me for saying that. Anyway, it was the four of us just sitting together, no one else was around, as there was a lull in the yard sale activity. I started to say something to Jennifer when she suddenly blurted out "jerk" very rapidly and then looked away.

Wah-huh? Everyone was quiet. Now I'm not easily offended and I've been called a lot of things by a lot of women…a lot. But it was the manner in which this came out that was peculiar. Then her friend Rachel quietly spoke up and said, "Jenny has this thing."

"Bastard!" Jennifer blurted.

"Thing?" I inquired.

"It's called Tourette's Syndrome." Rachel replied.

"Jerk!" Jennifer again.

"I see," I said. I was actually thinking that maybe my reputation had preceded me and she was just expressing her thoughts about me. It's happened enough in the past.

"Bastard!" Guess who. Technically, I am one of those as well.

This was the moment when my buddy Strap slowly turned to me and gave me a big smile. Great. He was already relishing the opportunity to harass me about this later. He was going to milk this one for all it was worth. He was laughing so hard on the inside right now that I could almost hear him. Me, on the other hand, I was letting out a big sigh on the inside. Why? Why me? It never fails, although it's not unusual for a woman to call me a jerk and a bastard at some point in the relationship anyway; it's just that it's usually at the end of it.

Okay, okay, let's get a grip; I can roll with this, right? People have all kinds of medical issues and whatnot all the time, right? Just be cool and casual like it's no big deal.

"Ah, okay, Tourette's, I've heard of that, no problem," I said as I was trying to sound casual, but I wasn't sure how I was coming off. I smiled at Jennifer and she smiled back.

"Jerk!"

"Yep, that's me," I said and nodded my head.

Well, this oughta be an interesting day. After all, she was still very pretty. The conversation picked back up and Jennifer ever cautiously chimed in more and more and I thought we did good, learning to ignore the verbal outbursts.

After a couple hours, it was clear that the brewery would have to wait another day, as getting to know these two girls a little better was looking promising.

After a while, the girls decided that we were somewhat trustworthy and asked us if we would mind keeping the yard sale going while they left to take care of something, promising to be back within an hour or so. Being the gentlemen that we are and having no ulterior motives in mind, none, none whatsoever, we agreed wholeheartedly.

After they left, it became apparent to Strap and me that we would be requiring a cold beverage in order to sustain us through the grueling labor of hosting the yard sale. And so with this in mind, I offered a young couple the items that they had picked out in exchange for making a beer run. I reasoned that Rachel and Jennifer would see the practicality in that and wouldn't have a problem with it.

We also figured that they wouldn't mind if we cranked up the stereo a bit either while we slogged away out in the yard. After a couple more hours had gone by, the girls still had not returned and we were getting hungry. Using the same logic, I approached a small group of people and made them the same offer, this time for food and more beer. They agreed of course and when they returned, they had food for themselves as well and stayed to eat with us. We also offered them beer, which they were happy to accept.

The afternoon stretched on and still no girls, but Strap and I, being the true Marines that we are, refused to abandon our post! Unfortunately, the wares for beers idea was working a little too well and several people stayed around to mingle as they were getting food, beer, and cool yard sale stuff and Strap and I were getting food, beer, and hammered! The yard sale began looking more and more like an outdoor party as yard sale shoppers stopped by and decided to hang out a bit and even neighbors started wandering over to see what was going on.

Some of the neighbors actually thought we lived there and thought it was a house warming party as people were coming and going to use the bathroom in the house. Evidently, someone found some margarita mix and broke out the blender. We were having a great time and I was beginning to wonder why we didn't do this yard sale thing more often!

Sometime in the late afternoon or early evening, Rachel and Jennifer finally returned. Noticing the large crowd of people, they were obviously very curious about what was going on. Now I'm not entirely sure how well we were able to articulate the events of the day because by this time, the alcohol was hindering my speech and memory a little. But evidently, we were able to explain to them why there was a party in their yard instead of the yard sale stuff due to our savvy negotiating skills. This was right about where the conversation went south, I'm guessing. You would think they would have been a little more appreciative of the fact that Strap and I stuck it out all day for them when they said they would only be gone an hour!

"YOU F***ING JERK!" It seemed Jenny had found her big girl voice and I wasn't just a jerk now; I had been promoted!

If you think that people with Tourette's can be a little verbally offensive when they're calm, you have seen nothing, my friend! I was impressed with how many expletives that girl could rattle off in one string. I mean, this girl became completely unhinged. Strap and I looked like we were doing the funky chicken, backpedaling through the yard and tripping over stuff while trying to get away from them as they were screaming and throwing anything they could grab! Now this was more like it; I was completely used to have a woman scream at me on the front lawn after she knew me, not before. All was normal now.

We grabbed the bikes and started pushing them down the road as fast as we could, but we were too drunk to ride them. Eventually, we coasted to a stop down the hill at an apartment complex with a parking garage under the first level and found a dark corner to sleep off the alcohol on the ground next to the bikes. And the day had started out with such promise.

The next morning, we woke up and went back to Joe's for breakfast again. Sitting there drinking coffee while waiting for our food, I looked at Strap across the table and said, "Okay, today we're going with my plan. Which is what we originally planned yesterday before your little det—"

"Jerk!" Strap blurted while wearing a big stupid grin. I had to laugh. And we sat there giggling like a couple of schoolboys as the waitress brought our food.

Chapter 12: Mushbrain

After a couple of days, I was thinking about taking a trip to Georgia to see Anna. She was on my mind a lot lately, which meant that it was time. As I was making plans, though, Strap and I got a call from the boss.

"You guys come by my place in the morning; I want to talk to all four of you about an idea," he said.

"Yes, sir, we'll be there," I replied. Well, I guessed I'd have to put that trip on hold for a bit.

The next morning, Strap and I arrived at the boss's house on Manhattan Beach, a nice two-story right on the Strand, overlooking the ocean. The Strand is a long bicycle/jogging path that runs along the beach from Redondo up past Santa Monica. Most of these homes are beautiful and situated perfectly on the beach with a guaranteed picturesque sunset every night. And the prices for many of them are in in the millions.

We found the boss out on the back deck, having coffee and reading the paper.

"Gentlemen, good morning. Please help yourself to some coffee and pastries on the breakfast bar and come join me. Sanchez and Tack should be arriving soon," he said.

As we relaxed on the deck, sipping coffee and watching the joggers and volleyball players, we talked about the last mission.

"So tell me about this guy and his plane down in the Galapagos." Strap and I chuckled as we told him about the tortoise and how drugged up the guy was. He laughed and traded a few stories of his own and he had some real doozies, as you can imagine. He had been shot, stabbed, survived a plane crash in the water, and spent a week in the jungle escaping from his employer's enemies once. I've always liked talking with him because he was a guy that really appreciated what we were doing, having been there and done that himself for so many years. He is also someone that I can admire a bit because he has found a niche in a market that clearly was going to be alive for a long time. And because he was smart about it and very careful about whom he did business with, he was thriving and making a nice living for himself.

Tack and Sanchez arrived a little later and the five of us lounged around the deck and threw around a few ideas for the plane when the boss finally got around to talking about why he summoned us.

"Gentlemen, I've gotten wind of a little war that might be brewing between a Central American and a Mexican cartel. I believe that the Central American bunch is getting ready for a giant push north with a lot of cargo in an attempt to flood the market. I'm considering having you guys stage down in Belize for a few weeks to be closer to the area because I think we might get busy soon." When he finished, he just looked at each of us individually.

"You guys can load the plane with extra supplies and equipment to hold you for a while down there until things calm down. I'm open to your thoughts," he added.

After a moment, Sanchez spoke first. "We'll need our boats and RVs looked after while we're away."

"Done, what else?" he asked.

"Where do you want us to stay while we're there?" This was me asking.

"Your choice. I can make arrangements for you or let you guys decide when you get there," he replied.

The four of us looked at each other and, after a brief discussion, we decided we would rather scope out our own digs for the stay.

The boss nodded his head thoughtfully and said, "I figured that you would prefer it that way. Any more thoughts or questions? Okay then, I'm having wi-fi installed on the aircraft as we speak. This way, we can communicate through an onboard laptop as well as the cell and satellite phones. In addition, I'm giving each of you a ten-thousand-dollar cash bonus today for the inconvenience."

This last gesture brought a round of nods and thank-yous from all of us.

"How soon do you want us to leave?" asked Strap.

"As soon as you're ready, a couple of days to prepare to be away for a while. You and Del can keep your bikes in my garage here if you like. Put some thought into extra parts and supplies for the plane and put it all on the expense card. Give me a list of any additional weapons or gear that you might want on board and I'll take care of it," he said.

This time, it was Tack that spoke up. "I think the four of us should give the plane a little service check before we leave also. Go over the engines real well, hit all the lube points, and perform a few systems ops checks." The rest of us nodded in agreement.

The boss stood up and said, "If you want, you guys can hang out here for the day and discuss everything. I have to go pick up a few things for a little get together that my girlfriend is having here tonight. She has invited several people from her salon college, employees and students, I think. The four of you are welcome to stay for that as well; as a matter of fact, I'd prefer that you did. These aren't the kind of people that I'm used to hanging out with."

A salon college meant ladies and the four of us, being the single men that we are, had no trouble with the boss's request.

After refreshing the coffee and grabbing another muffin, Strap, Tack, Sanchez, and I sat and made lists of everything we were going to do and get for the next two days. In addition, we pulled up an internet global map website to get an idea of how Belize was laid out. Tack and Sanchez were the only ones that had been there before and had a better idea of where we should set up shop for a while. Obviously, the tourist areas were better because the locals see new people through there all the time. If we suddenly appeared in a more remote area not frequented by foreigners, then it might raise suspicion and prompt people to ask questions. Even though we use false identities and a story to go along with it, it's still better to fly under the radar, so to speak. In this case, the idea was to hide in plain sight. "Nothing to see here, people; just four lazy Americans taking a little vacation and enjoying the scenery."

At some point, the coffee in our mugs magically transformed into beer in our mugs as we told lies and invented stories. We talked more about Tack and Sanchez moving out to the RV lot, complained about the Marine Corps, and relationships gone south. My past relationship stories seem to be the most popular for some reason. Tack and Sanchez were in tears when we told them about the yard sale incident the other day.

Later in the day, the boss returned with his girlfriend and people started to arrive. He had the perfect setup for a party. His house is a two story with the bedrooms upstairs with large sliding glass doors opening to a deck overlooking the ocean. Then downstairs was a huge kitchen and family room area with large sliding glass doors as well that opened to an even larger deck looking out over the beach and ocean. I could definitely get used to a place like this!

It was clear from the beginning when people started to arrive that there would be a contrast in the type of guests at this party. First you had Strap, Tack, Sanchez, and me sporting cargo shorts, faded t-shirts, and flip-flops. Then you had the other guests and it seemed there were just as many males as there were females. Notice I didn't use the term "men." The first fruitcake to sashay through the door was wearing really tight skinny jeans with a form-fitting button-up shirt and looking like he just got freshly manicured, waxed, and spray tanned. As far as I'm concerned, skinny jeans could not have been designed by a man because they're like a cheap hotel— no ball room!

"Now I see what the boss meant." This was Tack's observation. It was clear that the people in this crowd were the typical Hollywood socialite types who were all about their looks and the latest fashion. My idea of fashion is giving my t-shirt a sniff check before I put it on in the morning.

At least the ladies appeared to be attractive and, therefore, the evening had some potential. It turned out be a fun time because most of the guys were the flamboyant type and fairly entertaining if nothing else. It also turned out that most of them were interested in each other and not so interested in the women, which was perfect for those of us that were!

Later in the evening, I was approached by an attractive woman that appeared closer to my age than the rest of the twenty-something year olds that seemed to dominate the party. She was probably about five foot five, thin, with dark brown, shoulder-length hair and green eyes.

"I don't believe I've seen you at the salon before. My name is Janelle," she said as she stuck her hand out.

Taking her hand, I smiled and said, "I've never been in a salon in my life. I'm Del."

She chuckled and said, "Yes, I can tell that you aren't the type." She had a slightly British accent when she spoke. "Fancy yourself as a rough and tumble type, I'm guessing. Save the prettiness for the ladies?" she said, smiling back at me.

"Nope, nothin' fancy here, just don't like complicating the morning routine with a bunch of monkey-motion in the mirror. Throw on a hat, grab a cup of coffee, and I'm ready to roll," I said.

My outlook on relationships has really gone south lately and I think I'm going to come up with a whole new philosophy on the idea. I've given up on trying to impress women anymore. Why bother? It's like false advertising. They're going to see who you really are eventually, so why go through all the fake B.S. in the first place? If she sticks around, you're good to go, and you don't have to worry about disappointing her later by showing her what a scumbag you really are from the start.

"Gargle with a beer and give the underarms a sniff before heading out the door, I suppose? My, aren't you the ladies' man," she said with a raised eyebrow and a smirk on her face.

"For the record, I would like to mention that I had my weekly shower this morning," I said with the biggest grin I could muster. "Care to take a whiff?"

"No, but thank you for that wonderful offer, Mr. Del. I believe I've met my whiffing quota for the day," she replied with the most sincere smile that she could muster. She was teasing me. I think I like this girl. Maybe it wouldn't hurt to turn on a little Del charm.

"So, Del, how do you and your lot fit into this little soiree?" she asked as she scanned the deck. She led me over to a couch and we sat down.

"Well, we work for the owner of the house. We were here earlier today to discuss some company matters and he invited us to stay," I said.

"I see, and what is it that you gentlemen do exactly?" she asked as she watched me over her wine glass.

"We're troubleshooters for his company. We fix problems," I replied.

"Ooh, vague yet intriguing!" she said with mock wide-eyed excitement.

"It's really not that big a deal; we just keep things on the down-low because of the competition. You know how technology companies are these days," I said, shrugging. This will make her think we're a bunch of nerdy techno kids instead of gun-toting knuckledraggers.

"Hmm, you want me to believe that you guys are techy nerds?" she asked with a raised eyebrow. So much for that idea.

"Techy nerds usually don't look like they bench press their desks. They have soft squishy little hands because they only use them to type on their keyboards. Your hands look like you've been swinging from trees," she said.

"Well, maybe we're not exactly your average techy guys," I admitted.

"And I'm willing to bet that all of you are ex-military, am I right?" I could see there wasn't going to be any bullshitting this gal.

"Okay, you got me. We aren't exactly techy nerds," I said.

"I don't really need to know what you do, Del. But I do want to know whether or not you're in a relationship with someone. I noticed you haven't been prowling too much, unlike your friends," she said. *Wow, I thought, not only is she smart, but she's also direct.*

"Nope, no relationship," I replied.

"Gee, I can't understand why not. What girl in her right mind doesn't love a guy who takes a shower once a week and his oral hygiene consists of gargling with beer in the morning?" she said as she smiled at me again. I don't think I've ever met a woman who harassed me like this one did.

"I try not to advertise myself," I conceded.

"Like a diamond in the rough?" she asked.

"Or in something," I said, smiling.

"Or is it because you're just getting out of a relationship? Heart still on the mend?"

"Nope, no broken heart. Just tired, I guess," I admitted.

"Ah-ha, you're frustrated with women. Haven't had a lot of luck in the past?" she asked while eyeing me coolly.

"You don't happen to have a cat, do you?" I asked while remembering how my last relationship ended.

"No, that's a curious question. Why do you ask?" she said, eyeing me with an expectant look.

"Never mind. So tell me about yourself, Janelle. You-ins ain't from 'round here, is ya? I can tell by that there aanglish acksent you got," I said with my best hillbilly twang.

"Oh, I love American southern accents, Del! Will you do it some more? It really turns me on!" she said playfully. Now she was turned and facing me directly as she said this and I was struck by how pretty she really was.

"Really? That's what turns you on, huh? How about I knock out a couple my teeth and go shirtless under a pair of overalls?" I asked jokingly.

"Oh dear, I think you got me a little moist with the missing teeth idea!" she said with mock seriousness.

"Okay, as soon as I find some pliers, it's on, baby!" I said, smiling. We refreshed our drinks and stepped out to go for a walk on the Strand.

"So where are you from?" I asked.

"I grew up in England. I had an American father and a British mother. My father was a captain in the U.S. Air Force and flew fighter planes in Vietnam. He was shot down and killed when I was two. He and my mother met when he was stationed in England before the war," she explained.

"Sorry to hear about your dad; that must have been hard," I said.

"Thank you, but I didn't really know him. My mother took it hard, though. She eventually remarried when I was ten," she said.

"So what brought you to the States?" I asked curiously.

"Stardom, Hollywood. I wanted to go into acting. I was young, of course, but Hollywood forced me to grow up and face reality," she said.

"I think this town is probably full of stories like that," I said.

"Oh yes, definitely. I finally realized that an acting career wasn't going to happen for me. I had been working at an upscale hair salon in Hollywood and realized that there was money to be made out here. Everyone out here wants to look like they just stepped out of a camera shoot. So I got smart and started the college," she explained.

"Oh, so you're the owner of the salon college?" I asked in surprise.

"Yes, I am, and I have worked very hard at it to make it what it is now," she replied.

"Must be the American in you," I quipped teasingly.

"Oh, you think so? Don't forget where you Yanks came from," she fired back. "And what is your last name, by the way?"

"DelRio," I replied.

"Ah, so Del is short for DelRio. And what origin is the last name DelRio?" she asked.

"Not sure really, but it doesn't matter because my last name was given to me. My true family heritage is unknown to me," I said.

"I see. You'll have to tell me that story one day," she said, smiling up at me.

We walked and talked for a while. She was easy to be with and I felt like I had known her a long time.

"So, Del, are we going to see each other after tonight?" I was going to have to get used how direct she was. I appreciated it, though, because it certainly makes things easier.

"Umm, yeah, I guess, but I have something coming up," I said.

"Really? Getting right to the point, aren't we? Already planning breakfast for us in the morning too?" she said with a bashful little smile.

"What? I didn't mean that, I mean, I wasn't trying, what I mean is..." I stuttered. She had me backpedaling.

"I'm just teasing you, Del," she said and then she looped her arm inside mine.

"So do you live here in Manhattan Beach?" she asked as we started walking back to the party.

"No, I live a bit closer to the airport. How about you?" I replied.

"I live in Santa Monica. Which side of the airport do you live, El Segundo or Playa Del Ray?" she asked.

"Umm, neither, really. I'm closer to the runway side, I guess," I replied.

Dang it! Here's the downside to living in the lot. Nothing will impress a lady more than showing her your really cool digs on wheels in the middle of a parking lot. Well, I do have the philosophy about showing a girl what a scumbag I really am from the git-go and all that. Alright, so here I go.

"I guess I should tell you a little more about me," I admitted.

"You live with your mom," she said.

"Huh? No, no, that's not it," I said.

"You're gay," she said, smiling.

"No, nothing like that," I said. She was harassing me again.

"You're in jail and out on work release?" she asked again.

"Are you through?" I asked, giving her a blank expression.

"I suppose; go ahead." She was smiling at me again.

"I don't exactly live in a typical house in a typical neighborhood," I admitted.

"And?" she asked, looking at me with a raised eyebrow.

"And I sort of live in an RV," I said.

"And?" she continued.

"And I live in a parking lot." Okay, I said it. If she walks, then she walks. Not a problem; I've been doing fine without complicating things with women for the past few years since I've been out here. So why was I holding my breath?

"You live in an RV in a parking lot? How posh! Again, I just can't understand why some lucky girl hasn't scooped you up yet. You're practically L.A.'s most eligible bachelor, Del! How on earth could the tabloids have missed this one?" she said. Boy, she was really having fun with me now. She was just grinning from ear to ear.

"Are you through?" I asked.

"Oh no, Del, this takes the biscuit. I'm just relishing this!" I think she was actually bouncing on her toes while she was ribbing me.

"I want to go see it!" she said, beaming.

"No you don't," I said flatly.

"Yes I do," she said.

"The place is a mess; the maid didn't come this week." *Or ever, for that matter,* I thought to myself.

"Okay, if you're too embarrassed. What do you have coming up, if you don't mind me asking?"

"I have to leave to go on a business trip for a few weeks," I said apologetically.

"I see. Well then, will you walk a lady to her car?" she asked.

"Absolutely. Can I get your number before you go?" I asked as we strolled out to her car.

"Only if you promise to show me your RV when you get back," she said, smiling at me.

"I suppose we could talk about it, I guess," I said as I rolled my eyes.

"Not good enough," she insisted.

"Okaaaay, I'll let you see it." I sighed.

"See? That wasn't so hard. Here," she said. Then she wrote her phone number on my shirt with a pen, planted a big, fat, wet kiss on my lips, climbed in her Beemer, and drove off. She smelled good.

Dang it, what was I doing? This was no good; I'd been fine without a girlfriend for a while now. Sure, there had been times when I thought it might be nice, but then I remembered how badly most of my relationships have ended. I didn't even want a female dog again. Getting into another relationship was only going to cause me problems. And my line of work doesn't really lend itself to a good relationship scenario anyway. It was just better if I didn't think about her or call her.

I think, I don't know. Dang it.

Chapter 13: Doinkin' Doug

I used to have dog that I got as a puppy from a guy I used to work with. She was a great dog and a loyal companion for years. I had been living with a girlfriend for a while and she really loved that dog and actually took better care of her than I did. Well, one day, my girlfriend and I had a little falling out after I sorta kinda lost her mom.

So as I was loading my stuff in my truck, my now ex-girlfriend and my dog were watching me from the front porch. When I was finished, I whistled for the dog to come hop in the truck to leave and she just looked at me and then turned around and walked back into the house. Then, my now ex-girlfriend just shrugged her shoulders, smiled, and followed her into the house and closed the door. Now how do you like that? Betrayed by my own dog! Granted, she might have been getting a little tired of having to abruptly leave whatever place we were residing in from time to time. But that's no excuse; they're supposed to be man's best friend, right?

Okay, I didn't really lose her mom; it was just a little misunderstanding that could have happened to anyone. You see, her mom was flying in to visit for the holidays and my girlfriend asked me if I could pick her up from the airport. Being the nice boyfriend that I am, I said, "Sure, no problem" because she had to work and I was already at the airport because I was working there anyway. Well, I had never met her mom before and so I was working off of a description and a name. She told me that her mom was a little older and slightly senile and she didn't want her driving around and I was to pick her up at arrivals. When I pulled up at arrivals and saw a woman standing out there that matched the description, I got out and introduced myself, put her luggage in the car, and brought her home.

I really liked her mom; we really hit it off and we had a great chat while we were waiting for her daughter to get home. She told me that I looked a lot younger than what she thought and wasn't what she expected. I wasn't really sure what that meant, so I just blew it off.

Later on, my girlfriend came home from work, walked in the door, looked at her mom, and said, "Who's she?"

This was the moment when I was really hoping that maybe Mom had just colored her hair or something and maybe her daughter didn't recognize her for a second.

"This is your mom, honey," I said, smiling.

"No it isn't! Where is my mom?" she replied with a very concerned look on her face.

This is one of those moments where your brain just kind of locks up for a second and all you can do is sit there with a stupid look and blink once or twice. And then the little hamster started walking again on the little wheel that powered my little brain and I started processing the situation. *I picked up the wrong mom? How does that happen? Crap! Now I had just kidnapped somebody!*

"Uh, at the airport still?" It was more of a hopeful question than a statement.

This scene was the equivalent to driving down the road and hitting a patch of black ice. One moment you're in complete control of the vehicle and everything is fine when, suddenly, you're viewing the tail end of the car beside you. You're gripping the steering wheel in an attempt to control the car, but there is none to be had. Outside forces have now taken over and you can only watch as everything around you goes spinning by. All you can do now is wait for the crash.

"Oh my God! You lost my mom?" Now she was yelling.

"It's okay. I'll just return this lady and pick up your mom," I replied as casually as I could. I was trying to make the matter seem like an easy problem to fix.

"This isn't a pair of shoes that you're returning; she's a person!" Now she was yelling louder.

"Do you mean you're not Doug from the online dating service?" It was the imposter mom asking me.

"Huh? Doug? No, I'm Del. Del, not Doug, and I'm not from a dating service," I replied as realization of the situation started oozing over my little brain like warm oatmeal.

"Oh, well it sounds like you're about to be single. Do you want my number?" she asked with a smile. *Oh God. Is she serious*? I just hung my head.

"What? Ah, no thank you, ma'am. I'm good," I replied as I stared at her incredulously.

"Suit yourself. Can I use your phone please?" she asked.

"Well, while you two are getting acquainted, I'm going to the airport to get Mom!" my soon to be ex-girlfriend said as she stomped out of the door. And that was the proverbial crash.

So that was how I lost Mom, my girlfriend, and my dog, all in one day.

Trying to shake that memory and a few others was why I was shaking my head as I watched the taillights of Janelle's car disappear down the road.

Chapter 14: Raggedy Stumblebums

The next morning found me at my usual roost, generator running and having a weird Jesus moment. With the way my life has gone, sometimes I think God just keeps me around to use for experiments, like the fuzzy piece of meatloaf in the back of the office fridge that he takes out to poke with an electrode every now and then.

This happy thought quickly evaporated as soon as I heard the generator shut off, followed by a loud slap on the side of my RV.

"Morning, ball-bag! Pinch it off; we got things to do!" he said, laughing as he walked away. Sigh. *I really need to find better friends.*

The rest of the day saw us running around gathering additional supplies for the plane and then the four of us gave it an intensified service check. We gave the boss a small list of a few more toys that we thought could come in handy like flash-bang and smoke grenades and a portable grill.

Strap kept asking me questions about the woman that I disappeared with the night before. He was convinced we were rolling around under the fishing pier in the sand or something. He couldn't believe that we just walked and talked the whole time. I thought about calling her before we left for Belize, but I was still wrestling with myself about it. I don't know why, though; I should know myself by now. I'd end up calling her because I'm dumb and then I'd screw it all up at some point for the same reason. That's what I do. Alright then, it was all settled. I'd call her tomorrow.

* * *

The next morning, I was up early, taking care of a few things before we left later that day. Evidently, at some point during the night, a very inconsiderate person had the audacity to steal Strap's keys and park his own truck right up against his RV so he couldn't open the door! I just can't believe some of the things that people will do these days. Being the good buddy that I am, though, I decided to let him sleep in.

After running a few errands, I finally called Janelle and she suggested that we could meet for lunch. We met at a little café on Venice Beach and sat outside and watched the unique mix of people that frequent the area.

"How long did you argue with yourself before you finally decided to call me?" she asked, smiling at me. *How does this woman read me so well?* It was a little unnerving in a way and I was not sure if it was a good sign or a bad one.

"Pretty much the whole time since I last saw you," I admitted.

"And what made you decide to do it?" she asked.

"Sucker for a pretty face, glutton for punishment, looking for love in all the wrong places; you pick," I replied.

"I hope you aren't ever planning to be a salesman, Del. You'll starve." She was shaking her head this time.

"Sorry, I try to be realistic," I replied.

"Del, do you expect everything to always work the first time that you try it?" she asked.

"Yes. No. I mean, it would be nice if it did," I admitted.

"But does it?" she insisted.

"No. I know what you're saying," I said.

"No you don't. Stop expecting and just go with it," she said.

"Yes, ma'am." I smiled at her.

"Good. Now come see me when you get back or I'll come find you and your little RV. Remember, I know who you work for, Del," she said.

After lunch, she gave me a big hug and another kiss and told me to be careful, like she knew my job was a little dangerous. She definitely had that women's intuition thing going on, that's for sure. The problem was that I also saw the look. The look is something that I'm all too familiar with because it's the look that women get when they find a stray dog that they think is cute and has the potential for making a nice companion. I'm okay with this because I've been that stray dog all my life, but the problem is that women think that with a little love, patience, a good bath, and a haircut and a shave, they will have something presentable to tow around. They will also be able to feel good because they've done a nice charitable thing by taking in a stray animal and giving it a good home. And it usually works out fine until the dog poops on the proverbial pillow and then the deal is off.

After we parted, I drove to the corporate ramp at LAX and as I was walking through the security checkpoint, I heard a familiar voice.

"Del, why yo got dat big ole duffle bag?"

"Wussup, Huggy? We'll be taking an extended trip this time, so I need some extra lingerie to wear," I said sarcastically.

"Lingerie, huh? I s'pose ah ain't spoda look in it either," he said as he eyed me suspiciously.

"No, sir, you can search all you want. You can even try something on if you like, big sexy," I replied.

"Nah, man, 'fraid you ain't be jokin'. Might not be able to look at you da same no mo'," he said, smiling and waving me off.

"Suit yourself. I'll try and remember to pick you up something sexy this time," I said over my shoulder as I was walking through.

"No you won't," he replied.

When I got to the plane, Tack was the only one that was already there.

"Hey, man, where's your partner in crime?" I asked as I heaved my duffle bag up into the plane.

"He's at the laundromat finishing up; should be here in a few. Where's yours?" he asked.

"Probably using my name in vain and conspiring against me," I said.

"Uh-oh, what did you do now?" he asked.

"Let's just say that I returned a favor by ruining his morning routine," I said, smiling.

"Who was the pretty lady you made friends with the other night?" he asked.

"Her name is Janelle; just came back from having lunch with her," I said.

"Very classy-looking girl. What does she see in you?" he asked, smiling.

"Must have been the faded Led Zeppelin t-shirt and the swarthy unwashed look that I was sporting," I said.

"Yeah, I'm sure that's what it was. Did you show her the rolling man cave?" he asked.

"No, but I told her about it. Says she wants to see it. Go figure, huh? How about you? Saw you talking to a couple of young ladies," I asked.

"Nah, it was like talking to high schoolers. They acted like they've been sniffing too much hairspray," he replied. As we were talking, Strap came strolling up to us but was staring at me the whole time.

"Hey, buddy! How's your day been?" I asked him cheerfully.

"Jackass," was his only reply. Tack shook his head and just laughed.

"I don't even want to know," he said.

"Wait until you move out there with us," I said, smiling.

"Not sure if I want to," he replied.

Sanchez walked up with a big sea-bag over his shoulder.

"Laundry is done, golf clubs are already in the plane, and I'm ready to go! This is going to be a great trip!" he said enthusiastically.

With that, the four of us gave the plane a walk-around, secured all of our gear, and started the engines. Before we even took off, Strap had Gary Clark Jr.'s "Numb" playing on the audio system and was mixing Seven &7s in the galley while I got the cards out.

Chapter 15: Me Love You Long Time

We flew east until we were over Texas and then turned south, stopping for fuel twice along the way. During the planning stages of this trip, it was decided that the small coastal town of Dangriga would be an ideal place to stage for our little operation. It wasn't too big or too small and, with a couple of resorts in the area, there should be enough tourists around to blend in with.

There was a small airstrip on the north end of town that didn't see too much air traffic, which would allow us to fly in and out without too much notice.

We landed and taxied over to a flat grassy area next to a small hangar/terminal. After shutting down, the four of us climbed down to survey the area.

"Let's find a car and a hotel and then come and get our stuff," I suggested.

All in agreement, we locked up the plane and headed off in search of a place to rent a car. We rented an old Toyota van that looked like it had been compiled from five separate vehicles. It was ugly, but it ran, and that was perfect for us. We didn't want to drive around in anything new or flashy; better to keep a low profile.

The guy at the rental car place gave us a couple of hotel suggestions, all of which were the most popular for the tourists. We told him we weren't looking for that type of hotel; we were looking for something a little more off the beaten path.

"Ah, I know just the thing for you. My wife's cousin Gregos runs a place on the outskirts of town. I never recommend it to anyone because it's a dump, but he's cheap and he owes me money," he said.

"Sounds perfect. How do we find it?" asked Strap.

After we got the directions, we drove around a little to get an idea of the town before we found it and he was right; it was a dump. We were staring at a small two-story building with dirty white stucco on the outside with six rooms on the second floor and a little general store on the first. There were only three bathrooms, one located between every two rooms so that you had to share it with whoever was staying in the room next to you. That must have been fun for some people but worked fine for us. We rented four rooms for the week. Even though we knew we were staying longer, we didn't want them knowing that. The guy behind the desk initially gave us the hourly rate for the rooms, which gave us an idea about how the hotel got most of its business.

After going back to the plane to get our stuff, we went in search of a good meal and a beer. Since it was nighttime at this point, we figured we could find a fun place to hang out with the tourist types for a bit. Strap was intent on finding a local girl to make friends with and I got the feeling he was thinking that they all ran around in grass skirts and coconut bras down here.

"Just don't go sleeping around with the whole family this time, knucklehead. We don't need to get chased out of here just yet," I said, slapping him on the shoulder.

"Yeah, well, you try not to get us thrown out of any bars, then, cheesebag!" he replied, slapping me back.

"I'll see what I can do," I said, smiling. I do have a habit of getting us ejected from various establishments. Once, I got us thrown out of the same bar twice in one night. It's a personal record that I'm quite proud of.

We found what appeared to be a little indoor/outdoor bar and grill that had a lively crowd and Caribbean music spilling out onto the beach.

"This looks good!" Sanchez said as he led the way while he eyeballed one of the waitresses. We settled in while we ate and drank and got a feel for the local atmosphere. The people seemed pretty laid back and casual around here, which was good. I hate touristy areas where they want to nickel and dime you everywhere or try to hustle you out of money. I was starting to feel comfortable with the idea that we could lay low in this town and not get hassled.

Over dinner, we decided that we should get a good layout of the town and surrounding area the next day. We stayed and mingled with the crowd and had a few drinks before we returned to the hotel to get a little shut-eye. Instead of going straight to bed, we decided to go for a little stroll, just to see what the other nightlife looked like around the area. There was a seedy-looking little bar a couple of blocks away with a few locals hanging around but other than that, this side of town seemed relatively quiet. After walking around, we returned to the hotel for some much needed sleep. It turned out that our hotel got a little more late night business than we were expecting as it came with all of the telltale sounds of alcohol-induced love that only money can buy.

The next morning, I went downstairs to question Cousin Gregos about this area and his hotel a little more. He said that this just happened to be an area where you could find whatever you wanted for the right price. I got the feeling that maybe this country was popular for all types of vacationers from all over the world, and not just those looking for sun and surf.

Strap and I shared one of the bathrooms and I could hear him in the shower as I walked in. I needed to pee anyway, so I went in and used the toilet and deliberately flushed it so the cold water would temporarily stop and make his shower too hot. Then I stole all of the towels and turned off the lights. Satisfied that I was able to irritate him this morning, I went to go see if Tack and Sanchez were up.

Sanchez opened the door immediately when I knocked and told me that both of them had been up for hours already because of the noise in the hotel. Tack said he had been out walking around the town around dawn because he couldn't sleep. After Strap came out of his room and called me several names, I told them about my conversation with Gregos.

"Well, we can find another place today if y'all want. I'm okay either way," Strap said.

"I'm good for now," Tack agreed. I nodded in agreement.

"Alright, then let's slide outta here, get some breakfast, and check on the plane," Sanchez suggested.

It appeared that the plane wouldn't be bothered if we were away from it for a while. The local airstrip was pretty quiet and we didn't see very many people around. There weren't even any homes close by to speak of; just a lot of forest beyond the runway. As a matter of fact, looking west, all you could see were forest-covered mountains, and east, all you could see was ocean. I am always amazed at how beautiful it is down here in Central America with the tropical forests and crystal clear ocean.

We climbed back in the van after securing the plane and set out for food. We found a little mom and pop joint that looked promising and grabbed some breakfast. Afterwards, we decided to roam around for a while to get to know the town.

"Try to act like a nice tourist out to see the sights instead of a creepy pedophile like you usually do, pinhead," I said as I gave Strap a shove.

"I'll try my best. Don't walk too close to me. I don't want anyone thinking we're a couple, jerkweed," he said, pushing me back.

The town wasn't showing all of the signs of a major tourist town. The streets were narrow and most of them weren't even paved. Many of the homes were on stilts and either plywood with rusted tin roofs, cinderblock, or stucco, or some combination thereof. The locals seemed to be happy small town folk that took pleasure in the simple things life has to offer and it looked to me like fishing and tourists were the primary sources of income. It had all the ingredients for enterprising entrepreneurship, good and bad. The town had the potential for exploding into a major tourist town one day once the global economies got up and running again.

Our little trek through the backstreets of town was fairly uneventful, but the people were very friendly and willing to stop for a conversation when asked for directions. It was a nice change from some cities in the States where people can be the exact opposite sometimes.

I decided that I could get used to living in an area like this, where I could kick back in quiet comfort and simplicity, away from the hustle and bustle of life in the States. I'd almost be willing to trade it for that rockin' shoebox that I call home, something to think about. After a couple of hours of meandering around, we decided to work our way back to the hotel.

"Whaddaya say we go check out that little bar over there for a little refreshment?" Strap suggested, pointing at the seedy little joint we noticed the night before.

Other than the bartender, there were only a few people in the place. It was a typical bar, dimly lit with walls covered in old beer posters, wood floor and barstools, but the bar itself was kind of cool in that it looked like it was made from the wood of

---

an old boat. The four of us slid onto barstools, ordered a round, and struck up a conversation with the bartender.

"Hey, man, where are the best diving spots around here?" Tack asked as we sipped our beer.

"All of them! There is a reef a few hundred yards off the beach that offers some excellent scenery. Are all of you here to do some diving?" the bartender asked.

He had a different accent that I hadn't heard before. It had a little Hispanic and maybe some Jamaican or something. A lot of the people here seemed to have that sort of accent when they spoke English to us, but they spoke something else to each other sometimes. It seemed their local language included a few different varieties.

The beer was going down smoothly because the humidity was picking up, as it is a constant down there so close to the equator. We were approached by a few very young females who tried to get us to buy drinks for them at over-inflated prices in exchange for their company. Being all too familiar with this game, we politely declined.

"Shove off baby-san, we ain't buyin' you a drink," Strap told one of them while shaking his head. Even Strap didn't want any part of this, being the walking hard-on that he usually is. This is the same game you'll find in bars and clubs throughout the world, especially outside of military bases in poorer countries.

The girls work for the bar. They get you to buy them drinks at double or triple the going rate. The bar makes extra money and gives the girl a small percentage. Usually at some point, the girl will then ask you if you want to pay her bar fine. This is an amount of money that you pay the bar to take her home for the night. Or sometimes they'll ask you if you want to pay for a "short-time" or a "long time." A short time can mean a quickie in a room in the back of the bar or the whole evening. A long time can mean a week or maybe as long as you want, depending on what you're willing to pay. There are variations to this, but you get the idea.

In some countries, these girls are underage sex slaves that are forced to do this over and over again throughout the night. These are basically kids being forced to drink with grown men and let them have their way with them afterwards. All too often, these girls are drugged up in order to counter the alcohol and to make them dependent upon whoever owns them. Worse than that, many of them live in deplorable conditions and are beaten if they try to escape or refuse to comply with demands because they are basically prisoners. I was disappointed to see this going on here but not really surprised. We had witnessed it all too often when I was deployed overseas in the Marines. Sometimes local governments turn a blind eye to it because the corruption is so rampant.

We finished our beer and left the bar after deciding that it was time to do the tourist bit and have some fun. There is a barrier reef just a few hundred yards off the coast here that runs for miles, second only to the Great Barrier Reef off of Australia. So with that, we drove to a local dive shop that rented gear and a boat ride out to the reef. Diving in the Caribbean has always been my favorite. I just think that the variety of different species of fish and coral here are the most spectacular and this reef was no exception. The water was clear and warm as we dove along the plant life and brightly colored coral. I found a little octopus that I harassed for a while before he found a hole and disappeared. Large barracuda could be seen hovering in the current, moving just enough to keep themselves in one spot. All varieties of vividly colored and exotic-looking fish call the reef home and there is no shortage of eye-catching splendor.

After the dive, we found ourselves at the same little bar and grill that we were in the previous night. The place seemed to be the primary hotspot for the tourists. We found a couple others earlier in the day, but this one was the favorite, probably because it opened out onto the beach. The food was good, the drinks were tropical, and the staff was very lively and fun. Someone ordered tequila and, after a few shots, the proverbial hair found its way up the dark side of the moon, so to speak, and I started harassing Strap.

"Hey, did Strap tell you guys about his new friend Tonya? If not, I have a video!" I said, grinning at Tack and Sanchez. Strap just hung his head in silence.

"Or was it Tony? I got confused in all the commotion," I said, looking at Strap. I told them the story about her and then showed them the video on my phone. Tack and Sanchez laughed and made all kinds of fun of Strap.

"You said you wouldn't show that video!" he blurted.

"No, I said I wouldn't put it on the internet, ya big yard-ape! Besides, what difference does it make? If she wasn't already a guy, she could have just whipped out the old Strap-on anyway! Bahahahaha!" And then he tackled me while I was sitting in the chair.

"Get off me, you freakin' inbred. I'm not your relative!" I said as I tried to push him off. Tack and Sanchez were laughing as they helped us up and made a few apologies to a concerned-looking staff.

"You two idiots are gonna get us thrown out!" said Tack as he was straightening the chairs back up.

"Tell that to him. He's the one with the poor social skills," I said.

"Well, at least I don't go around humping gumball machines!" Strap replied. I knew that comment wouldn't be long in coming.

"It was mutual consent, and besides, just because it was short, doesn't mean it wasn't a meaningful relationship," I said, smiling as I took another sip of beer.

"Whatever works for you," he said, chuckling.

"You're just hateful because your parents didn't like you," I said as I flipped a bottle cap at him.

"Well, at least I can narrow my parents down to about a dozen people!" he said, throwing it back. He had me on that one.

Tack and Sanchez always get a kick out of this drunken banter and usually just sit back and laugh at us.

The part about Strap's parents is somewhat true. His parents were part of a close-knit group of carneys that traveled quite a bit. According to him, he was never really sure which of them were his actual mother and father because many of them seemed to sleep around with each other. There were several other kids besides him and they were all cared for by all of the adults in the group. We frequently like to rib each other about our unusual childhoods.

After dinner and several, several drinks, the four of us set out on foot back to the hotel. Then the phone rang.

"Uh oh, bad timing," observed Strap as Sanchez answered the call.

"Yeah, boss?" He stood there listening for a moment while swaying back and forth.

"Okay, let me call you right back for the coordinates when I find a pen and paper. Oh, okay, we'll head back to the hotel and pull it up on the lap-top, then." Then he hung up.

"We're going to Honduras," he said with raised eyebrows.

"And we're all too drunk to fly," observed Tack. The four of us stood there looking at each other in the middle of the street, then started laughing.

"Well, aren't we the model employees?" I said sarcastically.

"Oh yeah, we're awesome. Let's get back and get a little shuteye and be at the plane at first light. We're not going to find anything flying around in the dark anyway," Sanchez suggested.

After a few wrong turns, we finally found our way back and crashed in our rooms. Fortunately, the alcohol and the previous night's lack of sleep ensured we slept through the sounds of the hotel's usual late night festivities.

Chapter 16: Goat Roped

The early morning flight south to Honduras was refreshing as the cool air entered the aircraft, a nice break from the humidity. It was going to take us a bit to get acclimated to the region because L.A. doesn't get very humid. The coordinates we were given put us north and east of a village named Guarizama on a mountainside.

We overflew the area a few times to get a look at the surroundings before we landed. It wasn't even an airstrip as it was just a grassy field with a couple of dirt roads and a few trails leading down and away from it. We could see two aircraft, a few small pickup trucks, and about a dozen men standing around. I didn't like the looks of this because anytime there were more people than us, we were at an immediate disadvantage.

Even though the idea was that we were coming there to help them, you just never knew what they might be planning. Keep in mind that we were not dealing with the local church ladies annual fund raiser groups out here; these were drug smugglers.

"Let's get the M4s locked and loaded and make sure we've got plenty of loaded magazines handy," I said to Strap, who was way ahead of me. He was also getting the shotguns out and positioning them for easy access in the plane before we landed. Both of us checked our handguns and put them in pants holsters under our shirts.

I went up to talk to Tack and Sanchez to see what they were thinking.

"This doesn't look promising, but here we go," Tack said. "We're going to land south to north into the wind and that field looks short, so we're going to be hitting the brakes and reverse the props pretty quick, so you guys hang on."

They brought the plane in low and slow and touched down on the very bumpy and grassy field, then taxied over by the other two airplanes. After we shut down, I opened the door as a smiling individual was approaching the plane. I had my hand wrapped around the grip of the .45 in the small of my back as I watched him approach; smiling is a bad sign sometimes. He rattled off something Spanish that I didn't quite understand, but Sanchez answered from behind me as we were climbing out of the plane.

"His name is Esteban." He walked over to him and shook hands as their conversation ensued.

Sanchez motioned us to follow as they started walking off toward the other two planes. Tack made like he was busy inside the aircraft in order to watch our backs and guard the plane. I knew that he would have one of the M4s within easy reach at any given time. Strap and I followed behind acting casually while we surveyed the area and tried to gauge the other guys that were standing around. Most were just smoking and talking in little groups; some had handguns or a rifle on them and some did not. Just as we were approaching a group of about five or six, one of them with an AK47 slung over his shoulder turned and faced me directly and raised his hand up at about face level, giving me the indication to stop.

"Godsmack!" he shouted.

"Huh?" I stopped and looked at him in bewilderment for a second before I realized what he was saying. Then I looked down at the old Godsmack concert t-shirt that I was wearing.

"Yeah! Godsmack!" I said. He wasn't telling me to stop; he wanted to give me a high five!

"Yeah, man! Godsmack! Sully Erna!" he said enthusiastically and the rest of his buddies chimed in and started talking while they gathered around us. Head-bangers on the mountainside in Honduras—sure, why not? Most of them were pretty young, in their teens or early twenties, I would say, with dark complexions and wearing various assortments of clothes and sandals. Some of them spoke broken English, which worked well with our broken Spanish, except Sanchez, who could speak it fluently.

We stood around and smoked and talked with them for a few minutes and we let them check out our plane. Tack saw that everything was cool and had climbed out to join us by then. We finally got back to the subject of their planes, which was what we actually came here to do. I could see that one of them was loaded to the gills with burlap sacks packed with whatever. Coffee, I was sure it was just coffee.

"Hey, Sanchez!" Strap called out. "Ask them what's going on with these planes!" Sanchez turned to some of them and started talking. One guy, whom I assumed was one of the pilots, replied while pointing at the planes.

"He said that one is broken, so then they brought in the other one to take its place, but the engine quit when it landed." We walked over to a Piper Seneca twin-engine airplane that he had been pointing to as the original plane. The left engine cowl was open, so I nosed around the engine while Strap went to poke his head in the cockpit. I couldn't see any obvious damage to the plane, so I turned to Sanchez.

"Ask him what's wrong with it," I suggested. Sanchez was still standing with Esteban, whom I was guessing was the other pilot or the guy in charge of this little rag-tag outfit.

"He says it doesn't fly," he replied.

"Wow. Can you ask him if he can be just a little more vague?" I said as I stood there with my hands in my pockets. He looked at me and spread his hands open and gave me the "what do you want me to do?" look. Then he turned to him and they spoke some more.

"He says it doesn't turn on," he said while shrugging his shoulders. Yep, that was definitely more vague. Careful what you ask for, I guess.

"It ain't got no battery power," Strap yelled from the cockpit.

"Well, that's probably why it won't turn on," I said. "So they called us for a jump? What are we? AAA now? I thought we're supposed to fix damaged planes, not be a roadside service!" I said to no one sarcastically. "This is B.S. I got out of bed early for this?" Now I was venting a little.

"Quit whining and get some tools so we can pull the battery out!" Strap said to me.

"Okay, whatever," I grumbled to myself as I trudged off to our plane. I was starting to get a little grumpy because I didn't get my morning coffee. And this is coffee country down here! Here I was standing on a mountainside in Central America where some of the finest coffee in the world is grown and I was jonesing for a cup of coffee? That just didn't seem right! I thought that maybe I should go see if it really was coffee that they were smuggling in the plane. Fat chance, right? I think we had some instant stuff somewhere in the plane, but I really hate that crap. Then I thought that maybe these guys might have coffee with them. They drink the stuff all the time down here anyway, right?

Okay, maybe I should try to explain myself a little bit. I guess in a way I'm sort of an enigma in that I'm generally just a bum, but there are a couple of exceptions to my general lack of decorum. I'm willing to live in an old used travel trailer in a parking lot, I ride an old Harley, drive an old Chevy pickup, and I wear cheap clothes. But I will spend the money for good beer, good cigars, and really good coffee.

"Hey, do you guys have any coffee?" I asked, looking back at the Godsmack fan club.

"Café?" one of them replied. "Si, we have cafe."

"Why the hell are you asking them if they have coffee? We're not here to form a coffee-of-the-month club, hose-bag! Just get some tools so we can fix this thing!" Strap yelled at me. Of course, Strap is a little different in that I think the only thing he will spend money on is a good blow-up doll.

"Hey shaddup!" I yelled back. "I was just asking a question! And I got yer friggin' tool right here, skippy!" I said as I gripped my crotch.

The guy standing with Sanchez turned and said something to him.

"Oh yeah, this is normal," Sanchez replied to him in Spanish. "They'll probably start wrestling on the ground before the day is over."

We took the battery out and started charging it from a little gas generator that we keep on our plane. We gave the Piper a once over to see if we could see anything obvious that might be wrong with it. It was in rough shape but until we got some power on it, we wouldn't be able see if it had any electrical issues. We decided to have a look at the other plane while the battery was charging. As we were walking, a guy came up to me with a canteen cup full of coffee.

"Really? Awesome, dude! Thanks a lot, I really appreciate this," I said, smiling at him.

"Hey, where's mine?" Strap asked while looking at my cup.

"You don't get any 'cause you were being a big poopyhead!" I told him, but the guy told him he would be right back. I took a sip. And then another. Sweet Mother of Jesus! I couldn't believe how good this coffee was! It was intensely dark and strong (the way it should be), but the flavor was so smooth and full. It was so good, I swear that the clouds parted ever so slightly to allow a faint beam of sunlight shine onto this cup and I think I could almost hear angels singing.

"Holy cow! This stuff is really good! Taste this," I said, handing it to Strap.

"What the heck? We gotta get some of this stuff! Maybe we can bargain with 'em or somethin'," Strap suggested. I nodded my head in agreement. My mood just did a complete one eighty as I was savoring every sip of this heavenly nectar. The guy came back with another cup for Strap and we walked over to Tack and Sanchez to let them try it.

"Wow, this is good stuff!" Tack said, looking intently at the coffee and then he turned to Sanchez.

"Hey, ask him where they got this stuff." Sanchez started talking to Esteban and Esteban responded while pointing down the hill and making a lot of gestures that I didn't understand. But evidently, Sanchez did because he just stood there staring at him without saying anything. Then he slowly shifted his gaze over to us and started laughing.

"This isn't a good sign," I said quietly to Strap, who was now looking at the coffee with a raised eyebrow. The Godsmack crew and the rest of the guys were now standing around with us and laughing too.

When Sanchez finally regained his composure, he wiped his eyes and proceeded to tell us what Esteban had said.

"They get the coffee beans from goat poop!" he said, laughing again.

"What?" I asked incredulously while looking at all the guys standing around who were also drinking coffee. "Get outta here," I said.

"Seriously, the goats eat the coffee berries and then poop out the seeds and then they clean 'em and roast 'em," Sanchez explained. "He said they've made it like this in his village since he can remember." Esteban nodded and the rest of his band of misfits agreed with him. Actually, I had read that some of the best coffee in the world comes from coffee farmers over in Sumatra who do the same thing with the Asian Palm Civet and it is extremely expensive. But I hadn't heard that Central American coffee farmers were doing it with goats.

I took another sip. Goat poop or not, this was really good coffee. I looked over at Strap, who was still looking at the coffee with a raised eyebrow.

"Look at it this way," I said. "At least now you can use the coffee as an excuse for why your breath always smells the way it does." Sanchez translated out loud what I had just said and they started laughing again. For a bunch of drug smugglers, these guys were fun to hang out with.

"How about I eat some beans and take a dump in yer coffee pot?" Strap suggested to me.

"That's not very nice," I said. "Why can't you be polite when we have company over?"

"I'm always polite," he replied. "Except for when I'm not."

"Which is most of the time. Besides, you can't even spell polite much less know how to act like it," I said.

"Are you through with your little coffee break now or are you going putz around and socialize?" he asked.

"Who pooped in your coffee this morning, grumpy?" I asked. I couldn't resist. "And no, I'm having another cup. The caffeine and enjoyment that I get from having a cup of coffee in the morning helps to ensure that I won't shoot you at some point during the day," I said, smiling.

We walked over to the other plane, which was another small twin engine, and walked around it.

"Ask them which engine shut down when he landed!" I yelled back at Sanchez. After a brief discussion, he shouted back.

"He said the right engine propeller hit the ground when he hit a hole on landing and it stopped immediately," Sanchez replied.

"That ain't good. If he bent the shaft, this plane ain't goin' anywhere," Strap observed.

He was right; a sudden engine stoppage as a result of the propeller hitting something usually causes severe damage internally and is no quick fix. Besides, we don't carry replacement props or the parts for a complete engine teardown. In any case, these drug cartels threw planes away like most people do an old pair of socks. Usually, the only reason we even get a call is because they either can't get another plane to take the cargo fast enough or the cargo is worth so much that they don't want to abandon it. Cartels aren't dumb; they lose money all the time when shipments are discovered or lost due to accidents. So if they can save a plane full of cargo worth a lot of money in a relatively short period of time, then it's worth it to them to do so.

"See if it'll turn over. Maybe we'll get lucky," I said. Strap climbed in the plane and, after a minute, gave it a crank. I could hear it trying to engage, but it wouldn't turn over.

"No sense wasting any more time on this thing, then," I said, and we walked back over to the guys hanging out by the other plane.

"That engine is junk, chief," I said. "We can't fix it out here. We'll see if we can get this other one up and runnin' as soon as we get a charge on the battery."

I went and piddled around with the battery while it was charging and put a tester on it. I decided it would need a little longer, so I walked back over to where the other guys were.

"We'll give it a little longer," I said. "So do you guys have any more of that coffee you might want to trade for?" I asked the group of drug smugglers. The irony wasn't lost on anyone because they were chuckling. These guys were transporting either marijuana or cocaine worth hundreds of thousands of dollars and we were trying to negotiate for coffee made from goat excrement.

After several minutes of wheeling and dealing, we traded one used Godsmack concert t-shirt (mine), four boxes of Twinkies (Sanchez's), two bottles of vodka, four bottles of whisky, a pair of combat boots (Tack's), a pair of imitation Ray-Ban sunglasses (Strap's), and a half a dozen *Easy Rider* magazines for eighty lbs. of their finest goat poop coffee beans. I'd say we made out pretty good.

After the battery was charged, we put it back in the plane and it cranked right up and was ready to fly, although after looking at its overall condition, I wouldn't fly in the thing. I wasn't sure where this thing was going and I didn't want to know, but I wouldn't take bets on it making it there. These guys just loaded 'em and flew 'em, Very little attention, if any, was ever given to maintaining the plane; getting the cargo moved was all that mattered.

We loaded up the coffee and the generator, closed the door, and cranked up the plane. I was sitting right seat this time because I needed some takeoff and landing practice. We taxied to the south end of the grassy field to take off to the north into the wind as it was still blowing the grass slightly from that direction. Landing and taking off in remote areas like this can pose an extra challenge as opposed to landing at airports where you have a nice, smooth runway and wind indicators. This field was a little short and sloping down slightly because it was on the side of a mountain and very bumpy with a few holes hidden in the grass. This is the reason why we use a plane such as this because it was designed for such conditions.

Once we were up in the air, I was struck by the serenity that seemed to exude from the lush green mountains and meandering valleys. We kept it low and hopped over the hills and snaked around some mountains and blasted through a few canyons. We had nothing else to do, so I figured why not take the scenic route?

"Are you reliving your Top Gun days over there, Del?" Sanchez quipped. I just shrugged and gave him a big toothy grin.

"I think I should pick up a mad bomber hat and goggles to wear from now on when I sit up here," I replied. "You know, to complete the look."

"Yes, I think you should," Sanchez agreed while giving me a concerned look.

We continued to head in a northeasterly direction toward the coast, and once we reached the ocean, I was going to hang a left and follow the coast back to Dangriga. We cruised at around one thousand feet over the water just off the shore and view was spectacular again. Clear blue Caribbean water meeting a dramatic coastline broken up by a few coastal villages and towns. I could get used to this scene on a regular basis for sure.

The rest of the trip was uneventful as we landed back at Dangriga's very small, single-runway airport and parked the plane where we had before.

"Time for beer and grub, boys!" Tack announced as we all clambered out of the plane. Having voiced everyone's general thoughts, he received no objections as we made our way to what was becoming our usual hang-out for such a need. The beer and grub turned out to be beer, then grub, then beer, beer, beer…well, you get the idea. And that was where we spent the rest of the day, sad but true. The bar closing down was our clue that it was time to go and we found ourselves exactly where we were the night before; drunk and stumbling around, trying to find our way back to the hotel.

Chapter 17: Front toward Enemy

After about two weeks of nothing, I was getting a little bored. Don't get me wrong; we were doing plenty of diving and fishing, and went on a couple of hiking and road trips just to explore a bit. The three of them were determined to teach me how to play golf and they would have probably succeeded if I actually tried and took it a bit more seriously. We took some of the guns out in the woods and did a little target shooting and I was thinking about getting out and doing some hunting real soon.

We even worked on the plane for a couple of days just because there was always something that needed attention and we wanted to prevent any corrosion issues caused by the salt air.

I was getting bored because we weren't getting the action that we were actually down here for and I was wondering if it was worth it. Then again, why did I care? There were plenty of people in the world that would gladly trade places with me if given the chance. We talked about finding another hotel, but we hadn't done anything more than just that, talk. It was not that great, but it wasn't that bad either really, I guess we'd gotten used to it. We checked in with the boss daily to see if he'd heard anything. He still thought we were going to get busy soon and told us to hang loose for a few more weeks.

One development that was a little disturbing was that Tack's boat was broken into, but nothing was stolen. The boss had someone keeping tabs on our RVs and boats for us while we were down here, but Tack and Sanchez were concerned that it wasn't a random break-in but someone that was looking for them. Tack asked the boss if he could make the boat go away because he thought it might be too dangerous to go back to it in case someone was watching it.

"Guess I'm moving in by you two slugs for sure now," Tack observed.

"That ain't necessarily a safer option," Strap replied as he gave him an evil grin.

"Just try not to lower the property values in our neighborhood by living like a backwoods redneck, okay?" I said. "It is a gated community, ya know."

"I'll try not to let you down," Tack said, smiling and shaking his head. I could tell that he was still bothered by the news of the break-in. He was smart enough not to leave anything valuable or anything that could tie him to his previous life. It didn't matter; we all know that our own government has long-reaching arms and endless resources. Tack and Sanchez are still two loose ends that lead back to a very embarrassing scandal involving a presidency and our own military.

This incident had Sanchez on the fence for sure now and he was weighing the idea of doing the same thing.

I felt for these guys because their only crime was following orders and keeping their mouths shut and that wasn't enough of a guarantee to let them live. That colonel died because he wanted answers. Tack and Sanchez were just guilty by association.

Another thought being tossed around was that they could just come back down here and live like they did before. They weren't actually living here in Belize but in Guatemala, but that had its risks as well. It also posed a few logistical problems that our boss probably wouldn't be willing to deal with. For lack of anything better as far as ideas, we just decided to wait and evaluate things a little closer when we got back.

We had gotten to know some of the locals fairly well and they were used to seeing us hanging around by now. I really like it here as there seems to be a complete lack of pretentiousness because everyone comes from the same place and has the same story. There is a commonality that seems to be prevalent among small-town folk in any corner of the globe. This is the way that I see it anyway. I guess what I'm saying is that the American big city arrogance has not found its way into the mindset here and that's what makes it appealing to me.

This little town kind of reminds me of the time I spent in the Philippines in a village north of Olongapo. I had met a girl at a female mixed martial arts match that was held every night at a club on the outskirts of town. It turned out that she was a local martial arts instructor and had trained one of the girls that was fighting that night. I bet her dinner that I could pin her without spilling the beer in my hand and when she accepted the challenge, I pinned her in thumb wrestling. After several hours of alcohol and my goofy entertainment, good judgment on her part did not prevail because she decided to take me home. I say this only because women tend to question their own good judgment after really getting to know me.

She lived in a little community of houses on stilts built out over the water of a small inlet off of Subic Bay. These little shacks weren't more than ten feet away from each other and were connected by two by twelve planks running between them. Try walking across wood planks in the dark after a night of drinking while following a girl that keeps stressing to you not to fall. Her house was just one open room; four walls made of plywood and a rusty tin roof, wood slats for a floor, no drywall or insulation. The kitchen area was along one wall, the sink and counter was just cinder blocks stacked up to waist high with two of them removed from the top to form a sink area. A water hose with a clamp that ran down the wall from the ceiling served as the faucet and the water just drained through the separations between the stacked bricks and through the floor. The bathroom was the ledge outside next to the front door, where a small privacy wall was erected and a plywood bench with a hole cut in the middle. There wasn't any plumbing; just a hole that opened straight down into the water. Now I knew why she warned me not to fall.

None of this really became apparent to me until the next morning when I woke up to the sounds of pigs directly underneath me. I was lying face down with one arm hanging over the side, and as I peered over the edge of the bed, I could see them through the slats in the floor, wallowing around in the water.

I stayed out there with her for a week before I had to go back to base and then I got deployed to Okinawa. I never saw her again after that.

We had been keeping tabs on the news agencies on the internet and there was definitely an increase in drug trafficking incidents as well as cartel-on-cartel violence. More aircraft, boats, and now small submarines were being used to move product north from South and Central America to the U.S. It seemed the boss was right about his suspicions and we were in a good spot for some business. It was kind of like finding a good fishing hole in a lake; all we had to do was wait until they started biting. After a couple more days of waiting around, we finally got another call from the boss.

"Check the email," was all he said and then hung up.

This time, the mission was in El Salvador and I was looking forward to going because we hadn't been there too much in the past. Although I don't know why it really mattered; it's not like we were frequenting the local tourist spots anyway. One remote airstrip looked like any other no matter where we were on the map.

We took off early the next morning again, but this time, I didn't leave without enjoying another excellent cup of goat poop coffee, as we'd so fondly taken to calling it. We hadn't missed a morning without a cup since we had been back from the Honduras mission, as a matter of fact.

Tack and Sanchez were at the controls as we made our way south for the flight. Strap was mixing Bloody Marys to the sounds of Flogging Molly before we even left the ground, while I broke out the cards; no sense breaking tradition. The coordinates looked like they put us in an area close to a river several miles south of the little town of San Isidro. A low pass over the river valley revealed a flat open field that looked like it got used quite a bit as an airstrip.

A plane was parked under some trees and we could see three people standing outside of it. Strap and I made sure we were ready for the unexpected before we landed again as a standard precaution. Because the valley was a little tight for a standard approach, Tack and Sanchez brought the plane in low over the river and then banked it at the last minute before leveling off and touching down.

Once we were down, we taxied over to where the other plane was parked. It looked like a Cessna Conquest II, which is a twin-engine prop. It also looked like they had clipped something with the left wing, as it was obvious that it had been damaged. I opened the door again with one hand gripped around the .45 in the small of my back while the other three waited behind me with their weapons of choice. Tack played tail-end

Charlie and watched our backs again while the rest of us climbed down for the meet and greet.

Again, Sanchez did all of the talking while Strap and I pretended to look over the plane as we surveyed the area. It appeared that there were five of them as two more climbed out of the plane and they weren't acting as casually and friendly like our buddies did in Honduras. These guys looked older and more serious than that bunch and all of them were carrying rifles at the ready. I didn't like the fact that three of them started to circle the Cessna that we were looking at while Sanchez spoke with the other two.

"I don't think these banditos are gonna be interested in joining yer coffee-of-the-month club this time around," Strap observed while watching the three as they were watching us.

"Yep, they're looking at us like they're a little unsure of us right now," I said as I poked at the wing. A good foot or so of the outboard leading edge of the left wing was destroyed and would need to be cut out and completely rebuilt. Just then, Sanchez came walking over with one of the other gentlemen.

"He said that one of these guys hit the plane with a truck when he was turning around to back it up to the plane," Sanchez said.

"Steel vehicles and aluminum planes; the plane loses every time," I quipped while craning my head to get a better look at the underside of the wing. "Probably around eight hours, give or take. You guys could go catch us some lunch in the river while you're waiting if you want."

"Gee, I seem to have forgotten my fishing pole. There's peanut butter in the galley, though. Help yourself," Sanchez replied as he walked back over toward our plane.

Strap and I took tools and equipment off of our plane to get started on the Cessna. One of the three that were guarding the plane and watching us never moved from the plane's entry door.

"Must be proud of what they got in there," remarked Strap as we were walking back.

"Yep, I think they've got some very expensive cargo by the way they're acting," I replied. I think they started to relax a little after they saw that we were really there to fix the plane and weren't interested in what the plane was carrying. The two guys that weren't guarding the plane kept to themselves away from us and out of earshot, but their discussion appeared to be very animated and heated. We brought out our little generator and plugged in some power tools to start cutting away the damaged metal. As Strap was doing that, I walked back over to our plane to speak with Tack and Sanchez.

"What are you guys thinking?" They knew I was referring to our hosts.

"They're nervous about something. The guy I talked to was asking a lot of questions about us like he wasn't given a lot of information as to who to expect," Sanchez replied. As we were talking, the two that had been in deep discussion came walking over toward us and were acting very tense. Sanchez stepped off toward them to see what they wanted and I went back over to help Strap.

After a minute or so, their conversation with Sanchez grew louder and it was obvious Sanchez did not like what they were telling him. Strap and I stopped what we were doing and started walking toward them just as the three that were guarding the Cessna started pulling their rifles up toward their shoulders a little tighter in anticipation of something. Out of the corner of my eye, I saw Tack kneeling just inside the door of our plane with an M4 up to his shoulder. I didn't know what was being said, but everyone's body language suggested that they weren't sharing their favorite chili recipes.

"What's up, man?" I asked as Strap and I approached the three of them. Strap was almost walking backwards as he watched the three around the damaged plane very intently.

"They don't want to wait for us to fix their plane; they want us to fly their cargo," Sanchez replied.

"That ain't happenin'!" I said, voicing one of our major rules while looking at the two standing in front of Sanchez. Just then, one of them started to level his rifle at Sanchez. Oh great, I thought, and I was beginning to think that we might have to go through the whole day without someone pointing a gun at us.

As soon as he started moving his rifle in the direction of his shoulder, my .45 was out and coming up. Sanchez had his Glock up, Strap dropped to one knee and had his .45 up and pointed back toward the three by the Cessna, and Tack had the safety off the M4, covering all of us. And then no one said anything.

This is why I have taken the steps that I have to make sure that Anna gets the letter and the map to my little retirement savings. Because if this goes down, we're going to die out here and no one will ever know what happened or why. We just wouldn't come back one day and that would be it.

Sanchez very calmly started talking to the two in front of him. He had his Glock up in a two-handed grip, pointed directly at the other guy's face while the guy had his rifle pointed directly back at him. Nobody would walk away from this gun battle, except maybe Tack. He was the only one that was partially shielded inside the door and had a pretty good vantage point; the rest of us were completely exposed. Sanchez said something again and both of the guys looked over toward Tack, obviously considering their own likelihood of walking away from this as well. I was standing directly behind Sanchez and slightly to the right with my .45 leveled at the guy standing next to Sanchez. Just then, the guy said something out loud so the other three could hear and he lowered his rifle, the rest of his men following his lead.

Me, Strap, and Sanchez started walking backwards toward our plane with our weapons still at the ready. Once they realized that we were about to leave, the one that seemed to be in charge started talking to Sanchez. By now, we were all back at our own plane and Tack was handing Strap and me each an M4 through the door.

Sanchez spoke to us while still facing toward our hosts.

"He said that they are desperate to get their cargo out of here because we are all in a lot of danger right now. They have enemies close by and are afraid our presence will be discovered soon. He apologizes for trying to take our plane, but he thinks eight hours to fix theirs will be too long."

"Well, we ain't hauling no drugs in our plane. That ain't our gig." Strap voiced what we were already thinking. Hauling drugs in our plane was not an option.

"Well, we have the option of leaving and these guys can just fend for themselves," Tack said.

"Let's vote now. Do we stay and fix it or do we bug out?" Sanchez asked.

"I'm willing to stay to fix it," I said. "If you guys act as our gofers, we can shave off some time."

"I'm good with that," Strap said.

"Tell him we'll stay to help them, but they need to be watching for company instead of us," Tack said. "I'll help them establish a perimeter to give us some better security."

All in agreement, Sanchez laid out our proposal to these guys and made it clear that we would help them if they helped us or we would leave and let them figure it out for themselves. Obviously, they agreed because nobody else was offering anything better. Me, Strap, and Sanchez got to work on the plane while Tack set out with the other guys to position them two hundred to three hundred yards out to watch for anyone approaching.

Some of the little goodies that we keep on board for just such occasions are claymore mines. These are nasty little surprises in the form of an explosive device molded in the shape of an arc and imbedded with steel balls. They're designed as antipersonnel mines that are manually operated and can be mounted on the ground or affixed to a tree or just about anything. They set them out to cover the most likely avenues of approach, like trails and dirt roads with the arc facing out where it says "front toward enemy." Tack grabbed the sniper rifle and positioned himself on a slightly elevated position that allowed him to cover the area. In addition, he pulled out the walkie-talkies so we could all keep in communication.

Strap and I got back to work with new intensity while Sanchez played gofer by running tools back and forth (Gofer – go fer tools). Since we didn't have the luxury of time that we thought we had before, we decided on a different approach. Now we were just going to straighten out the frame and ribs as best as we could, cut away the damaged skin, and just use speed tape in its place. Speed tape is just aluminum tape that can be used as a temporary repair until a more permanent one can be made. I didn't really care if they got it repaired later or not at this point; we were just going to cover the hole and vacate the premises ASAP. We're already pretty loose about being safe while working, but getting shot at doesn't really fall under my idea of safe workplace practices.

Just as we were wrapping up, we could hear the sound of an aircraft approaching in the distance. Just then, Tack came over the radio.

"You guys hear that?" Sanchez acknowledged him and then asked the other guys over the radio if they were expecting any friends by plane. Of course they said "no," which meant we needed to go right now.

"Tack, get back here. We're loading up!" Sanchez told him and then set out to help him get the claymores while Strap and I loaded up our tools. When we were through, I jumped into the cockpit and started the right engine while Strap helped Tack and Sanchez. Just then, a King Air flew low over the field and banked a hard left and dropped his gear like he was trying to land in a hurry.

"Let's go, you guys; I don't like the looks of this!" I yelled back through the cockpit door. I could see that all three were now piling into the plane, so I cranked the left engine. The other five guys were running around their own plane that we had just repaired. They kept watching the King Air as it was landing and it didn't look like they were excited about its arrival.

As far as I was concerned, our job was done and they were on their own. We didn't know who or how many were in the King Air and we weren't going to hang out to find out their intentions either. For all we knew, it could be someone who didn't even care about us or who we were, but something about the way they were in a hurry to land gave me a bad feeling.

Sanchez came up to the cockpit and then I climbed out to let Tack have my place. Those two were much more proficient at the controls, especially if we needed to perform some evasive maneuvers to get away. Sanchez released the parking brake, goosed the throttles, and whipped the plane around just as the King Air was taxiing straight toward us very quickly. Sanchez threw the coals to the fire as soon as he lined up the plane and I almost cartwheeled down the aisle when he did. Strap grabbed my shirt as I went by him and slammed me into a seat.

"Thanks, buddy!" I said as we both tried to see what was going on through the windows, but the props kicked up a dust storm behind us as we raced across the field. Just then, the plane jumped off the ground and yawed to the right. We heard and felt a *thunk* as I saw a tree go by the left wing.

"Sorry!" came a voice from the cockpit.

"Did we just hit a tree?" Strap asked, peering over his shoulder from the other side of the cabin.

"Evidently," I replied as I was trying to see if there was any damage to the wing, but I really couldn't tell. We banked to the right as we gained altitude so we could see the other two planes now as we were coming around and we could watch the drama unfold below us. It looked like the guys we had helped had the plane started and were trying to taxi, but one guy was still out of the plane and running for the door, which was still open. We could see three men spilling out of the King Air and shooting at him and the Cessna.

The guy that was chasing the plane gave up on catching it and dove to the ground and started shooting back at the three that came out of the King Air. We saw two of them drop almost immediately from being shot and a battle ensued between him and the third one. I was cheering for the guy that we had just helped, obviously. He was taking on that other group and kicking butt even though he just lost his ride. We watched the Cessna as it was gaining speed, even though it looked like it sustained several hits from automatic rifle fire. Surprisingly, it kept going across the field and lifted off, although it looked pretty shaky at first. We could watch its progress as we kept our plane in a slow right bank overhead. The pilot of the Cessna kept it low in the valley and followed the river for quite some time. We guessed that this was an effort to throw off the direction of their escape from the King Air, once it took off again.

The third guy from the King Air gave up on the gunfight and ran for the door of the plane, only to get gunned down from behind by the guy we helped. I'm guessing the only people that were left in the King Air was the pilot or pilots because no one else came out to help.

We watched our friend get up from the ground, change magazines out of his rifle, and start walking toward the King Air as he was firing.

"This guy is a bad-ass!" Strap said as we continued to watch from above. Our friend shot out the cockpit windows before he climbed into the entry door, presumably to finish off whoever was still alive in the plane.

"Should we go back and give the guy a ride or something?" I asked Strap, who just shrugged his shoulders. We went up to the cockpit to talk to Tack and Sanchez. All of us agreed that the wise thing to do was to put as much distance between us and this scene as possible. But no one has ever accused us of being wise men. I was okay with at least giving the guy some supplies so he could hike his way out to wherever he wanted to go.

After a brief discussion, we decided to land again to help the guy out, as all of us were impressed with his combat discipline. And besides, we had already helped the guy once by fixing his plane and he helped us by guarding it while we worked.

After we landed, we taxied up close to the King Air; our friend was leaning against the wing and smoking a cigarette with his rifle slung over his shoulder. When we stopped, he flicked away his cigarette and casually strolled over to the door when I opened it.

"Need a ride?" I asked. He looked around, shrugged his shoulders, and climbed aboard. Strap came out of the galley with three cold beers and gave one to him as he sat down.

"Cheers, dude. You earned it," he said as we all took a sip.

"Thanks, man," he replied in perfect English. "It's been a bad day."

"You speak English." I said as more of a statement than a question.

"Never said I didn't," he replied.

"Hey, where are we dropping him off?" Tack yelled from the cockpit as Sanchez throttled up the engines again.

"Where to, chief?" Strap asked.

"Eduardo, but everyone calls me Ed," he replied. "And I don't know because I was just there to guard the shipment and help load it on the plane when it arrived."

"Okay, Ed, where do you call home?" I asked. We were off the ground again and flying in no particular direction while we figured out where we were taking this guy.

"Wherever they're paying is where home is," he said as he took another sip of beer. "I'm out of a job now because of that mess down there. I have people in northern Costa Rica; can you take me there? There is an airfield there that belongs to some old guy that had a crop-dusting service," he said, smiling.

"Costa Rica? That's probably over three hundred miles away," Strap observed.

"Hey, you asked," Ed replied.

"Come on," I said as I motioned him to follow me up to the cockpit. "Tell these guys where you're talking about." As Eduardo explained where this airfield was, Tack pulled out a map and fingered it.

"I know this place," Tack said. "This strip was used a lot when the U.S. was flying guns down to the Contras years ago."

"Is it far?" I asked. I was really kind of asking if it was too far to take this guy. I don't know what I really expected him to say when I asked him if he needed a ride. I was thinking something more or less across town, not two countries away. Relatively speaking, I guess it really wasn't that far.

"Nah, I didn't have anything planned for the rest of the day anyway. Did you? We probably shouldn't mention this to the boss, though. We're not really in the air taxi service," Tack said sarcastically.

Back in the cabin, the three of us grabbed another beer and relaxed.

"Hey, Ed, where did you get your combat skills?" I asked. "We watched that gun fight after we took off and I was impressed by the way you handled yourself."

"El Paso, Texas, where I grew up. We were always getting into shootouts with rival gangs," he said in a matter-of-fact tone. Strap and I just stared at him for a second.

"Wait, you're from Texas? That explains the English. Why the hell are you down here?" Strap asked.

"Me and my homies in El Paso used to move crack for some major players down here. I got a warrant out for my arrest for poppin' some punks tryin' to bust in on our operation, so I came to work for them down here so I could stay out of prison," Ed replied.

"Wow, small world. How long have you been down here?" I asked.

"At least ten years, I think. Let's see, I left when I was seventeen and I'm twenty-eight now. They just use me as muscle to help guard the stuff; that's what I was doing when they hit the plane with the truck. It's not too bad, I guess. I got me a girl down in Costa Rica where we're headed. They just call when they want me and I go wherever they want me to go and then they pay me." He shrugged as he was saying this.

"Sounds kind of like us; we get a call and just go where we're told and get paid," I said and then took another sip.

"So you guys just fly around and fix planes and stuff?" Ed asked Strap and me.

"Yep, we're your neighborhood roadside service for drug runners, gun runners, and for whoever needs a little help without a lot of questions, for the right price, of course," I said, smiling.

"Huh, I didn't know there was such a thing. I take it you guys aren't listed in the yellow pages," he said.

"Nah, they charge too much for a full page ad. We only advertise in public restroom stalls," Strap replied sarcastically.

"You guys looking for any help?" he asked.

"We'll let you know if we have an opening," I replied.

"Thanks for coming for me back there. I wasn't sure where I was going to go and I wasn't going to hang around there to see who showed up next," Ed explained.

"So what was that all about anyway? How did you get there?" I asked.

"We started moving supply out of El Salvador a short time ago, but that region is normally controlled by another cartel, I think. I'm just a hired gun, but I can put two and two together. I think something is going down because we've been real busy lately. Me and those other dudes have been there for almost a month living in the woods in a camp with the people that make the coke. Then we meet one of our planes and load it, but we have to be careful 'cause the other cartel has people watching the airstrips. That's why we were in that field. We would have gotten out of there today if that idiot hadn't hit the plane with the truck."

"So that's why you can't hang around because they probably know where you guys might be camped out now too, right?" I asked.

"Yep. I'll tell them what happened and that we got the plane and coke out of there in time. But we definitely can't use that area anymore for sure," he replied.

All of this made sense and fit right in to what the boss had told us. The problem was that because of this little war, we could get taken out simply because we were in the right place at the wrong time, like today. The four of us were going to have to talk about this and decide if we needed to be better equipped or differently equipped. Maybe come up with a few contingency plans for various scenarios. It was dangerous enough just dealing with these guys while we were trying to help them out, but we needed to stay neutral and not get ourselves caught in the crossfire.

This had never been an issue until today and helping this guy out was more akin to taking sides, which we weren't. It's kind of hard, in that part of me wants to help a guy out that's in a little predicament and I guess that's our nature. But then again, you've got to consider who these people are and what they're doing. They're shipping drugs, which I personally do not condone, but I'm not going to be able to stop it. But if there wasn't a demand, then there wouldn't be a supply, and as far as I'm concerned, drug use is a choice. A choice that just destroys lives, families, and neighborhoods, and I've seen it firsthand. And that's why I will never touch the stuff.

We touched down on a dirt airstrip in a valley that looked more like a farm in eastern Tennessee than in Costa Rica. It was a wide valley with lush green trees and grass and a stream running through it. The airstrip ran east and west in the middle of the valley floor with two large barns and an old house at one end.

As we taxied up close to one of the barns that had the doors open on both ends, a figure appeared from around the corner. We opened the entry door to the plane and I could see that the figure was an older gentleman, probably in his late sixties. He was probably a little over five feet, salt and pepper hair with a bushy mustache to match. His skin reminded me of an old baseball mitt that I used to have, deeply tanned and creased from years in the sun, but his dark brown eyes were sharp and alert. He walked around our plane, rubbing his hand along the skin as he did so, stopping every so often to examine a patch or a repair before he came over to us.

"Hi!" I said a little too enthusiastically.

"You have a tree branch stuck in your wing," he said flatly. His English was heavily accented.

We turned to look at Sanchez. "It just ran out in front of me, I couldn't stop," he said in defense.

"We can fix it," I said to the old timer.

"I know this plane. It was a different color when I saw her last," he said to no one in particular.

"Really, you remember the tail number?" I asked.

"Nope, had a different tail then. It didn't have the turbo-props either; still had the original Wasp radials at the time. But I know this plane, remember the guy that flew it too. Heard he disappeared with it sometime in the eighties," he said, looking at us now that we were all standing there listening to him.

"Huh, interesting. I'm sure this old girl has quite a story to tell," I said while thinking, *Oh crap, this guy knows the boss!* It made perfect sense, though; this plane was used down here quite a bit so it shouldn't surprise me that someone remembered it. Just like when a girl puts on new makeup and changes her hair; if you knew her before, you'll still recognize her.

"Any idea what happened to that guy?" he asked while looking at us intently. I could tell this old timer was no fool and there probably wasn't much that got by him.

"Living a different life now, I'm sure," I replied while looking directly in his eyes. He just nodded and turned to walk away while indicating for us to follow.

"I'm glad. I hope he's done well for himself," he said while walking. We followed him toward the barn where an old AG crop duster was parked and a 1940-something diesel fuel truck was sitting. At the far end of the barn, I could see an old biplane sitting that was covered with tarps.

"What kind of plane you got parked back there?" Tack asked.

"Stearman PT-17," was all he said as he kept walking.

"No kidding? A Stearman? Really? Man, I've always loved those old birds. Does it fly?" Tack asked enthusiastically.

"Sure does." This guy wasn't much of a conversationalist. He stopped and turned and said, "I expect you're needing some fuel. Am I right?" I turned to look at Tack and Sanchez and they both shrugged.

"Not really. We could top off, but we certainly have plenty to get back," Sanchez replied.

"Then what do you need?" he asked, looking at all of us.

"Ah, nothing really. This gentleman needed a ride and so we're just dropping him off," I said, smiling at him. And then we all just sort of stood there in a circle staring at one another.

"You mean you just stopped here to drop this guy off? You don't need fuel. You're not here to make a pick up or anything?" he asked while looking at us as if we all had two heads.

"Ah, yep, I guess so," I said while still smiling. I guess it did sound a little weird when you thought about it.

"What do you guys do when you're not delivering people?" he asked with a raised eyebrow.

"Ah, sir, well, we provide aircraft maintenance to clients in remote locations," Sanchez replied. The guy just nodded while looking at each of us individually. He seemed like he was weighing whether he thought we were full of it or not.

"I've heard of you guys. The guy that used to fly that plane did that too," the old man said knowingly. And suddenly, his whole demeanor changed and he was very relaxed now that he knew who we were.

"And you must work for my biggest customer," he said, looking at Ed. Ed just nodded in response.

"There's a phone in the office if you need to make a call," he said, pointing to a door with a window in the top half off to the side of the barn where a little office had been built. Ed headed off toward the door without saying anything.

"So, ah, do you still operate the crop-dusting service?" Sanchez inquired while pointing to the AG.

"A little, not so much anymore, though. I just sell fuel and service a few planes from time to time," the old guy replied. "Everyone calls me Miguel." The four of us introduced ourselves.

"Mind if I see what you've done to the inside of that old bird?" he asked.

"No, sir, help yourself," Sanchez replied as we all walked back out to the plane to show it off.

We showed him some of the handiwork that we had done in the interior and the modifications to the overall aircraft.

"I can tell you guys have put a lot of thought into this plane. It's perfect for what you do," Miguel said. "I was about to make myself some lunch when you arrived. Would you like to join me?" he asked as he looked at each one of us.

"We wouldn't want to impose on you and your family, sir," Tack replied.

"There is no family; it's just me and it would be nice to have some company. C'mon; follow me over to the house. I've got some pork that I smoked a few days ago that we can slice up," Miguel said as he headed off to the farmhouse. We just kind of shrugged and looked at each other.

"Sure, why not? It's not like we had anything scheduled for the rest of the day anyway," Strap said as we followed him toward the old farmhouse. Ed came trotting up behind us as we were walking.

"Somebody's coming to pick me up later; they're taking me to the villa to explain what happened this morning," he said.

"Villa?" I asked as I turned to look at him.

"That's where Calderon lives. I've only been there twice before, but it's a big estate, heavily guarded. It's about eighty miles south of here," he explained.

"Is this going to be bad for you?" I asked. I wasn't sure how things worked in this type of operation, but I knew these cartels were ruthless.

"No, I'm good. I've been a loyal soldier for them for many years and they trust me. They want the details on the people that showed up and what exactly went wrong. There's a rumor that there's a mole among us that is working for the other cartel. They're trying to find out if today was really an accident or a coincidence or if we were set up," he said.

We all stopped to look at him.

"You mean that plane could have been damaged on purpose so that you guys would be delayed long enough for them to get there?" Sanchez asked.

"Maybe. I'm not sure. There have been several incidences now, so they think that there's a pattern. I'm just a soldier, so I don't know about all that goes on. I just know of a few things that I've heard about," Ed replied.

"This could be real bad for us if that's what's going on. We could definitely get caught in the crossfire if someone is deliberately sabotaging planes so they can get caught," Tack said.

"Man, this ain't cool," Strap said. "Now we really have no idea what to expect when we drop in to help somebody. We could literally be flying into an ambush just because we were there at the wrong time."

Right about now was when I started wondering what Janelle was doing and thinking that it would be nice if we were all back in the lot, just kicking back and relaxing. The last thing I wanted was to get involved with this mess. I'm okay with just fixing the planes and leaving. I really don't feel the need to get mixed up in a drug war. I guess I really can't complain. I could have chosen to become a paper-pusher, stuck in a cubicle on the third floor of some building, working for some random company. Then my biggest concern at work would be worrying about my lunch getting stolen out of the break room refrigerator.

Actually, I think my ideal job would be a deck hand on a charter boat for vacationers on the coast somewhere. That way, I could just work on the boat, help the pale fat guy from Indiana bait his hook while I check out his wife, drink my day's pay away while I tell lies in the marina bar, then get up to do it all over again. Easy enough; no cubicles, no getting shot at, no worries.

"Hey, Buck Rogers, you with us?" Strap asked while snapping his fingers at me.

"Huh? Yep, what's up?" I replied as we were stepping up on the porch of the house.

"Sorry to interrupt your space flight. I asked you if you wanted a beer. I'm going back to the plane to grab some. Or would you rather run around out in the yard and play rocket man for a while?" he asked.

"I might later, but a beer sounds good right now," I replied.

The rest of us followed Miguel into the house and helped him make lunch. He sliced up the pork and served it with leftover rice and plantains and coffee. The house was airy and simple, the furniture was all handmade, and the floors were wood. There were a few pictures of a family, Miguel smiling with a woman and two kids.

"Is this your family, Miguel?" I asked while looking at one of them.

"Yes, but they are gone now," he replied as he went into the kitchen for more coffee. I looked at the other guys and shrugged with an "I have no idea" look on my face.

When he returned, he walked over to the picture that I had been looking at and picked it up.

"This was my wife Dominga, my daughter Onya, and my son Tico. They are now resting in a small graveyard at the other end of the valley, under a stand of trees. Tico, my youngest, would have been twenty-nine next month." He placed the framed picture back in the spot that it had always been in and would always be. He turned and walked back to the table where we had all been sitting and sat down.

"Many years ago, there was much turmoil in this region. Various political parties were trying to gain control of governments and countries. Much larger countries like the U.S. tried to influence who they wanted in place by supplying them with money and arms, like Nicaragua and El Salvador. Other countries were flying guns up to them from South America as well in hopes of helping whoever they wanted in place. Many of those planes would come through here needing fuel and repair. I was paid well for my services and loyalty. But in the end, I was repaid for my services by a death squad sent down from an opposing political group from El Salvador. They made sure that I would no longer help their political enemies by murdering my family right here in this room," Miguel explained.

You could have heard a pin drop. What do you say to a man that tells you that? All of us just stared at him in silence.

Sanchez made the sign of the cross on himself and whispered something I didn't understand. The rest of us mumbled our condolences.

So many senseless deaths and for what? I remember watching the news on TV and hearing about whole villages getting wiped out and thought our government was trying to help. Now when I read about what happened in El Salvador when the government was fighting the FMLN and Nicaragua when the Contras were fighting the Sandinistas, I wonder if our government was partly to blame. I also never thought I would meet someone that was affected by it so directly like I was right now.

"Join me on the porch for an afternoon café and cigar, my friends?" Miguel said as he rose from the table. "Life is too short to sit around and cry like a bunch of old women!" We got up to follow as he went to a wooden box sitting on a table by the door. He opened the box to reveal a dozen or so hand-rolled cigars.

"These are made here in Costa Rica. I buy them at a market not far from here. Please have one," he said while holding the box out to us.

"Thank you, Miguel. You're a very generous host," I said as I took one.

The six of us sat and smoked on the porch in silence for a bit. The air was a little thick with humidity, but there was a nice breeze coming through from the west that kept it tolerable. I think I was finally getting used to the humidity down here.

"You men need to be very careful of what you do down here. Use my life as a lesson to you. This is a turbulent time again, as there are those who want to control this whole region with the drug pipeline. In my day, it was governments that were trying to gain control; now it is the cartels. You can get on the wrong side of one of them very easily for helping their enemy, just like me," he explained.

Miguel was speaking what we had already been thinking and discussing. It was beginning to feel a little weird to me that we came here. It was as if we were meant to meet him for some reason, but everything about today was an accident as far as how we ended up down here. It was becoming a little surreal.

"We were just talking about that earlier because of what happened today," I admitted. "We were going to sit down and figure out some strategies to help protect ourselves."

"Our biggest problem is that when we get sent in, we don't know who we're dealing with. It's the nature of the beast," Tack added.

Miguel listened as the four of us started talking more about it. The ideal situation would be to have someone on the ground scoping the area for us before we arrived, but we didn't have the resources for that. We talked about taking long, slow circles as we gradually spiraled our way into our destination so we could look for potential threats. This would be the extended version of our usual low and slow flyover the area that we do now before we land. Eddy, as we'd started calling him, kept volunteering to be ground security for us whenever we went someplace.

"Gentlemen, if I may make a few suggestions," Miguel said as we were discussing all of this. "Another man on the ground to help defend you while you're working makes more sense than anything else; safety in numbers." We all turned to look at Eddy. The guy was good in a gunfight, we had witnessed that. We had the room on the plane and the extra weight of another man would not be an issue. And he'd been volunteering to help since we met him. Why not?

"While you guys chew on that for a minute, here's something else; I can help you as well," Miguel said. "I can find out who you're dealing with before you get there."

"How's that?" I asked as all five of us turned to look at him squarely. This was the kind of stuff that we'd always needed.

"I still have many friends that use my airfield and services. I can make a phone call to ask if they have a little bird with a broken wing somewhere. If not, then we know whose it isn't and can probably guess whose it is," he said in a matter-of-fact tone. The rest of us just looked at each other for a moment.

"Miguel, we appreciate your offer, but we can't ask you to get involved with this. You've obviously sacrificed enough over the years," Sanchez told him.

"I am an old man now and I have lost all that is important to me," he said while looking at us very seriously. "You boys remind me of myself once upon a time. I can help to keep you from making the same mistakes that I have." Then he turned away and gazed off into the distance while he took a long draw from his cigar. I'm not sure why but that pretty much ended the discussion. No one else had anything to say because we just looked at each other and smoked, each to his own thoughts.

After the cigars, Strap and I went to look over the wing where we had hit the tree. Miguel was right; there was a small tree branch that was crammed through the skin where it had punctured the leading edge.

"We can speed tape this until we get a chance work on it back in Belize," Strap said. "It's getting a little late to start monkeyin' around with it now."

"Sounds good. I'll get a roll," I said as I walked around to get some out of the plane. When I came out, Tack and Sanchez were walking over to the wing where we were working.

"How's it look?" Tack asked as they walked up.

"It looks like somebody is trying to get into the tree trimming business, that's what it looks like!" I said very sarcastically as I gave Sanchez a light punch on the arm. He just shrugged and gave us a big grin.

"It's fine. We're just gonna tape it up for now and do a repair tomorrow in Belize," Strap replied. "What do you guys think of Yoda back there? Should we tie in with 'em and let him help us?"

"Yoda? That's what you're gonna call the dude? Why can't you have a little respect, meathead?" I said to him.

"Actually, he kind of reminds me of Yoda too," Sanchez said.

"Fuel your airplane, I can," Tack said in his best Yoda imitation. I had to laugh. They were right; he was short and older and did have a little bit of a Yoda quality about him.

"Y'all aren't right, you know that?" I said, still laughing. "The guy invites us into his house, feeds us lunch, offers to help us out, and you want to make fun of him. I'm ashamed to be associated with all three of you!" I said in the most admonishing tone that I could muster. It didn't work because I couldn't keep a straight face.

"Full of it, you are. Yes, hmmm?" Tack imitated again.

Chapter 18: Never Trust a Fart

After the wing was taped, we told Miguel that we would have to confer with the boss about his proposition when we got back to Belize.

"This is a better place to operate out of than where you are now," Miguel said. "It is more secure and I could use the help and the company around here." Then he just turned and walked into the barn with a backwards wave. "Until we meet again, my friends. Be well," he said.

"This guy doesn't leave you a lot of options to discuss things much, does he?" I said while we watched him leave.

"Not really, no," Tack agreed.

"Did he just offer to let us live here for a while?" Strap asked.

"I think so," Sanchez replied.

Just then, Eddy came walking up to us.

"Miguel offered to teach me some stuff about planes if I wanted to work for him around here in exchange for room and board," he said.

"No kidding? That doesn't sound like a bad gig, dude. Gotta have a better retirement plan than the job you're working now," I said.

"Yeah, man, and it would make the girlfriend happy. She doesn't like that I'm gone a lot," Eddy replied.

"Most girlfriends don't. I think you should do it. We'll be back in a couple of days and talk more about using you for security," Sanchez told him.

"Sounds good, man. I'll be here. Thanks again for coming back for me out there today," Eddy replied.

"You're welcome, sir. Glad we could help," Sanchez replied. The four of us shook hands with him and turned to climb into the plane. As we were taxiing, we saw two large SUVs approaching the airfield on a dirt road from the southeast. They stopped next to Eddy and he climbed in before they turned and drove away.

The flight back to Dangriga was uneventful and we landed with a couple hours of sun left. We sent the boss a semi-coded e-mail to let him know what was up: ...>Sit-rep - Green Manilishi found old crop-duster friend. Offers airfield as new base camp and intel support. Do you concur? Developing situation may require additional operator for security. Have prospect. Do you concur?<...

While we waited for the boss to reply, we decided to grab some beers at our favorite beachside watering hole.

"What do you guys think about staging down there with Yoda?" Sanchez asked while we were waiting for our drinks to arrive.

"Assuming the boss is cool with it, I'm ready for a change of scenery," I said, looking at the other three.

"I'm good with it, especially if he can provide us with some intelligence on what we might be flying into in the future," Tack said next.

"I'm still a little leery because we really don't know much about this cat," Strap said next. "If he's cool, then I think this could be a good gig for us, but I don't want to get too comfortable too fast."

"Okay, game plan. If the boss gives the okay, we fly down after we fix the wing and then play it day by day. Anybody gets an uneasy feeling about things, we bug out," Sanchez said while looking at us as we all nodded in agreement.

"You want to play it the same way with Eddy?" I asked.

"I think we should bring him in slow as well, make sure he's really got our backs," Strap replied.

"I get the feeling he's been looking for a change in life; maybe he's grown out of his gang-banger mentality and the reality of his lifestyle has been sinking in," I said.

"I got that feeling too. He can't go home and he's stuck down here and I'll bet that has worn on him a bit," Tack interjected.

After several drinks and dinner, we made it back to our favorite hotel for a good night's sleep. I wasn't going to miss this place if we did get a chance to vacate; the hotel part, I mean. Some nights, the sounds of romance just got a little too…romantic, I guess you could say. Strap, on the other hand, would probably miss this place as I'm sure some of those sounds of romance were probably coming from his room.

I had a hard time sleeping because I kept thinking about everything that went on that day. Some days just take a really weird turn in ways that you could have never predicted. I was still marveling at how we found Miguel down there, even though it happened by chance, I was convinced that we were supposed to meet him. There were no red flags going off or that little voice in my head warning me about any of it. I have learned to trust that little voice back there over the years and that voice was telling me that we needed to get back down there sooner than later.

Sometimes you will meet someone and everything on the surface will seem normal about them. But sometimes there is something, just something that is there that you can't quite put your finger on. That is that extra little sense that warns us. Call it a sixth sense or intuition or instinct or whatever you want but don't ignore it. It's there to keep you safe and alive and I firmly believe that when you're doing something that you shouldn't, you'll get a warning to stop. That warning will come in various forms, but there will be something that will happen that will tell you that disaster is looming if you don't change what you're doing.

I was getting the opposite from my extra little sense right now; it was screaming at me to get back there. I wanted to go wake the other guys right now and say, "We gotta go!" but they'd probably just look at me weird and call me names and I get that enough as it is.

The next morning, we met at our usual table on the little veranda on the side of the hotel. Strap was the last one down.

"Glad you could make it, sunshine," I said to him as he pulled up a chair. He just mumbled something unintelligible, but I think he suggested something rather rude to me.

"Was that a goat I heard in your room last night?" I asked. "I had trouble falling asleep because of the weird noises coming out of there." Tack and Sanchez chimed in to harass him a little also as Strap just ignored us and reached for the carafe of our favorite goat coffee. I had already a made a pot as I'm sure that I was the first one up. I finally fell asleep for a few hours after lying there for what seemed like half the night. Sanchez brought his laptop down with him to pull up e-mails while we sat. The boss had responded sometime during the night and his response was even briefer than our own.

….>Crop duster is trusted ally. Base camp and security your call<… was all it read.

"That's what I love about that guy; everything is short, sweet, and brief!" Strap said as he poured another cup for himself.

"I'm ready to blaze outta here as soon as we fix the plane," I said a little too enthusiastically.

"You know, I was up thinking about this a little last night and I think this will be good," Sanchez said next.

"Really? I was too. Yesterday was a little weird for me," I replied. Tack and Strap both nodded in agreement with us.

"Awright then, let's grab our crap and beat feet to the plane when we're through here. Me and Del will repair the wing while you guys get everything ready," Strap said to all of us. I was relieved; everyone was on board and felt the way I did, and I was really itching to roll now. I'm sure the five cups of coffee that I'd already had since I'd been up had nothing to do with it.

We piled in the van after we grabbed our stuff and checked out and set off to the airfield again. Strap and I took our time doing the sheet-metal repair on the leading edge of the wing where the tree branch had gone through. While we were working on the plane, Tack and Sanchez went and got us some breakfast and then loaded all of our stuff on board and then fueled it. The four of us sat and talked more about Miguel and Eddy and relocating down to Costa Rica and the situation that unfolded in El Salvador. We were satisfied with how we handled things and the decisions that we had to make on the fly. It's good to be able to talk about what each one of us was thinking and relay our thought processes to each other. This helps a team become more in tune with one another because it will help you know what the other guy will be thinking in a given situation.

With the wing repaired and plane fueled and loaded, we lifted off and said goodbye to Belize with Strap mixing drinks to Ronnie Montrose and Sammy Hagar cranking out "Bad Motor Scooter" on the surround system. And just as the wheels came up into the wheel-wells, we got a call from the boss and Strap answered the phone.

"Yeah," Strap said.

"Check the e-mail," was all he said and hung up.

Strap yelled up to the cockpit, "Hey, Sanchez, where's the laptop? We got something from the boss." We pulled up the e-mail and it had the coordinates for Honduras again but a different location than before. As Tack and Sanchez set a new course, Strap and I got busy in the cabin.

"Okay, kids, Disney World's gotta wait. We have work to do," I said.

"Hey, maybe you can start a chicken poop breakfast muffin club this time, butthead," Strap said to me as he was pulling the rifles out of their compartments. That made me chuckle a little bit.

"You complaining about the coffee?" I asked.

"Nope, no complaints here. I'm just looking forward to watching more of your famous international diplomacy skills," he replied.

"International diplomacy skills? Wow, those are some big words. I hope you didn't hurt yourself getting those out, peckerwood," I said.

As we got close to the location that we were given, we could see a low, grassy plateau bordered by trees and scrub on the north and east sides. There was just one winding dirt road that led up to the top of the plateau from the valley on the north end. We did a slow circle of the area, flying low around the plateau. We could tell that there was a Cessna 182 up under the trees, but we couldn't see any vehicles or people around it. Then we dropped down into the valley and flew along that for a bit, just to see what the neighborhood looked like. We couldn't see any activity in the valley at all; no vehicles or even a village close by. The plateau was probably a good mile and a half long and almost as wide, so there was plenty of room to land and take off. Actually, it was about perfect for an airfield because the elevation was at least three to four hundred feet above the valley floor. It looked as if someone just took a giant knife and cut the top of the hill off.

With everyone satisfied that the area looked cool, we circled back around to land from the south. Strap and I each had an M4 in our hands with a full magazine inserted and a round chambered; I guess we were both being a little more careful now. When we landed, Sanchez and Tack taxied the plane to within fifty yards of the Cessna and whipped the plane around before they stopped so it was already facing away for an immediate take-off.

When I opened the door, I was immediately greeted by no one, nothing, zip, zippo, nada, and that's bad. Strap placed his hand on my shoulder, giving me the go-ahead and that he was on my six. I climbed out of the plane and crouched with the rifle at my shoulder, looking for activity. Seeing nothing, Strap and I moved as one to the back of our plane so we could get a good look at the tree line where the Cessna was parked. Tack and Sanchez stayed in the plane, one in the cockpit ready to start things up while the other was ready to jump out with an M4 to come help us if we needed it.

Strap and I quickly moved across the open ground between our plane and the Cessna and stopped at the wing and crouched, looking and listening. I could see a guy leaning back with his hat pulled down over his eyes in the cockpit of the Cessna but no movement; I don't know how that guy could have slept through the noise of our arrival, though. Strap and I crept around to the front of the plane to get a better look inside and I could see cardboard boxes stacked in the back of the plane. As I approached the left side of the plane closest to where the pilot was sitting, alarm bells were clanging loudly in my head and that little voice was telling me to run, but I just froze. I looked at Strap, who shook his head, telling me that he knew something wasn't right either. I slowly started to peer inside the plane when BRAAAAAP! I was startled by the sound of a giant fart right behind me!

"Really?" I whispered.

"That's gonna stink too," he said as he was smiling at me.

"Give a guy a little warning, will ya?" I whispered. "And what the hell did you eat?"

"Just shaddup and check the plane," he whispered back.

"I think you need to check your underwear," I said.

I slowly peered inside the plane again to see if there was anyone else in there that may have been hiding but saw no one. Strap moved slowly and cautiously to the opposite side of the cockpit. After he looked in from his side, he gave me a nod. Very lightly, I tapped on the window next to the sleeping pilot so I wouldn't scare the living Bejesus out of him, but he didn't move. I tapped a little harder and then I reached out to open the door when Strap told me to freeze in a loud whisper. He was looking through the window from his side and motioned for me to come around. When I came around next to him, he pointed to the floor of the plane by the pilot's feet where we could see blood and what looked like a wire with one end twist-tied to the door handle and the other to the safety ring of a grenade wedged under the seat.

I pointed my index finger up and twirled it high in the air to give Tack and Sanchez the signal to start the engines. Immediately, an engine turned over as Strap and I backed away from the plane very slowly while watching the tree line and for any other surprises. The second engine started turning as we climbed back into the plane and closed the door. Tack and Sanchez were both in the cockpit and Tack was looking over his shoulder at us to make sure we were on board when Strap signaled for them to go now. Tack shoved the throttles full forward just as Strap and I got seated before we got tossed backward.

Strap went up to tell Tack and Sanchez what we had found after we were off the ground; I just sat there fuming at what had almost happened to us.

That was definitely meant for us, which meant we were being targeted, which was bad. When a drug cartel decides to make you a target, it's a little worse than them just taking you off of their Christmas list. Strap came back with a couple of beers and handed one to me as he sat down.

"Thanks for keeping me from blowing us up back there, man," I said as we toasted each other.

"Well, you are my favorite hemorrhoid, ya know. I ain't ready to put the boot heel to ya just yet, ole buddy!" he said, smiling as he took a sip.

"Thanks, I think. Are we headed to Yoda's place?" Now I was calling him that.

"Yep, and we're gonna need to figure out what the hell that was all about and whether or not that was meant for us!" Strap said pointedly.

"Oh, I already know that. I think we pissed somebody off yesterday, but who? Could someone have been watching what happened yesterday that we didn't see?" I asked while thinking out loud.

"That's what I'm thinking. Maybe Eddy can shed some light on that," Strap said. This is why we have always made it a point to keep things neutral, but going back to pick up Eddy showed that we had taken a side. That was the only thing that I could think of that would have given that impression. Maybe Yoda could make some inquiries and see what was going down.

The rest of the flight was spent by each man deep in his own thoughts; no music, no card game, and no alcohol other than that first beer. We could have burned our bridges down here yesterday and our little operation could be drying up right now. Time would tell, obviously, but we were not going to able to operate as we had been if one cartel was after us because they thought we were helping another one. We're not equipped for running gun battles every time we go somewhere to fix a plane. All of our weaponry is just for defending ourselves so we can get out of a bad situation if necessary. We were going to have to let the boss know what happened and hopefully he could set things straight from his end. This might be the "writing on the wall" for us, which could mean a career change or we'd just have to operate in another part of the world for a while. I hate to think that way because I like what we do, but we also have to be realistic about the possibilities and the ramifications of our own decisions.

Chapter 19: Barn Rats

When we landed back at Miguel's place back down in Costa Rica, we could see that Miguel had pulled the old Stearman out of the barn and was working on the engine. He came walking over toward us as we taxied to a stop next to the barn where we parked yesterday.

"Good afternoon, my friends; good to see you again," he said to us as we opened the door and climbed out. We all shook hands with him again.

"Do you have room at the inn for four wayward souls?" Sanchez asked.

Miguel just smiled and nodded as he looked at each of us.

"Of course. I've been expecting you. But something tells me that you are troubled; something has happened?" he asked.

He led us to the house, where he made coffee, and we sat on the covered front porch and told him about what happened this morning.

"That is disturbing, but that doesn't mean it was meant for you," Miguel said after he thought for a moment.

"Why doesn't it? We got the call this morning, so it looks like that plane was booby trapped for us," Strap said.

"It could have been a legitimate call, but maybe the people were attacked by a rival cartel while waiting for you and the booby trap was meant for any associates that might show up to get the plane. It could be that the attackers didn't know that you guys had been called and were on the way," Miguel explained.

The four us just sat and looked at him as we contemplated that possible scenario. Master Yoda had given his students something to ponder.

"That would be good for us if that were the case. I would rather that than us being the ones that were targeted," Sanchez said after a moment.

"We must still be cautious either way. I am going into town today and I will make some quiet inquiries. In the meantime, I will show you where you can bunk and then we can make some lunch before you help me pull a couple of jugs off the Stearman," Miguel said as he got up.

"This should be fun. I haven't pulled the jugs on a radial since A&P School!" I said as we stepped off the porch and followed him to the barn.

"Are we sleeping in the barn?" Strap asked as we were walking.

"Evidently, he must have heard about your propensity for courting farm animals," I replied. Tack and Sanchez started chuckling when Miguel turned to give Strap a strange look. On the opposite side of the barn from the office, there was another little rectangular building that was built inside the barn similar to the office except twice as long. We were surprised when we entered to find that there were four separate rooms and a separate full-sized bathroom with running water, electricity, and everything. The amenities were sparse, though, with wood plank floors, simply made wood furniture and beds, but it was perfect for us.

"I have well water here and there is a septic tank. Please make yourselves at home, gentlemen," Miguel said as he showed us around.

"How much do you want for rent and food and stuff, Miguel?" Tack asked when we walked back outside.

"Nothing. I have a vegetable garden that needs tending to from time to time. I have chickens, cows, and pigs, and I get a few things from the local market. You help me around the farm and work on the planes and that is your rent and food," he replied while looking at us. The four of us just looked at each other and back at him and nodded.

"I'm good with that," I replied. "At least we shouldn't get bored."

After lunch, which was plantains, shredded pork with rice, and coffee, we each picked a room and settled in to make ourselves comfortable. Strap and I got our tools and started helping Miguel pull the jugs off the Stearman.

"Why are you pulling these, Miguel?" I asked as we were working.

"Plugs are fouling real bad and I'm losing power," he replied.

"Sounds like a good reason to me," I said. I was thankful for the work and the distraction. It was peaceful out here and far away from the noise and congestion of L.A. Belize is fun, but after a while, there was a little too much free time, if that makes any sense. Here, there will always be things to do that weren't necessarily recreation but still fun and also productive. I could really get into living like this; part farm life, part aviation. I was beginning to hope that this could work out for us in the long run. We sent an e-mail to the boss giving him an update on our situation and what we came across this morning and asked him to make some inquiries as to what that was all about.

Later that day, Miguel went into town for a couple of hours to get some rice, flour, sugar, and a few other things. He also found a trusted friend and asked him if he could find out some things for us. It would be a couple of days before we heard back, Miguel told us. It didn't really matter because the next three days were quiet around the farm. The boss hadn't replied to the e-mail that we had sent nor did we get any messages to go on any missions either. It might have been because he didn't want to send us on any until he found out something also. Either way, I was having fun and enjoying the new surroundings.

We took turns learning to milk a cow and collect chicken eggs and pick vegetables. Miguel insisted on doing all the cooking, which was fine with us because he was a fine cook. Every morning was eggs, bacon, and coffee, which I was really enjoying. We got him to try our coffee, which he was reluctant to do at first, but he finally agreed that it was really good and possibly even better than his.

Tack accidentally called him Yoda one day and Miguel asked him who Yoda was. After describing the *Star Wars* character, which Miguel had never seen, along with Tack doing his best Yoda impression, Miguel laughed and said he liked the nickname.

We got the Stearman back together and Miguel took it up while the rest of us watched him. After a while, he landed and taxied over to us and yelled, "Who's first?" We all took turns riding in the Stearman with him, which was just a blast and a half as far as I'm concerned!

We had been there about a week and Miguel had since gone back into town to talk to his friend. There was no talk about us being targeted or anything relating us to the incident when we met Eddy. Maybe Miguel was right after all and that little booby trap wasn't meant for us, which was very good. But that didn't mean that we couldn't be any less careful because grenades and bullets don't care who they hit. The boss finally replied to our email and it was basically the same news; there was no talk about us being a target. These two bits of information relieved the tension that had been growing between my shoulders and I could sense a noticeable air of relaxation coming from the other guys.

One afternoon, Eddy suddenly showed up with a big smile on his face and a pregnant lady by his side.

"Guys, this is Elaina. Elaina, this is Miguel who owns this place and Del, Strap, Tack, and Sanchez, the guys that came back for me the other day," he said. She came up to each one of us and gave us a hug and expressed her gratitude for helping him. She was from Costa Rica, in her mid-twenties with long dark hair and very pretty. She was also very pleasant to be around and very pregnant; seven months, according to her.

"My dear, let me show you to the house where we can get you to a chair so you can get off your feet," Miguel told her as he led her off to the house, leaving the other five us just standing there.

"Wow, we didn't know your girlfriend was pregnant. Congrats," Tack said as he shook his hand and then the rest of us took turns welcoming him back as well.

"Thanks, man. So you guys are here now? All moved in and everything?" Eddy asked.

"Heck, yeah! We've been learning how to live on a farm all week. You'll get to learn how to milk the cow and shovel pig shit tomorrow, buddy!" I said, slapping him on the shoulder.

"Yay, sounds fun," he said as we helped him carry the few belongings that they had packed in their little car.

"How did things go with your boss last week after they came to pick you up?" Sanchez asked as we were walking.

"Fine, I guess. I told them the whole story and what you guys did. The other guys that I was with that got away in the plane told them the same story, but they didn't know that you guys came back to get me. They just nodded and told me that I had done well and gave me a nice little cash bonus. I told them that Miguel offered work for me and that I would like to come here to live. Because they know him and use his airfield frequently, they said that they know where to find me if they need me," Eddy explained.

"So does that mean they won't let you leave?" Tack asked.

"You don't just quit working for the cartel. If they don't want you around anymore, then they just kill you. If you try to disappear, then they'll assume that you're a threat to their operation and will hunt you down and kill you. This way works because they can keep an eye on me and still use me if they need to, but because I'm working for someone that they use frequently, they're not worried about what I'll be doing and where I am," he replied. "Over time, they will use me less and less and just forget about me. This is only possible because I have been loyal to them for so many years and they have trusted me enough to help guard some of their major players in the past," he explained.

"So everything will be good, then?" I asked.

"Everything will be good. Now what about that extra security guy that you guys need?" he asked enthusiastically with a big grin on his face.

"You're in, kid; we'll use you as we need you, but you may want to rethink this after we tell you about our latest little adventure," Sanchez replied. We told him about the booby-trapped plane and what we had assumed initially.

"That's not good," Eddy said. "These guys like to leave little surprises for anyone intruding on their operation. And we still can't assume that it wasn't left for you guys just because no one is talking." He was right, of course; we were just going to have to suck it up and treat every situation like we were a possible target.

"Well, thanks for brightening the day, Eddy," I said sarcastically as we walked.

"Sure, anything I can do to help," he said, smiling. I began to think Eddy was going to fit in just fine.

It became very clear over the next few days that Miguel was going to pamper Elaina and dote on her and the rest of us were going to be treated like the redheaded step-kids. It wasn't really that bad, but you could see Miguel was missing his family and was itching to play Grandpa. Eddy and Elaina stayed in the house and Miguel made every effort to make them feel at home. He wouldn't let her do very much work around the place, even though she tried very hard to show her appreciation. The rest of us fell into a pretty good routine around the farm and helped Miguel fix up a few areas that he hadn't been able to get to with him being the only one living here for quite some time. Miguel insisted that we sit and eat all the meals as a family, which was actually quite nice for a change, and the evening meals were always delicious and the conversation lively.

Elaina turned out be quite a cook herself and she was slowly moving Miguel out of his kitchen duties. It was nice having her around as she kind of rounded out the group by adding the female element.

Late one evening as we were sitting on the front porch having cigars, a message came through from the boss, another mission. The coordinates put us in Nicaragua this time and so we decided to get some sleep and so we were wheels up at first light.

"Are you up for going with us, Eddy?" Sanchez asked.

"Absolutely!" he replied very enthusiastically. We had given Eddy a quick and dirty on the Green Manilishi and showed him where we kept everything and went over the operation on a few of our toys just to make sure. We talked about how we operated, our procedures, our dos and don'ts, etc. We also told him that we would start teaching him some aircraft maintenance as well along with what Miguel would be teaching him.

In time, Miguel said he would teach him how to fly by starting him out on the Stearman and then we could work him up to learning to fly the C-47. This way, Eddy could have some real skills to use to give him more options in the future, but that would be down the road a bit.

The next morning, Miguel had made a call to one of his connections to see what they knew about the plane that we were about to go repair. Elaina was up and had already made us a nice breakfast and had made ham sandwiches for us to take along.

"How did a slug like you come across a nice girl like that, Eddy?" Strap asked him playfully over breakfast.

"I have no idea, man; my life has been full of lucky breaks, though," he said sincerely. Miguel came out and told us that this mission was legit as far as he could determine from his contact.

Strap and Tack started the left engine just as the sun was peaking over the hill while Sanchez, Eddy, and I broke out the cards with Edgar Winter cranking out "Frankenstein" on the surround sound. The flight to Nicaragua was relatively short from where we were in Costa Rica because the coordinates put us in a low-lying valley area called Bratera by the river Rio Grande de Matagalpa. A low and slow fly over the area told us that it was fairly remote with one small village a couple of miles upstream.

In a wide open grassy area on the west side of the river, we could see a twin-engine Aero Commander parked and several small boats pulled up on the shore with about a dozen or so people milling about. The length of the area was probably about a quarter of a mile long but only about two hundred yards wide before the terrain rose up to a hill. We snaked through the river canyon in both directions to scope out the area real well before we lined up for an approach from the southeast. When we approached the area, Eddy started pulling out M4s and handed one to me and one to Sanchez. I checked my trusty .45 that I keep in my waistband holster in the small of my back. We touched down on the grassy field by the water and taxied over close to the Aero Commander and positioned it for a quick take-off. I opened the door and stepped out with Eddy right behind me followed by Sanchez. I walked around toward the Aero Commander and stopped and stood there staring at it. It took me a minute to figure out why it was sitting kind of lopsided, and then I realized that the plane was resting on the bottom of the fuselage instead of the landing gear. Strap came walking up and stopped next to me while I was staring at the plane.

"What the hell?" was his only comment.

"The gear sank into the grass; it's sitting on the belly," I said.

"They called us here for that? Buncha morons!" he said. I started chuckling; this day was gonna be fun because Strap was already venting as we walked over to the plane. Sanchez was talking to some people that had been standing around it. None of them looked threatening in any way and I didn't even see any guns that were readily visible. I looked back at Eddy, who was just leaning up against our plane. He just smiled and shrugged at me as he shook out a cigarette.

Aero Commanders sit pretty low to the ground already and it was obvious that this big grassy field was relatively soft, being so close to the river. So the plane was probably fine when it landed but began to sink a little because of all the weight that these people were loading in the plane. I glanced back at the Green Manilishi to see if the main gear had started to sink yet. It didn't look like it, and besides, we weren't going to load it up with a bunch of weight either, so I figured that we would be fine.

Strap and I walked around the plane, and with what information Sanchez relayed to us, we figured out that they were going to have to unload their plane if they wanted it out.

"Tell these guys that they'll have to unload this thing and find another place to land and load it because if we pull him out, he'll just sink right back down again if they try to load it," I said to Sanchez.

"How are we going to get this thing out?" he asked while surveying the area.

"Hooking a wench to a tree would work great if we had a tree and a wench," I said. "But I think if we pound that five-foot crowbar that we have into the ground out in front of the plane about thirty feet, then we can tie some rope and a come-a-long to it and get all those people behind the landing gear to push, we just might get it." Strap and Sanchez looked at the plane and pondered the idea. Strap just started grumbling as he walked off to our plane to get what we needed.

"I can't believe this crap. What are we? AAA? Buncha morons couldn't figure this out for themselves? We oughta tell the boss to charge these idiots double for this one," he said. Sanchez just smiled and shook his head as he walked off to tell the people to stop loading the plane and start unloading it.

"He's starting to sound like you," he said as he looked back at me. I guess that meant we were going with my idea. I followed Strap over to get what we needed and explained to Eddy and Tack what the plan was.

"This is what you guys do?" Eddy asked as he grabbed some rope and followed me over to the forward landing gear of the Aero Commander.

"Not ideally, but we do seem to get called for something kinda dumb every once in a while. But I guess if they're willing to pay whatever the boss charges them for us to help them, then I guess it doesn't really matter what we do," I said.

"What does he charge?" Eddy asked as we finished tying the rope to the nose gear and he followed me to the main gear where I did the same thing.

"We're not really sure; he handles the monetary side of things, so we never see the cash transfer or however he handles it. But I'm guessing it's gotta be six figures or better at least because if you think about it, the people that call us are transporting millions in street value in whatever they're transporting, so a few hundred thousand should be like pocket change to these guys," I said.

"I know that's true. I've seen bedrooms in houses stacked floor to ceiling with stacks of money. Whole rooms completely filled with cash. It blows my mind," he said.

"I believe it." We ran the ropes from all three landing gear forward and tied them to the come-a-long. Strap and Tack pounded the five-foot crowbar into the ground until about a foot was sticking up and we hooked the come-a-long to it. Sanchez came walking over after spending fifteen minutes convincing the people loading the plane that they needed to stop and unload it.

"How can that not be obvious to them?" Strap started venting again. "Why do we even have to explain that? I would have given them about two minutes to believe me or I would have said 'we're outta here'! The morons can't figure it out for themselves? Buncha backwoods inbreds! That just goes to prove that stupid people are breeding all over the world!" The rest of us just stood there and listened and laughed at Strap while he was going off. We had to wait for them to unload the plane anyway.

"And another thing, we aren't doing the human race any favors by helping stupid people. We go too far when it comes to helping stupid people. Let them be stupid, let the natural order of things take its course. The cheetah goes after the ones in the herd that can't keep up! Protecting the stupid people from themselves gives them a chance to breed more stupid people and that's obviously what's happened here in this place!" Now Strap was so amped up that he was getting animated with his arms as he blathered on about being here to help them pull their plane out of the mud. It was rare to see him get worked up like this, but every once in a while, a wild hair will crawl up his butt and set him off.

Finally, after about twenty minutes, the plane was empty and we got them ready to push. We really only needed to move the plane forward a couple of feet and then it would be good. I was really hoping this would work because I didn't have any other ideas and the main landing gear tires on the Aero Commander were almost buried and the plane was actually teetering on its belly.

After about a half an hour of ratcheting the come-a-long while everybody pushed, we managed to slide the plane forward enough to get the weight back on the gear and there was actually about three inches of clearance under the belly.

"That dude better get that thing outta here before it sinks again," I said. "That's the wrong type of aircraft to be operating on soft ground."

We loaded up and closed the doors while they loaded all of their drugs back in the boats to take wherever. I didn't know and I didn't care. The pilot of the Aero Commander started the engines and we watched him take off and then Tack and Sanchez started up our plane and took off without issue.

We landed back at the farm just in time for lunch and spent the rest of the day working on the Green Manilishi. Strap and I wanted to service the engines and give the plane a little service check. Eddy was eager to learn about the plane and what we were doing, so we spent a lot of extra time teaching him about the aircraft. After we finished, we closed up the engines and cleaned up just as Elaina came looking for us to let us know that dinner would be ready soon.

"You're a lucky man, Eddy," I said as we were standing in the field between the barn and the house.

"Yeah, I know. Miguel is real funny; he treats her like she is his daughter. I mean, it's like we're family, like we've always been here," he said.

"You are, man. He needed you guys just as much as you needed him and this place. Just roll with it; it's all good, my friend," I said as we walked toward the house. Tack and Sanchez were hanging out on the porch drinking beer and smoking cigars and Strap was about to join them with his own beer and freshly lit cigar. As soon as he came out onto the porch, Elaina came out right behind him and gave him a bunch of grief!

"Strap, you don't light that stinky thing in the house, you light it outside!" she said in heavily accented English, and then she turned and went right back inside. There was silence for about the count of three and then we all started laughing at Strap as he just stood there looking at the closed door.

"Oh, buddy; you better not mess with her; she's the woman of this house now!" Tack said.

"I guess so," he said as he sat down. And that was exactly what she had become and you could see Miguel was enjoying letting her run it. She would make sure we wiped our feet before coming inside and that we washed real well before eating and made sure we used our manners at the table. Actually, I don't think Strap ever had any, but he was learning by watching everyone else. You could tell that she was going to be a great mom.

After dinner, we sat out on the porch again and talked.

"We need to make a beer run soon; the supply in the plane is getting low," Tack said. "And we're down to less than half of our coffee supply. Do we want to fly back to that hill and try to get some more from the village?" Tack, Sanchez, and Strap all turned to look at me.

"Why are you guys looking at me? You like the coffee as much as I do, right?" I said.

"Cause yer the Grand Poobah of the coffee-of-the-month club, pinhead!" Strap said.

"Okay, whatever. Sure, I'm willing to go back and get more whenever you guys want. We should gather up stuff to trade in the meantime, though," I said. Strap took pleasure in telling the others the story about how we came across that bunch with the coffee and how we ended up trading for it. Elaina was less than impressed with the coffee after she heard how it was processed.

"You guys are drinking coffee that is made from beans that have come out of an animal's anus?" she asked, looking at us incredulously.

"It's been cleaned and washed and roasted before it gets ground up," I said defensively.

"How do you know how well it was cleaned, Del?" she asked.

"They said it was?" I replied as sort of a question and rather sheepishly. Why do women have to ask these common sense questions like this? Things are much easier when the women let us men be stupid and do what we want.

"You guys can drink whatever you want, but I think that is disgusting," she said next.

"Okay, so we're good, then. When do you guys want to go back?" I said to the group. Elaina just laughed and threw a dishtowel at me. I liked her; she was feisty and outspoken and fit in well in this group. After about an hour or so of joking around, we decided to turn in for the night.

Knuckledraggers

Chapter 20: Barrel House Dogs

The phone rang after what only seemed like a couple hours of sleep. Sanchez answered in the pitch black of his bedroom in the barn.

"Yeah?" he said.

"Check the email." And then there was a click. He looked at his watch and saw that it was only a quarter after four in the morning.

"Don't these drug runners sleep at night?" he said to himself. He got up and turned on the light, turned on the laptop, and then walked down the short hall to the bathroom that the four of us shared and took a leak. When he came back, the computer was warmed up and he opened the mail. He knew from the coordinates that we would be going somewhere in El Salvador again. He got up and knocked on each of our doors, only to receive a rude suggestion in response to his troubles.

Once we were up and getting the plane ready, I saw lights on in the house, so we knew someone was up and Elaina would probably at least have some coffee brewing for us. To our pleasant surprise, she not only had coffee ready, but she was frying up some eggs as we walked in. Eddy was just making his way down the stairs when we were each pouring ourselves a cup.

"What's up, guys? Elaina woke me and said she saw you guys up and moving around, so I figured we got a call," he said.

"Yep, going to El Salvador. Wheels up as soon as we can see where the runway is," Tack said as he sat down at the table.

Miguel came in a short time later and we told him where we were headed. He just grunted in response. He poured himself a cup of coffee and as he sat down to join he said, "I do not like that region. Be careful. Give me a moment to make a call for you before you leave, just to make sure there aren't any surprises." We remembered the story that he had told us about his family. Elaina looked at him and then looked at Eddy.

"It's okay, babe. I'll be fine," he said. I looked at the both of them for a moment, trying to figure out why she was concerned.

"You're worried about him going on this mission after what he used to do for a living?" I asked and I looked over at Eddy, who was looking at me a little wide-eyed and shaking his head.

"What did you used to do for a living? You told me that you traveled around to hire yourself out to help farmers harvest fruit!" she said, glaring at Eddy.

"Whoops! Somebody's gonna be sleeping with the pigs for a while!" Strap said as Eddy tried to play dumb while he was eating. The rest of us just ate and chuckled while Elaina grilled Eddy about what he really did for a living before he met us.

"Just tell her the truth, dude. It doesn't matter now anyway; she's already pissed at you," Sanchez told him as we were getting up to leave.

"C'mon, Eddy; let's go. She'll still be mad when we get back. Don't worry about that," Tack said next. We pulled Eddy along with us as we left the house with his girlfriend glaring at him while she kissed him goodbye and handed him a bag full of sandwiches.

"Sorry about that, Eddy," I said. "I didn't know that she didn't know what you did."

"It's okay; she probably would have found out eventually anyway," he said.

"Anything else we should know just for future reference?" Strap asked as we were climbing in the plane.

"Nothing that I can think of," he said. We started the engines with me in the right seat and Tack in the left. The sun's rays were just starting to turn the sky from black to blue, which was enough for us to see where we were going. Without the aid of a taxiway and runway lights, we had to be careful about what we were doing. Fortunately, there weren't very many obstacles to watch out for; actually, my biggest concern was a cow or a coyote wandering out in front of us. A smile came across my face as we were taking off when I heard "Proud Mary" by Credence Clearwater Revival over the surround and I knew that Strap would be mixing Bloody Marys in the little galley behind us.

The morning was cool, but the sky was clear as we flew low over the hills and mountains in a northwesterly direction toward El Salvador. Miguel could not find out any information as to who we might be going to help. That wasn't necessarily good or bad, just that it was completely unknown and we needed to be careful. That's how we're used to operating anyway, but it would be nice to know if it was one of the cartels that have called on us before and we were on good terms with.

My mind wandered off to thoughts of Anna while we were flying, I was definitely going to see her when we got back to the States. I was overdue for a visit and she would be more aware of that than I would. She'd give me some lighthearted ribbing for it when I saw her, but I know it's only because she worries. Poor woman has spent her whole life worrying about me. I should take her on a vacation somewhere or something. She would probably like that. It would be kind of a nice way to say "thanks," even though that couldn't possibly even come close to repaying her for what she's done for me. I decided that I needed to quit daydreaming and get my head back in the game. We need to be sharp when we're on a mission.

"You want some more coffee? I'm going back to make another cup," I said to Tack as I got up.

"Yeah, man, I could use another cup," he replied. As I stepped out, I could see that Eddy, Strap, and Sanchez were deep into a card game and Strap and Sanchez were harassing each other over Strap's loose interpretation of the rules. This just meant that he was cheating. I stepped into the galley and poured Tack and me each a cup of goat coffee from a thermos that Elaina gave us.

As we got close to the area, Tack dropped us down low and slow and snaked up a very wide and shallow valley that would take us to where we were going. I looked back and gave the guys the hand signal to start looking out the windows for anything weird. There were a few houses and small villages/communities here and there. A larger town off in the distance, a few little fishing hamlets, and so on. There were some very poor areas in this part of the world; not just this country, but much of Central America.

The coordinates led us away from the valley and over a low-lying area that was heavily wooded and very dense with vegetation. Within a couple of miles, I saw a long rectangular area cut out in the heavily wooded area that was obviously meant for a plane to land. The strip was certainly long enough, but it was very narrow and it didn't look much wider than our wingspan, which meant it was made for smaller planes. A low fly over the airstrip revealed that there was a twin-engine plane parked at one end and we could see a couple of people standing just inside the tree line. After we passed over the area, we did a slow, wide banking turn away so we could line up for an approach from the other end. As I looked back at the strip while we were banking, I almost lost sight of it. The area was very well hidden in the dense forest, and if you didn't know to look for it, you would probably never see it. I was a little uncomfortable with this because of the close proximity of the trees to where we would be landing because trees can hide people, whereas an open field gives range and distance to see who might be coming.

I looked back to make sure that the other three were geared up and ready for action. Tack brought the plane in because he was definitely the more experienced pilot and this landing was going to be tight with not much room for error and we were going to have to spin the plane around in a very tight area so we could take off. As we came in for landing, there seemed to be only about thirty feet of room from each wing tip to the trees. But even with that much room, the distance seemed much closer at higher speeds and a plane doesn't fly on a rail. The lower we dropped; the pucker factor in my butt seemed to be directly proportional to the distance we got to the trees because I thought we were going to clip one with a wing at any moment. We touched down without incident and taxied up slowly to the other plane, which turned out to be a DeHavilland Twin Otter. When we got to about fifty yards away, Tack stomped the left brake and goosed the right engine throttle and whipped the plane around in a full one hundred and eighty degree turn and didn't hit any trees. I was impressed.

"Nice driving, dude," I said as I got up when we shut down the engines.

"Thanks, but I knew you guys would be able to fix it if I whacked a tree anyway," he replied.

"Right," I said while shaking my head. When I stepped out of the cockpit, Strap was opening the door with Eddy and Sanchez in tow. All had M4s at the ready. I adjusted my .45 out of habit and waited while they made sure the area was secure. I gave it a few minutes before Tack and I climbed out because we hadn't heard any shooting or anybody running around yet. When I walked around to the back of the plane, I could see Eddy walking around the area, just kind of making sure there wasn't anyone lurking in the trees.

Strap was looking at the tail of the other plane, which was obviously damaged, and Sanchez was talking to a couple of guys off to the side. I walked over next to Strap as he was poking at a very crunched left horizontal stabilizer.

"Looks like he hit a tree while trying to spin this thing around," he said without looking at me. You could see the brown scrapes and pieces of bark from a tree on the white paint.

"Yep, he nailed it pretty good," I said. We were going to have to repair about eighteen to twenty inches of the outboard end of the stabilizer. We guessed that it would probably take ten to twelve hours because it wasn't just the outer skin that was damaged but also the internal ribs and frame. While we were looking at it, the plane moved slightly, indicating that someone was inside moving around. Strap and I walked around the tail of the plane toward where Sanchez was talking and also to tell them how long it would take. Sanchez relayed what he had learned and it was just as we expected. Up to this point, I hadn't really gotten a look at the people he was talking to until now. There were three men in their mid-twenties, I would guess, all of them Latino and carrying AK-47s. They didn't seem hostile, but they didn't give us the impression of being very friendly either. They looked like they were a little wary of us, but we were used to that by now.

We told Sanchez what we estimated that it would take to repair the tail and that whoever else was in the plane would have to climb out so we could work on it without the plane bouncing around every time they moved.

Sanchez translated to them what we said, but they said that the people in the plane could not come out. When Sanchez said this, we all turned to look at the plane. *People? How many people are we talking and why can't they come out?* I thought to myself. Alarm bells started going off in my head as I glanced at Strap and Sanchez, who had curious looks on their faces as well. I walked over to the side of the plane to look in the window and my blood instantly went cold! Inside were what looked to be about a half a dozen girls chained to the floor like dogs in the back of the plane! They didn't look to be any older than their mid-teens at best and all of them looked unwashed, unfed, and unhealthy.

Oh crap! I thought. *Be cool,* I said to myself. *We gotta figure this out. There is no way in hell that we're going to help these scumbags, but we can't alarm them.* Immediately, I turned and looked at Sanchez, who was still looking at me as I tried to act very calm and collected like we see this kind of thing all the time.

"Tell them that they can stay in the plane as long as they don't move around too much," I said to him. Strap was giving me a curious look, so I just grinned like nothing was wrong.

"C'mon, man; we got a lot of work to do," I said to him as I motioned for them both to follow me back to our plane like we were going to get tools and stuff.

Tack was walking toward us after looking at the tail. "What do you guys think, will it take long to fix it?" he asked as we approached.

"We ain't fixin' squat and we need to have a little pow-wow," I said in a low voice. As we got back to our plane, I climbed in like I was going to start pulling equipment.

"Act natural while I'm telling you this and I'm going to hand out tools and stuff as I'm talking." Tack, Sanchez, and

Strap were standing outside of the plane, looking at me as I started handing them tools.

"That plane is full of young girls! They're trafficking sex slaves! We need to hash out a plan while we give the impression that we're helping them." I said as calmly as I could, but I could feel my heartbeat picking up and adrenaline start to enter my bloodstream. I was going to kill these guys and I wanted to do it now. My body was starting to vibrate with the anticipation. I hated this kind of thing and I know it goes on all over the world, but this was the first time that we had ever come across it and I damn sure wasn't about to let these scumbags live to do it anymore!

The three of them just stared at me. I gave each of them something to carry over to the tail of the DeHavilland.

"Here, carry this stuff over and I'll follow and then Strap and I will start working on the plane while you guys let Eddy know what's going on." None of them said much as they turned to walk away. I jumped out of the plane with some air hose to start uncoiling.

"Hey, Eddy!" I said. "Mind giving me a hand with this?" I motioned for him to come over towards me as he was just standing and watching from a distance of about twenty-five yards away. Eddy slung his rifle over his back as he strolled over.

"We have an issue. Stand here and uncoil the air hose for me while I drag it out to the plane. Tack and Sanchez will fill you in. Act normal," I said as I walked off with the end of the hose and some tools. I glanced over at the three human smugglers to see if they were looking at us or anything. One was standing by the door to the DeHavilland speaking to the girls inside, one was taking a leak in the bushes, and one was smoking a cigarette and barely paying any attention. That was good; we hadn't alerted them yet.

When I got to the tail, the other three were discussing a game plan while Strap started making noise by pulling on damaged skin with a pair of pliers to give the impression of work.

"Del, do you still have your .45 on you?" Sanchez asked as I approached.

"Yeah, it's under my shirt," I replied.

"Was there anyone else in the plane with the girls?" he asked.

"No, these three are the only guys that I've seen so far. I saw Eddy scoping the tree line, so it doesn't look like he has seen anyone else yet either," I said.

"How about this? I walk back over and tell Eddy what's going on while I act like I'm getting more stuff. Then I'm going to walk over to those guys and act like I need to talk to them again. When I approach them, you three take out the guy by the door to the plane and the guy standing off to the side. Eddy and I will pop the guy that I walk up to and the guy off to the side if you guys haven't gotten him already." Sanchez looked around at the three of us and we all nodded. Then he turned and casually walked back over to our plane and spoke to Eddy while he climbed back into the plane to act like he was getting more tools. Eddy was the only one that was still carrying his M4 as the rest of us had put ours back in the plane when we started getting tools and such, but all of us still carried our handguns of choice as we were accustomed to do. After a couple of minutes, Sanchez climbed back out of the plane. By now, he would have explained the game plan to Eddy and they were ready. At that moment, I was standing behind the horizontal stabilizer facing forward with Strap in front me with his back to the front of the plane and Tack was next to us. I lifted the back of my shirt up over my .45 so it would be out of the way when I went to draw it.

Just as Sanchez was about to start walking, there was a commotion in the plane as one of the guards started yelling at one of the girls and then he pulled her out of the plane and started walking her toward the tree line, holding her by her hair. Sanchez froze and then turned back to the plane as if he wasn't concerned. Watching this made my blood boil and I could feel my hands start to shake a little because I wanted to run up and shoot that guy in the head!

"Easy, cowboy," Strap said in a low voice. He had been watching me and could obviously read the emotions in my face. I didn't say anything but watched them over his shoulder as they walked. It was obvious that the girl needed to pee and he wasn't happy about the inconvenience of having to take her. She stepped behind a tree and squatted as the guard just stared and watched her. *What a freakin' pig!* I thought. *Doesn't even let her pee without staring at her?*

After a minute, he started yelling at her and the three of us at the stabilizer turned to watch. The guard grabbed the girl by the hair and started dragging her on the ground back to the plane while she was screaming and crying. All of a sudden, we jumped as two rifle shots rang out from right behind us. The guard that was dragging the girl dropped like a sack of potatoes and then the rest of us jumped into action. As I pulled out my .45, there were two more shots from behind me and by now I knew it was Eddy because I could tell the shots were from an M4 rifle. Tack, Strap, and I started running toward the front of the plane where we could see the other guard leveling his AK-47 at Eddy and Sanchez, who were now running toward him from the other side of the plane. I stopped and dropped to one knee and shot him twice as Strap and Tack fired at him at the same time. The guy didn't have time to get one round off before he was thrown backwards from getting hit. When it was obvious that he wasn't moving, the five of us all loosely gathered in front of the DeHavilland and looked around to see if we had drawn any attention from all the gunfire.

The second set of rifle shots we heard was Eddy taking out the guy that Sanchez was going to walk up to as he was just lying where he had been standing when it all started. The girl that was being dragged was lying on the ground, crying, a couple of feet away from the guard that had been dragging her. She was looking at us and visibly shaking, as I'm sure she thought that she would be next.

"Sorry about jumping the gun, guys, but that dude was pissin' me off," Eddy said.

"Don't apologize, buddy. I like the way you handled that!" I said as I clapped him on the shoulder.

"Absolutely, man. You took advantage of a good moment where those guys were distracted by watching that," Sanchez said to him.

"No problem here, dude; it was a good call," Tack said next.

"You can drop guys like that in front of me any day, man. Nice shootin'!" Strap said while shaking his hand.

Tack and I walked over to the girl to get her up and calm her down while the other guys went to the plane to get the rest of them out. All of them had their wrists tied to each other and to the inside of the plane.

Sanchez was speaking to them softly in Spanish and assuring them that we were going to help them. When we got them out of the plane and huddled together, every single one of them looked like they were ready to bolt into the woods. Tack came up with an idea to keep them from running off and that was food and drink. Sanchez asked them if they wanted food and persuaded them to follow us over to the Green Manilishi, where we started pulling out all kinds of snacks and sodas and handing it to them. These girls wolfed down this stuff like they hadn't eaten in weeks. While we were all standing by the plane and watching them eat, it was obvious that they were all very young like I had suspected. Young as in early to mid-teens at the most and very thin and malnourished. There were eight of them and all of them looked like they were from Central or South America except one.

I've read about human trafficking and the numbers are astonishing. Even in the United States, where you might think that it shouldn't be so bad, it is surprisingly high. Countries like the U.S. are the source for much of the demand, but women are recruited from modernized countries as well. Many poorer countries wind up being the supply for much of it and sex traffickers will go into poor towns and villages and lure young girls by offering work, clothes, and lives of luxury or whatever. In many cases, a family member or friend of the family will sell a girl into the sex trade. The stories are all over the board and it's a sad reality and it's unfortunate that so many countries will turn a blind eye to it because so many officials will actually be a part of it themselves.

The five of us were standing there discussing what our next move should be and the obvious answer was to load them up and get them back to the farm and start caring for them. Then Miguel could help us get them back to their families and homes. The girls kept a wary eye on us while they huddled and ate, but none of them spoke; not to us or each other.

We decided that we probably didn't need to hang around much longer and discussed what we should do with the plane. Take it, leave it, or burn it were basically our choices. It was a nice plane and it would be nice to have, but keeping it and selling it or just keeping it would present a few issues. After a while, we decided that we would burn it and say that it was on fire when we showed up, so we never landed to see what happened. Basically, we were going to tell everyone that we were never here. My favorite story!

Sanchez spoke to the girls and told them that we were going to take care of them and then help them get home, but they were going to have to come with us in the plane. I thought that there would be some reluctance and they wouldn't believe us, but to my surprise, they climbed in the plane without saying a word. That probably meant that their spirits had been broken and they had just become accustomed to doing whatever they were told.

Eddy and I each taped a grenade to the underside of each wing of the DeHavilland where the fuel tanks were located. Once Tack and Sanchez had our plane fired up and ready to roll, we pulled the pins and ran! Eddy and I dove through the door of the plane just as Tack shoved the throttles to the firewall and we watched the DeHavilland Twin Otter explode into a glorious ball of fire as we raced across the field and into the air.

On the plane, Strap, Eddy, and I sat at the table where we normally play cards, but the girls stayed huddled together on the couch, seeking comfort from one another. I asked them if any one of them would like more to drink or eat. All of them accepted the offer, so Strap and I went into the galley and made peanut and jelly sandwiches. Nothing like a good ole fashioned PB&J to chase the hunger away! When we were handing out the sandwiches to the girls, one of them looked at me and asked, "Where are you taking us?" Again, I had assumed that they only spoke the local languages down here and didn't speak any English.

"Well, sweetheart, we're going back to where we live and get you guys cleaned up and taken care of. My name is Del. What's your name?" I asked as I sat down in a chair across the aisle from her.

"Katelyn," she replied.

"Nice to meet you, Katelyn. How old are you?" I asked.

"Fourteen, I think, or almost fifteen. I'm not sure," she said.

"Where are you from?" I asked next.

"Toledo," she said flatly.

"You're from Toledo? As in Ohio? How the heck did you get to El Salvador?" I asked incredulously.

"I don't where El Salvador is," she replied.

"You're in Central America right now. Do you know how long you've been down here?" I asked. By this time, Strap and Eddy had moved closer to us because they had become very interested in the conversation.

"Not really. I kind of figured that I wasn't in America anymore a long time ago," she said. I could only stare at her in disbelief. Eventually, I left her alone to eat her sandwich and went back to the table with the other guys.

The rest of the flight was quiet and uneventful as it seemed that everyone was deep in their own thoughts. I was glad that we came across these girls, but I wondered how easy or hard it would be to get them back to their real homes. I know that women and children that have been subjected to abuse like sex slavery can suffer from long term or even permanent psychological, physical, and emotional damage. I didn't have any answers for this one, but I knew that we had done the right thing. I think the girls started to relax a bit because they started talking quietly to one another and looking around the plane a little more, where before, they just looked down and didn't speak. When we started descending for the approach, they became very curious and started looking out the windows to try and see where we were going.

When we landed and could see the farm as we were taxiing, they started chattering more with a little excitement. I caught Katelyn looking at me and I just smiled at her and said, "This is home!"

We pulled up next to the barn and Elaina was already standing there waiting with Miguel. After we shut down the engines, Strap opened the door and climbed out, followed by me and Eddy. I stuck my head in the door and told the girls it was okay to come out. As they started emerging from the plane, I watched the expressions on Miguel's and Elaina's faces. They went from curiosity to concern and to surprise as all eight girls were now out of the plane and were standing there staring back at them.

"Back to delivering people again?" Miguel asked.

"More like we've started adopting them," I said. We gave them the quick and dirty on what happened in El Salvador and that we wanted to get them back to their homes.

Miguel and Elaina didn't waste any time introducing themselves to the girls and started directing them to the house where showers and clean clothes would be made available. The rest of us just stood there watching them walk away until Elaina stopped and turned toward us and started barking orders.

"What are you guys standing there for? We need fresh milk, eggs, and some vegetables for dinner; we have more mouths to feed now! Now get to it!" she said and then turned and followed the girls into the house.

"Yes, ma'am!" Tack said sarcastically before we started doing what she wanted.

Chapter 21: Hung Start

The next couple of days went by without much going on, at least for us anyway. Elaina got the girls cleaned up and found some old clothes that used to belong to Miguel's kids. He could never find it within himself to throw them out and I guess now we knew why. She had to spend some time working through some issues with them, emotional and physical. She said a warm safe environment, good food, a lot of love, and time would go a long way toward helping them heal.

We sent a cryptic e-mail to the boss letting him know what happened and what we did. He got the gist of it and relayed back to the people that called him to hire us that the plane was on fire when we got there. Miguel and Elaina were able to figure out where most of the girls were from and we started to figure out how to get them back home. Most were from various regions in Central America, two from Mexico, and of course Katelyn from Toledo, which still blows my mind.

Eventually, we would end up flying some of them as close to home as we could. Some did not want to go back to where they were from because the conditions were so bad there or it was because the family or a family member were the ones that got rid of them or sold them in the first place.

The third day after we found the girls, Katelyn found us in the barn working on Miguel's old AG crop duster.

"Hi, Del, what are you guys doing to that plane?" she asked. It was Strap, Tack, Sanchez, and I that happened to be in there at the time and all four of us stopped and came over to talk to her. She looked completely different now that she was all cleaned up and her hair brushed and was wearing clean clothes. She had brown eyes and dark brown shoulder-length hair that framed a thirty-year-old face. She lost her innocence long ago and you could see it in her face, but she still had a youthful glint in her eyes. We really hadn't seen much of them since we got back because Elaina had been so busy with them. Dinner had been soup and sandwiches on the front porch for us guys for the last couple of nights as well. We didn't mind, of course, and we understood completely, so we were a little surprised when she showed up in the barn that day and came over to us.

"Hi, Katelyn, we're just fixing a few things for Miguel," I said. "By the way, this is Strap, Sanchez, and Tack." All three of them shook her hand.

"Miguel and Elaina are really nice," she said.

"Yes, they are. Are you doing okay? Can we help you with anything?" I asked.

"I'm fine. I was just getting bored and I wanted to see the farm animals. Elaina said it would be okay," she replied.

"Well sure, we can take you over to see them. C'mon; we can all go," Strap said next. We took her over to see the cows and pigs and chickens and gave her a tour of the farm. I really wanted to ask her more questions about how she got down here, but I didn't want to bombard her too much.

Later on that day, all of the girls were out and about around the farm and we were able to get to know all of them a little more. Some could speak some broken English, which was okay because Strap, Tack, and I were the only ones that weren't really fluent in Spanish, but we each knew a little. Everyone else was fluent in Spanish, including Eddy, so there weren't any language barriers that we couldn't deal with.

One night after dinner, the adults sat around on the porch. We needed to discuss what we were going to do with the girls that didn't want to be taken back to their homes. This included Katelyn as well. She told Elaina that she ran away from home because her mom did a lot of drugs and she constantly had boyfriends or guys over that would try to molest her. She knew a girl from school that told her she could stay with her for a while because her mom was never home and wouldn't even know the difference. Her friend's boyfriend was a little older than both of them and was apparently tied in with a gang that was into human trafficking and sex slavery. From there, she was taken and was forced to work in various cities around the U.S. Eventually, she was sold and brought south of the border and had been down there for quite some time. She didn't really know how long she'd been away by now and that was why she wasn't even sure how old she was. Unable to speak Spanish, she wasn't able to communicate with any other girls that she was kept with and therefore really had no idea where she was.

As I sat back and absorbed this new information, my only thought was *"my God, how does this happen in the U.S."*? But unfortunately, it's a huge problem that we haven't even begun to get a handle on in our country, much less around the world. *America! Home of the free! Yeah.* No wonder she didn't want to go home. I wouldn't either. Our only real option was to let them live here on the farm, which was a pretty good option if you asked me. Taking them back to the States to live in the parking lot definitely wouldn't work out. Besides, they would probably think that we were homeless too if they saw that! This little rag-tag family was growing by the minute and it seemed like we were the ones that kept bringing home all the strays to live.

Miguel made it clear that he wanted the girls to live there as long as they wanted. We might have to add some rooms onto the house before long, but that would not be an issue.

So it was decided that we would do just that, add rooms onto the house, make a bigger vegetable garden, raise more chickens, pigs, and cows. Miguel said he knew some locals that were good construction workers and could hire them to help us make the additions on the house. Tack, Strap, Sanchez, and I decided that we would cover the cost for that.

We started to make plans to fly five of the girls to their homes, but that presented a few difficulties because some of them couldn't exactly show us on a map where they lived. A couple of these girls had received little to no education and didn't understand maps or had ever even seen one. Miguel and Elaina were able to piece together what clues the girls could give them and, from there, we were able to get an idea where they were from. The other problem was that few people have an airstrip next to their house, so dropping them off could present additional challenges as well.

The two girls from Mexico made it easy as they were able to tell us exactly where they were from and both of them lived in relative proximity to a real airfield. So all we needed to do was fly in and figure out some ground transportation from there. We had to be real careful about where we flew into sometimes because Mexican customs can be unpredictable at best. This is the reason why we try to stay out of most of the "real" airports in Mexico except Cabo, of course. Although Strap seems to be slowly making that town a little more unfriendly, one girl at a time.

Over about a two-week period, we were able to return four of the girls to their homes. Miguel went with us to help with local language and get directions and so forth. There were some teary reunions as expected and extremely grateful family members. The fifth girl, Yanina, could not find her family. She was from Panama and when we took her home, which was a small community next to a bend in a river called Rio Tabasara, several miles east of Chichica, her family was not there. According to the locals, her family moved after she was abducted and they didn't know where they moved to. This was going to be a real problem because this region was so remote that finding them would be a significant challenge. Just getting to this area required us to land in a field and hike several miles to the village by the river where she was from. We decided that it was possible that her family moved to Chichica because that was the next closest and larger town. Of course they didn't have an airfield there either, so we had to do the same thing, find a flat field to land and walk.

After spending a couple of hours walking around Chichica without any luck, we had to call it a day. I felt really bad for her, but we were pretty much out of ideas for the moment. She thought that she was taken about two years before and it wasn't like they could've just left a forwarding address because there weren't any post offices there.

We decided to go home and let Miguel use his contacts to try to track them down. Even though it could take some time, it was really our only option at this point. Fortunately, Yanina was tough and accepted this and didn't seem too disappointed. I think it was because she liked it on the farm. She seemed to have taken a special liking to Miguel because he was the grandfatherly figure and, for some strange reason, the girls started calling him Yoda. We had no idea how they might have picked up on calling him that, none at all. I'm not sure how the girls viewed the rest of us, though. Obviously, Eddy and Elaina were their own thing and were about to start a family within the family. But as far as Strap, Tack, Sanchez, and me, they probably just looked at us like the weird uncles.

I can sort of relate to the weird uncle bit in a way because Anna has an older brother named Billy with a stuttering problem. That's not why he was weird, but it didn't help. Anna said he got hit in the head when someone threw a fruitcake at him when he was a kid and was never quite the same after that. He was definitely one of those guys that marched to the beat of a different drummer. I don't think he was dangerous, but if I was a parent and saw him hanging around the playground, I would definitely call the cops.

I never knew where he lived because I think he just kind of drifted around and sort of showed up from time to time. As far as jobs, I was never really sure what it was that he did for a living either except I remember that he showed up at the boys' home once trying to sell vacuum cleaners. If you've never witnessed a vacuum cleaner salesman with a stuttering problem, it's a painful experience. I pretended that I didn't know him.

Once when I was about twelve or thirteen, I was out with Anna and her brother came with us. She needed to pick up some stuff at the grocery store for her mom because the family was having a big cookout. I think it was because it was Memorial Day weekend or something and that was why she came to pick me up that day. Anyway, the three of us walked into the grocery store and went straight to the meat section because she was going to buy steaks. Anna and Billy were discussing which type of steaks would be best for grilling and the conversation slowly turned into an argument. This was where I learned that her brother's level of stuttering was directly proportional to his level of agitation. Normally, I would have vacated the area until brother and sister worked things out, but it was becoming mildly entertaining. Noticing this, the butcher came around from behind the counter to ask if he could offer any assistance. When he began speaking, he started stuttering as well, which I thought was funny because I thought that he was making fun of Billy! Evidently, Billy assumed the same thing and he just exploded at the butcher for having the audacity to make fun of him. The butcher was shocked by the outburst and immediately became infuriated because he now thought that Billy was making fun of him! Both Anna and I stood there dumbfounded at this scene because neither one of us knew what to make of it.

It wasn't long before the commotion started to draw the attention of several other shoppers in the grocery store, as I'm sure few had ever witnessed two grown men with stuttering problems get into an argument. I can tell you that had I not already been there, there was no way I could have ever figured out what the heck they were arguing about because neither one of them could complete a sentence.

It wasn't long before Anna and I figured out that the butcher's stuttering problem was legit, but neither one of those two idiots were ever going to figure it out. Just as Anna was about to step in to try and calm things down, her brother shoved the butcher. The butcher backed into the meat freezer, at which point he turned and picked up a foot-and-half-long pork loin and slapped Billy across the face with it.

Anna screamed for me to help her, but I couldn't stop laughing long enough to be of any use. It didn't matter because, by this time, the store manager had arrived in time to witness his butcher assaulting a customer with a pork loin and separated them. Needless to say, the butcher was fired on the spot and we were thrown out of the grocery store. Anna was so angry and embarrassed that she wouldn't speak to either one of us after that. Her brother for obvious reasons, but she was mad at me because I just laughed at the whole thing and didn't help her.

When we got to the next grocery store, Anna made us both sit in the car and wait.

Chapter 22: All Jacked Up With No Place to Go

I got to know Katelyn a little more over the next few days because she became my little tag-a-long. I can't say I minded the extra company; she was very curious and had lots of questions and just sort of bounced along beside me as I did chores and worked around the farm. It seemed to me that her real personality was started to reemerge and she could finally be who she really was after being oppressed for too long. She was very interested in me and where I came from, how I got started in life, and she saw a few similarities that she seemed to latch on to. I did my best to show her that all that didn't really matter and that it didn't have to change what kind of person you were in life and that you can make that a part of your strength and become successful and not use it as a reason to be loser in life as so many people tend to do.

"Hey, Del, do you think I could go with you guys sometime?" she asked. I looked over at Strap, who just shrugged.

"I guess you could go if we knew it wouldn't be dangerous. As you know, we tend to run into a few bad guys every once in a while," I replied and winked at her.

"Do you think you could teach me about planes and how to fly one day?" she asked next.

"Absolutely, kiddo," I replied. "Speaking of learning things, I understand Mr. Miguel and Elaina are going to start some home schooling for you guys."

"Yeah, I guess," she said with a little less enthusiasm.

"You'll be fine. Make sure you learn all that you can because they are only trying to help you. You've had a rough time, but we can get through that. If you promise that you'll study and learn everything that they teach you, I promise that we'll teach you all about airplanes and even how to fly. Deal?" I asked, putting my hand out.

"Deal!" she said, shaking it enthusiastically.

"When do you guys have to go back to L.A.?" she asked next.

"Not sure, kiddo. Why? Are you ready to get rid of us already?" I said jokingly.

"No," she replied quietly. It was obvious that she was worried about losing people that she had begun to care for. I could relate to the fact that she had gone several years without having anyplace to call home or anyone to call family. And just when she was able to find people that actually cared for her, the thought of them going away would be heartbreaking. I turned to her and noticed that she was watering up and was about to get the lip trembling.

"Ah jeez," I said. I didn't realize that this conversation was going to be this high on the drama scale. What is it with women; do they go to some sort of school for this stuff when they're toddlers or something? It's like flicking on a switch and boom, here come the waterworks. I stepped over to her and leaned over to give her a hug and tell her it would be okay and all of a sudden she had both arms wrapped around my neck and she was bawling! I'm mean, she was really crying hard; all the years of abuse and loneliness came pouring out right there by the barn. She sank down to her knees and pulled me down with her because she was still holding on to my neck like it was tree in the middle of a raging river! I didn't really know what else to do except hold her while the front of my t-shirt got soaked. She shook while she cried and her whole body reverberated like she was taking blows to the torso. To be honest, I had never witnessed a person cry this hard and for this long and I have been to a few funerals before. This was not faking; this was an entire childhood of pent-up emotion stored up because there was never an opportunity to let some of it go. Every scraped knee, every bump in the night, every little thing that a kid may come crying to their parent about was stored up in her because she was never given the opportunity to let it out little by little along the way. And Del gets the whole swimming pool full in one shot. I wonder if she and Anna are related somehow.

I looked up to see Strap kneeling down by her and Tack and Sanchez walked over as well. I think all of us had developed a soft spot for the girls because they were still just kids that had been dealt a bad hand in life. The four of us gathered around her and calmed her down after a few minutes and even I had to wipe my own eyes when she was done. Her emotion was so strong that I could feel it while she was gripping me. There was no denying the depth of her pain as she tried to release it in its entirety right there and I was truly affected by it.

Elaina had noticed what was going on and came running over from the house. She recognized the situation for what it was, as I think she had been expecting some of the girls to have an episode from time to time. She gathered Katelyn up and walked her back to the house to clean her up and let her lie down for a while. Strap slapped me on the shoulder after they went in. "I knew you were a big softy."

"Shaddup," I said.

"Poor kid; can't imagine what she's been through," Tack said next.

"What brought all that on?" Sanchez asked next.

"She was wondering when we were going to leave. I get the feeling that she doesn't want us to go," I replied. He just nodded.

"I guess that means we'll have to visit pretty frequently from now on once the boss pulls us out," he said.

"I'm beginning to suspect that things may be slowing down a little down in this region. He may be telling us to come home before long anyway," Tack said next.

"Yep, we've already been down here longer than originally anticipated as it is, I think. I don't even know what day it is much less the date by now," Strap chimed in. I could relate; I couldn't tell you if it was a Tuesday or a Saturday at this point.

"Are you guys ready for a trip back to L.A.? I mean, we could tell him that we're ready to come back for a few weeks and then come back down," Sanchez asked while looking at the rest of us.

"You know what could possibly work out well is that we split our time equally between here and L.A. We could bounce back and forth on a regular basis as the missions dictate. I think it would give us better flexibility overall and we could help Yoda and the bunch as well," I said next.

"Also, Sanchez and I could use this place to lay low if we think someone might be getting close to us in the States," Tack said thoughtfully as he looked over at Sanchez, who just nodded in agreement.

"I had thought about that also since we still don't know anything more about your boat getting broken into," Sanchez said.

"I agree. I think we should get RVs and join these two slugs in the lot and use this place as our fallback position now. That way, these two can help watch our backs and we won't be so isolated out on the boats," Tack replied. That finally put this issue to bed because it had been weighing on all of us a little since we'd been down here. Sanchez had been on the fence for a while, but now with our little base down here in northern Costa Rica, this option made much more sense.

"Okay, so am I telling the boss that we're ready to go back to L.A. for a bit?" Sanchez asked while looking at the three of us. Strap and Tack nodded, but the thought of leaving Katelyn right now didn't sit well with me.

I guess it was obvious what I was thinking because I glanced back toward the house before I replied. Before I could say anything, though, Strap said, "I think maybe we should give it a couple more days to see how she's holding up."

"Yeah, you're right. We need to think about them as well before we make some of these decisions. Let's talk to them tonight after dinner and get their input," Tack said.

When Strap, Tack, Sanchez, and I walked into the house for dinner, Katelyn was just walking down the stairs looking freshly washed and rested. No words were necessary as she came over and gave the four of us each a hug. The conversation around the table was lively as we passed around servings of baked chicken, potatoes, and fresh vegetables. Elaina was an excellent cook and we had gotten spoiled for sure by now. I think even Yoda had finally become comfortable with relinquishing his kitchen by now and was enjoying the benefits as well.

I don't know much about women and having babies, but she looked like she was ready to download that thing any second. I was amazed at how a person could walk around with all that hangin' out in front without flopping over and doing a turtle impression.

"Hey, Eddy, have you checked to see if her turkey button has popped out yet?" I asked jokingly.

He just chuckled a little nervously and patted Elaina on the belly. "Yeah, man, I think she's ready. Got me a little nervous, ya know?" he replied.

"We take her into town tomorrow to see the doctor again," Yoda said next.

"When is the due date again?" Tack asked Elaina.

"Yesterday," she said matter-of-factly. We stopped eating and just looked at her for a minute.

"Really? Oh crap!" Strap blurted as it looked like he was about to jump out of his chair. "What do we do?"

"It's okay, Strap. The baby will come when it is ready. We are ready when the time comes," Elaina replied very softly with a smile. "We are just going tomorrow so the doctor can listen to the baby's' heart beat and make sure that I am doing okay, but it will be very soon." Strap seemed to relax a bit with that.

"But it could be tonight," she said next with a smile just to tease Strap, which worked because he stopped eating and looked at her wide-eyed. This brought a chuckle around the table.

I slapped him on the shoulder and asked, "What's wrong, buddy? It's not like you're the one that's going to be the one playing catcher or anything."

"Nah, man, I'm cool. It's just that uh, this is kinda big, right? We gotta do stuff, right? What are we supposed to do exactly?" he asked, looking around the table a little nervously. Elaina just chuckled at him and shook her head.

"Strap, you don't have to do anything. It's okay," she said. He just nodded his head with his eyes real wide while looking at her. I smiled and shook my head and went back to eating. This was an interesting side of him that I'd never seen before. He was clearly nervous about this whole newborn baby idea. Obviously because he had zero experience with it, I'm sure. I had a little because I got to hold Anna's babies when they were little from time to time when I could come over.

After dinner, the adults gathered on the porch. We held off on the cigars when Elaina was with us because we didn't want her to have to smell them. It was another beautiful night as usual down here and there was a steady rain coming down that had a very calming effect.

"We need to talk to you guys about when it would be a good time for us to go back to L.A. for a while. We want to split our time between here and there, but we want to make sure that the timing doesn't put a strain on things here," Sanchez said. Yoda nodded softly because everyone was looking at him for his reply. He was the quasi-patriarch of this little rag-tag family here, so all matters went through him obviously.

"I know you boys have been away from home for a while, but I knew it would be time for you to return soon. You are part of us now and we want you here as much as possible, of course. I have no doubt that you will be here when needed." That was it and it was clear that was all he needed to say. This guy reminded me of an old Indian chief; at least what I perceive an old Indian chief to be like anyway. He didn't blather on about things; he said what made sense and left it alone. And of course what he said was true; we were not going to leave 'em hangin'.

The conversation continued as we talked about improvements to the house and farm. We planned out a few little projects here and there and so on. After a while, Elaina said she was tired and wanted to turn in. Eddy took her upstairs and made sure all of the ladies were okay. The rest of us broke out some whiskey and cigars and just sat and listened to the rain, each man deep in his own thoughts. Then the phone rang.

"Gee, I wonder who it could be at this hour," Strap said sarcastically. Sanchez went inside and retrieved the laptop after he got off the phone.

"Panama," Sanchez said flatly. "That's a little interesting; we haven't been down there in a long time." Yoda just grunted and got up to make a phone call.

"Should we bring Eddy with his girl about ready to pop?" I asked rhetorically but was answered with four heads shaking "no."

"We'll leave at first light as usual," Sanchez said, closing the laptop. We finished the cigars and headed off to the barn to get some shuteye. Yoda didn't find out anything but said he would try again in the morning.

Chapter 23: Suzy and the Trunk Monkeys

For some reason, I didn't sleep well that night, which is unusual for me because I can usually sleep like a baby when it's raining. Maybe it was Katelyn or the baby that was about to arrive or that we were going to go back to L.A. soon. Of course Strap rattling the walls with his snoring in the room next to me didn't help either. When I did finally get to sleep, it must not have been very deep because I heard Sanchez getting up to wake the rest of us before he knocked on the door.

We kept the plane loaded and fueled, so there wasn't much for us to do to get it ready. Fortunately, the rain stopped finally and we trudged over to the house when we saw the lights were on. To our surprise, it was Yoda and not Elaina in the kitchen making coffee when we came in.

"I think she had a bad night, didn't get much sleep," he said when we came in.

"That makes two of us," I said. He wrapped a few day-old biscuits in a towel and handed them to us and shrugged.

"Breakfast," he said. "I don't have any information on who you're helping today either."

Just then, we heard quick steps running down the stairs followed by Katelyn rounding the corner with a panicked look on her face.

"Relax, kiddo; we're just going to fix somebody's plane. We'll be back later," I said, giving her a hug. "Go back to sleep and help Elaina today."

"Okay," she said, looking relieved as she turned to go back upstairs.

"So do you mean to tell me that there is one person in this world that actually likes you?" Strap asked as we were walking out of the house.

"Nah, she's just low on friends right now, but she'll come to her senses before long," I said.

"Let's hope," he replied.

"Who's flying this rig this morning?" Tack asked as we were approaching the plane.

"Not me. I didn't sleep well and I'm not sharp this morning," I said.

"You and the word 'sharp' should never be used in the same sentence," Strap said next.

"Wow, Del, Strap's all over you this morning," Tack said, chuckling. "What'd you do to him?"

"Let him have his fun. I let him jab at me about once a month so he can feel smart too," I said, climbing into the plane. I plopped down in a chair and leaned my head back; I needed this coffee to take effect soon.

Tack and Sanchez started the left engine as Strap pulled the chocks and climbed into the plane. He went straight to the surround system and plugged in a CD before going into the galley. Just as Rob Halford and Judas Priest started cranking out "Victim of Changes," Strap stuck his head out of the galley and said, "I got the just the thing to wake your dead ass up, buddy!" I drained the last of my coffee right as he came up and handed me a glass of Bloody Mary with Tabasco and Worcestershire sauce mixed with an energy drink.

"BLEH!" was my only response.

"Shaddup and drink it, weenie!" he said.

We flew south and east deep into Panama while Strap and I played cards as I choked down his concoction. Actually, it didn't taste too bad once I added more Tabasco sauce, but it definitely had the desired effect because I was wired for sound by the time we were over our area.

It was pure jungle down there with lots of hills and valleys, but oddly enough, we were looking down at an actual airfield this time. It wasn't much of one, but it was definitely more than a patch of grass that had been hacked down with machetes. As we circled back around for a landing, I could see a large twin-engine King Air sitting off to the side of the runway and a small Cessna 172 parked about fifty yards away from it. There were two small pickup trucks and a land Rover parked close by and about a dozen guys or so dressed in military green with AK-47s slung over their shoulders.

"This looks like it's going to be fun," Strap observed while looking out the window. "What do you make of this?"

"I don't know, man, but they definitely look like they know who we are and why we're here," I replied. Which I usually take as a good sign. Nonetheless, Strap and I had our usual assortment of party favors loaded and ready, just in case things went south. Our last couple of incidents didn't really go so well and all of us were going to be a little tense for a while as a result. That isn't necessarily a bad thing, though, because being on edge helps alleviate complacency, which can get you killed just as easily.

We landed and taxied up slowly toward the King Air, which was obviously the one that was damaged. It looked like the nose gear had collapsed while either landing or taxiing as the plane was sitting with the nose on the ground. Sanchez swung our plane around so it was pointing toward a speedy takeoff and also so that the entry door to our plane was close to the damaged plane for ease of getting out tools and equipment.

As the engines were winding down, I looked out the window while unconsciously adjusting the .45 in my back under my t-shirt. Everyone out there was just standing around casually, waiting for us to open the door and come out, which was another good sign. Sanchez came out of the cockpit and followed Strap and me out when I opened the door.

"*Buenos diaz!*" he said to no one in particular as we stepped out. An older gentleman smartly dressed in civilian clothes came walking over from behind the military types and introduced himself as Alejandro. Immediately, Sanchez engaged him and introduced everyone before we started walking back toward the King Air. He seemed to be the one in charge of the military types, even though he wasn't in uniform himself. There were three other guys in civilian clothes as well that were just leaning against a Land Rover smoking cigarettes. They seemed to be eyeing us a little more closely than the others as we walked and it gave me an uneasy feeling.

"What's with the stink eye from Miami Vice over there?" I asked Strap quietly as we followed Sanchez and Alejandro.

"Dunno, but they're definitely watching me and you pretty hard," he replied.

"Think maybe they have a sister that you ruined?" I asked. He snorted and looked back over at them again before replying.

"I don't think so; it's been a long time since we've been down in these parts. But you never know," he said with a smile. I just shook my head. I was kidding with him, of course, but those three over by the truck were definitely watching us with evil intent in their eyes.

As we approached the King Air, I looked first at the props because if they were spinning and hit the ground when the nose gear collapsed, there wasn't much we would be able to do for them. What I didn't realize until we came around to the front of the plane when we got close was that the nose gear was pulled forward and not collapsed backward under the plane as I had originally assumed. That means it was pulled out by someone towing it improperly, which meant that the engines might not have been running at the time. The rope lying on the ground still tied to the nose strut confirmed my suspicions. As Strap and I knelt down to stick our heads up under the wheel well, Sanchez came over to us.

"Alejandro says they were going to tow it with a truck and the guy hit the gas before they released the parking brake on the plane and yanked the nose gear forward," he said.

"Yep, he did a nice job too; totally destroyed the down-lock actuator attach point. We'll be able to see more when we get it jacked up," I said as we started back to our plane to unload equipment and tools.

"Alejandro says he is willing to compensate each of us handsomely for a speedy repair on top of the fee that our boss is charging him," Sanchez said to the three of us when we got back to the plane.

"Sounds good to me. I'm all about additional compensation!" Strap said with a big grin.

"Must be itchin' to move whatever he's got loaded in that bird," I said next.

"Gold," Sanchez replied flatly. "He has a lot of gold in there that he's worried about." All three of us stopped and looked at him when he said that.

"Guess that explains his little army out there," Tack said while looking out the door.

"Did you notice how interested that little trio by the pickups are in us?" I asked Sanchez.

"Not until you just mentioned it. What's up with them?" he asked.

"Not sure, but I think we need to watch 'em closely," I said next.

"I'll keep an eye on 'em while you guys are working," Tack said while handing us some tools.

The four of us started carrying tools and equipment from our plane to the King Air and Alejandro ordered some of his troops to help us carry stuff as well. Before long, we had the plane jacked and Strap got in there with a cutting torch and a few other tools of destruction and started cutting out broken and twisted gear parts that were no longer of any use. In the meantime, I went rummaging through our collection of various airplane parts that we keep on board in hopes of finding some that we could use. My hopes were high because I knew that we had some from having fixed a few King Airs in the past. They seemed to be popular with many of the drug runner types because they had turbo-props, were fast, and could carry a large payload for their size.

I got lucky in that I found some gear parts that would probably work with some modification if needed. There are different models of these types of planes and so therefore do not all use the same parts. But close is sometimes good enough in our line of work, especially if they're paying extra to get this plane in the air.

Unfortunately for us, the heat and humidity were in full swing and the white people were suffering badly. That would be me, Strap, and Tack, and we were soaking ourselves with bottled water every so often, which always works well. Everyone else took shelter under some nearby trees and watched Strap and me work from a distance. Fortunately, we were having some good luck in getting the gear back in working condition and I was surprised that we would even be able to get it to retract with the parts that we had. I was initially thinking that we would have to settle for just bracing it in place like we did with the kumquat cowboy on the turtle island.

It took us almost five hours from the time that we arrived until we were finally done. Both Strap and I were filthy from sweat and the water and crawling around in the dirt under the plane all day, but we got it. Sanchez and Tack dumped several bottles of water over us as we took makeshift showers with our shirts off. When we were packing up the tools and equipment, a very satisfied-looking Alejandro approached us by our plane. He handed us a small cardboard box about the size of a small brick that weighed about three or four pounds.

"Thank you for your help," he said in heavily accented English. "Please accept this as a token of my appreciation." The four of us thanked him in return and watched him leave as he and another gentleman climbed aboard the King Air. Tack took the box inside the plane and came back out with some cold beers.

"You guys look like you could use one," he said as he passed them around.

"Thanks, dude," I said as I inverted the bottle and drained it without coming up for air. The second one I drank a little more slowly but not much. We stood there and watched the King Air start up and start taxiing, as did the small platoon of military guys. I don't really know if they were actually Panamanian Army or Alejandro's personal little army. Also watching were the guys dressed in civilian clothes, but they weren't watching the plane. They were still watching us.

"Those dudes might be waiting to make a move on us when this guy takes off," Tack observed. He had been keeping a close eye on them all day. "If they start coming at us, I have all the rifles ready right inside the door."

"There's only three of them unless this platoon gets in on it, but they don't seem to be associated with 'em," Sanchez observed.

The King Air whipped around at the end of the runway and immediately the engines spooled up to take-off power and the plane lurched forward. About halfway down the runway, it lifted off and we watched the landing gear retract with much satisfaction. The pilot did a lap around the airfield and waggled his wings at us as he went by, letting us know that he was good to go. We waved back and watched the platoon of soldiers climb into the back of the two pickup trucks and leave. That left the other three guys and the Land Rover and they weren't giving us the impression that they were ready to leave just yet.

"Here we go," Strap observed as he drained the last bit of his third beer and tossed the bottle in the dirt. Evidently, a wild hair had just crawled up Strap's anal orifice because he reached inside the plane and grabbed an M4, made sure a round was chambered, and flicked the safe off. He adjusted his shades and spun his hat around backwards, then turned and faced the three guys with his rifle on his shoulder, obviously ready to level it at them.

"Let's get it on, you sonsabitches. I'm too hot and tired to have any patience for yer bullshit!" he said loud enough for them to hear and they were probably at least a hundred yards away. Tack snorted and chuckled as the three of us looked at each other in a bit of humored surprise.

"Oookay then," Sanchez said next as he grabbed the other three M4s and handed one each to Tack and me. Then we spread out in a line with Strap facing them like we were getting ready for a shootout at the O.K. Corral, which was essentially what we were expecting. All three of them seemed a little surprised by our actions as they just sort of looked at one another but made no sudden moves.

"Let's go see what they want," Tack said next and then the four of us started walking toward them with our rifles at the ready. We kept our spacing from each other to no closer than about fifteen feet apart and closed on them with a quick stride as to reduce their time to be able react to our advance. At about thirty feet away, we stopped and spread ourselves a little more in a half circle around them, which would ensure that they would not be able to take cover and defend themselves effectively in time.

By this time, these three guys were clearly looking very uncomfortable as opposed to the imposing looks that they were giving us earlier. They were in their mid to late twenties, thin with black, longish hair almost to shoulder length. One was wearing his in a ponytail, but all three were wearing sunglasses and dressed fairly well with loose, lightweight kakis and button-up shirts.

Sanchez started the conversation in Spanish by telling them to put all of their weapons on the hood of the vehicle. I have a habit of wrapping my upper arm once through the sling of my rifle, which allows me to pull it in tighter to my shoulder. When Sanchez gave the order, I assumed the classic Marine Corps off-hand rifle stance and leveled my rifle at the head of the guy closest to us. Then I very carefully and deliberately adjusted my cheek on the butt stock while I lined up the front and rear sights and placed the front sight post midlevel on his face. Like Strap, I too was in no mood right now and was more than ready to cut loose and get a little gnarly after sweating my balls off today. This did not go unnoticed by them, as I was making it clear who was first if they decided to get squirrelly.

By now, they went from looking uncomfortable to being frozen in place with eyes wide with concern. The guy that was about to have the pleasure of tasting my first bullet spoke without moving a muscle. All of this was probably a little unnecessary, but after a couple of incidences that we've had, we weren't taking any chances.

"We are unarmed and do not want any trouble, gentlemen," he replied in perfect English.

"All three of you lift your shirts and make a slow turn so that we can make sure you aren't lying," Sanchez said next in English. After we verified that they were unarmed, the four of us relaxed and lowered the rifles to their obvious and visible relief.

"What do you want?" Sanchez asked next. The one that was closest to Sanchez took off his sunglasses and approached Sanchez with his hand extended.

"My name is Senobio and we represent Mr. Alejandro Echevarria, the gentleman with which you just conducted business. We are his consultants, if you will, and he has tasked us with evaluating you with the possibility of making you a lucrative offer," he said.

"We don't fly drugs, chief. We just fix planes," Strap replied.

"Absolutely, gentlemen, and that is exactly what we want to discuss with you. That aircraft that you just repaired was not the first of which you have repaired for us. Our employer would like to keep you on retainer, in which you would be on call to assist with our aircraft and our aircraft only. That way, you won't be preoccupied elsewhere and unable to reach us," Senobio said.

Well, this was interesting. We had never been propositioned like this before and so we just looked back and forth at one another for a moment.

"We'll have to run this by our boss first. What's the catch?" Tack asked.

"No catch. You operate on call as you do now, but we contact you directly for expediency purposes. Our operation extends all the way from the southernmost tip of South America, all of the Caribbean, the whole United States and up through Canada and into Alaska right now. The amount that Mr. Echevarria is willing to pay to keep you on retainer far exceeds what your boss is charging for your services now," he explained.

"Holy globetrotters, Batman. That would be a lot of territory for us to cover!" Sanchez replied with a low whistle.

"You would not be expected to cover that entire area yourselves. We would be interested in using you in the Central and South American region only, as you are now," Senobio responded. "And just to clarify, we do not transport drugs. We deal in the precious metals black market."

"Really." This was more of a statement than a question by me. "I guess I never thought about there being a black market in precious metals."

Senobio looked at me squarely and said, "Sir, there is a black market for everything."

"Learn somethin' new every day in this line of work," Strap said flatly.

"Obviously, we already know how to contact your employer, which we are in the process of doing as we are having this conversation. We felt that we should speak with the four of you as well to ensure that you understand what we are offering." He looked at each of us individually as he spoke. "This is a very generous business proposition, gentlemen. Even if your employer chooses not to do business with us, we may be able to work out a separate agreement with just you as contractors. Here is my contact information, but we will be in touch," he said as he handed each of us a business card. Then the three of them climbed in the Land Rover and drove away.

"Well tie me up and call me Suzy!" Strap said out loud as we watched them drive off. "What the hell do you make of that?"

Chapter 24: The Duke of Dazzle

I've never been very good at pickup lines when it comes to hitting on women. That's not to say that I never try. I think it's my delivery that needs a little polishing. The last one I tried was when I told a female motorcycle cop that I was The Honorary Chief of the Slap-A-Hoe Tribe and asked her if she wanted to see my "peace pipe"! That was right before she shot me with her stun gun, which was right before she arrested me for public intoxication, disorderly conduct, and tampering with a police vehicle (aka; molesting her motorcycle). Evidently, I was dry humping it from behind while singing AC/DC's "She's Got Balls" as loud as I could.

Strap is absolutely no help when it comes to these types of situations because he just lies on the sidewalk and laughs. And then when he tries to get up, he yells, "The floor ain't working right!"

This happened right out in front of the bar that he and I had just gotten ourselves thrown out of again for the second time that night. I can't remember how we talked our way back in after getting thrown out the first time because I had slapped the bartender for displaying a big Jägermeister flag on the wall behind the bar. The second time was because I ripped it off the wall and pretended to surf/fly it like a magic carpet on top of the bar with Steppenwolf blasting in the background.

Sometime the next day, I was released from jail, but Strap was still being processed, so I set off on foot back to the bar where we had been arrested in hopes that our Harleys were still parked in the back.

As I was walking, a car pulled over to the side of the road next to me and stopped. When I peered inside, I was somewhat surprised to see that it was the very same female cop that had arrested me the night before. Except now she was off duty and driving home in her personal vehicle after her shift had ended and happened to recognize me walking down the road.

She asked me where I was going and why and I explained to her that it was her fault that I was walking because had she not arrested me, I probably would be passed out somewhere in close proximity to my bike. I knew this because I have tested this theory on numerous occasions. Even though she was a cop, she was still a woman and women seem to see something in me that tends to pull at their instincts or something because I've got what I have learned to recognize later in life as "the look." Of course, at this point in my life, I had not yet learned to recognize this for what it was and just assumed that she thought I was really cool and studly. Anyway, against her better judgment and probably some cop rule that says they shouldn't pick up people that they just arrested the night before, she offered me a lift back to the bar to get my bike.

As we were driving, she asked how I was feeling and admitted to me that she felt bad about the taser, but she needed to get cuffs on me and wasn't really sure how else to do it. I told her that I understood and really didn't blame her because I know I can get a little wild when I drink tequila. Then I suggested that she should probably give her bike a pregnancy test and told her that I would forgive her if she let me buy her breakfast.

Unable to resist my perverted humor and dazzling charm, she relented and had breakfast with me. Either that or I just happened to catch her at a very weak time in her life. Most likely it was the latter because she probably just saw me as the proverbial stray dog that she literally picked up on the side of the road in hopes of turning this mutt into a purebred show hound.

Strap just smiled and shook his head later when she and I pulled up in her car to pick him up after he was released from jail.

"How is it that you get released before I do and you're the one that got us arrested?" he asked.

"April, Strap. Strap, April," I said, making introductions.

"Hi, April, nice job tasering his butt last night! I loved the flounder impression that he gave us on the sidewalk! Bahahahaha!"

April giggled a little when he said that and looked at over at me. "Sorry," she said.

"It's okay. Can I borrow it to shoot him with it?" I asked.

I dated/lived with her for about a year until she tasered me again when I broke up with her.

Note to self: Don't date cops.

That was when we decided it was time to leave town and give Denver a try because Seattle was not a good place for me to live anymore.

That's why going back to L.A. wasn't sitting well with me right now. It doesn't feel normal for me to leave town unless it's on bad terms; it seems to be my *modus operandi*. Pissed-off females with tasers and lighters is like the modern day equivalent to villagers with pitchforks and torches. I knew we'd be coming back before long, but it still felt like we were abandoning our little hippie family down here. The place was kind of feeling like home, even though the lot in L.A. is the longest I've ever stayed in one place other than the boys' home when I was a kid.

Back at the farm, we were mum about our new employment offer. We needed to pow-wow with the boss in person about this one, so we were just going to sit on it until we got back. Katelyn was sticking to her promise by helping Elaina, as were the other girls. Eddy understood why we left him behind, but I think he would have preferred to stay back with Elaina to take her to the doctor today anyway. The doctor gave her the "thumbs up" and said everything looked good and that she was dilated.

"What does 'dilated' mean?" Strap asked later when we were alone.

"They check the pupils in their eyes to see if they're dilated," I replied.

"Really? What for?" he asked.

"It's like a pressure indicator; they build up pressure inside 'em so they can shoot the kid out. The docs can tell by their eyeballs when the pressure's high enough." I am so full of it. I love messin' with his head.

"Yeah, makes sense. She looks like she's ready to explode," he said.

"Yeah, like having a giant fart pushing it out," I said, chuckling. "How would you like being the doctor down there trying to catch the kid when it slides down the ramp and then you get blasted in the face with all that wet air?" He started shaking his head with his lip curled as if he smelled something foul.

"No thanks, dude. I don't mind getting pissed on by airplanes, but human body fluids and odors and stuff are no *bueno!*" he said. "By the way, I think we should pop open the cowls on the Manilishi and go over the engines a little."

"Sounds good. I'll grab some beers," I replied. We were already dirty, so we might as well get a little more work done for our own benefit before we grabbed a shower before dinner.

The brick-sized box that Alejandro had given us contained four ten-ounce gold bars, one for each of us. Nice little tip, if I do say so myself. That guy was slick; that little tip was just a little enticer for the proposition that he knew we were about to receive. I was beginning to think that being on retainer for Alejandro might not be a bad idea. The problem was that if the boss didn't go for it, then all four of us would have to agree together to work for him as a team. Just one or two of us going it alone would be difficult but probably not impossible. I'm not sure that I would be willing to break off and go solo because it wasn't like we were hurting financially anyway. All of us were stashing a fair amount of cash away already by living on the cheap.

Just as Strap and I were finishing up and closing the engine cowls, Katelyn came sprinting across the field from the house, yelling.

"Del, Strap, Elaina's water broke. She's going into labor!"

"Here we go!" I said. As I said that, I saw Eddy run out of the house and jump into the pickup truck and go speeding off toward town with a big dust cloud in his path behind him, obviously going to get the doctor.

"Okay, let's go see how she's doing, kiddo," I said as Strap and I jogged back toward the house behind Katelyn.

When we entered the house, we saw Elaina sitting on a couple of towels at the kitchen table, drinking a glass of water. As we walked in the kitchen, she turned to us and smiled.

"Everything is okay; the labor pains are very mild right now. But you two need to get showers before you can meet your new nephew or niece!" she said while pointing toward the front door.

Without saying anything, we turned and walked back outside with our marching orders and went to the barn to get cleaned up.

"I guess we know what we'll be doin' tonight," Strap said.

"What's that?" I asked.

"Sittin' around waitin' fer the kid to make an appearance, I reckon," he replied.

"That's okay; we have beer, cigars, and cards," I said. "We'll just hang out on the front porch while they're all inside dealing with all that."

Eddy arrived about a half hour later with the doctor, and Tack and Sanchez were inside the house cooking dinner with Yoda when we came back from the showers. Katelyn and the other girls were helping and waiting on Elaina and just doing anything they could to be useful. Eddy, Elaina, and the doctor were upstairs getting things ready, I assumed. Not finding anything obvious that needed our attention, Strap and I just sat out on the porch and hung out while everyone else did their thing. At one point, Katelyn came out to see where we were and asked if we needed anything, which we did not. Before returning inside, she gave Strap and me each a big hug and a kiss on the cheek without saying anything.

"What was that for?" he asked after she was inside.

"I'm guessing she's happy we bathed," I said sarcastically. We both knew what it was about and it didn't help me swallow the fact that we were going to have to go back to L.A. soon. Poor kid hadn't had a real family her whole life and she was latching on to this one as hard as she could. I didn't blame her. She didn't know that I knew she would be fine from here on out. There was no way we would let anything happen to any one of these girls ever again. But they couldn't be so sure and how could they be? They just knew that they were being loved and cared for now and not being used and abused. I was guessing that it would be a long time before they would truly be able to relax and feel like they belonged and be able to care and let people get close to them. It would take time, but time was something that they definitely had now.

I didn't want Katelyn to regress or get upset when we had to leave in a couple of weeks. I'd start talking to her about it more and more so she could get used to the idea and get comfortable with it. I really needed to convince her that we would be back and be back a lot.

After dinner, we all pitched in to clean up. Eddy took Elaina a plate upstairs and ate with her. We made the doc a plate and he ate with us as he knew it would probably be a long night. It was kind of a nice thing to see that doctors still made house calls in some parts of the world. You didn't see that kind of thing in the U.S. much anymore. One reason was that there really wasn't a hospital per se for a couple hundred miles from where we were here. So local doctors had little clinics but also made house calls mostly, as this area was fairly rural.

We camped out on the porch and relaxed in the cool night air and talked. We taught the girls how to play Rummy and I taught them how to tell when Strap was cheating. They laughed and giggled as the night wore on because we teased them and made jokes. We got to know all of them a little more and learned more details about where they were from and their families. All of them told us that they loved it here and wanted to stay and asked us questions about where we lived and when we were leaving. I kept an eye on Katelyn during this conversation, but she seemed to be okay.

They were curious about our families and where we grew up and so forth. We told them how we knew each other in the Marines and how we got started doing what we do. Sanchez told them stories about when he was a bull rider when he was very young living in New Mexico. Tack told them about where he grew up in Utah and things he did as a kid. We didn't tell them about the fact that they couldn't go home or have any contact with their family for fear of our beloved government wanting to make them disappear.

The night wore on and the girls started dropping off and going to bed. Elaina's labor was going slowly and the doctor dozed in the chair beside her bed upstairs. Yoda went to bed a short time after the girls and Eddy stayed with Elaina. That left the four of us to break out the cigars and the alcohol now that the girls went to bed. We could hear Elaina from time to time as the night wore on as her contractions got closer. Sometime around four in the morning, we heard the telltale sounds of a baby and the girls came bounding down the stairs with excitement to tell us the news.

"It's a boy, it's a boy!" they kept yelling. Yoda came down the stairs to inform us that all was well and we could go up to see her in a little while. Then he went into the kitchen and started some coffee. The house was buzzing like Christmas morning with all the excitement that the girls were creating. The doctor came downstairs after about an hour and sat down at the table to a cup of coffee and a sandwich that Yoda prepared for him.

"You guys can go upstairs for a visit now," he said as he took a sip.

I followed Strap, Tack, and Sanchez up the stairs and the four of us quietly entered the bedroom where Eddy and Elaina were sitting with the baby.

"Congratulations, you guys," Tack said quietly as we eased around on both sides of the bed to get a look.

"What's the little bambino's name?" Sanchez asked.

"I think you oughta name him The Duke! You know, like John Wayne. Or you could name him John Wayne and we'll just call him the Duke anyway," Strap blurted. I just looked at him.

"It's not a dog, you friggin' cow pie!" I told him. "What's wrong with you? They're not gonna want to name their kid Duke."

"It's not Duke. It's '<u>The</u> Duke,'" he replied.

"Oh, well, that changes everything. How about instead of moron, we call you '<u>The</u> Moron'?" I said.

"Will you two idiots shut up?" Tack said. Elaina was smiling and shaking her head at Strap and me.

"Thank you, Strap, but we have already named him. His name is Eduardo Severino Guerrero," Elaina replied softly.

"A little Eddy Junior, huh?" Sanchez said.

"Hey, we can call him 'Little Eddy Munster'!" Strap chimed in again.

"That's nice. And you wonder why people pretend they don't know you in public," I said.

"They do? Who does that?" he asked with a curious look on his face. I just shook my head.

"Strap, would you like to hold the baby?" Elaina asked. Strap froze in place with an "Oh God what do I do?" look. Kind of like you do when you're in a grocery store and you're alone in an aisle, so you figure it's safe to fart, but then some really hot chick comes around the corner and you just polluted the area and you're the only one there, so she's going know it was you.

"Uh," was the only thing that he could say. *This is going to be entertaining,* I thought.

"Come here. I will show you how to hold him. Come sit here on the bed," Elaina said, indicating a spot next to her. Strap did as he was told and sat down. Elaina demonstrated how she was holding the baby and showed him to hold his arms like she was. Then she carefully passed the baby to him and he sat there holding him rigid like a statue.

"You don't need to hold it like it's about to explode, onion head," I said.

"I know that. I just don't know what I'm supposed to do with it now," he replied. Elaina laughed softly.

"It's a he and you can talk to him. He won't bite you," she said as the rest of us quietly laughed with her.

"What's up, little dude? Nice to meet you," Strap said, looking down at Eddy Jr. "Hey, he's looking at me!"

"You may want to rethink this one, Elaina. Are you sure that you want Strap to be one of the first people your son has contact with in the world?" I said. Strap managed to extend a middle finger while holding little Eddy.

"See? He's already teaching him bad habits," I said.

We chatted with them for a few minutes longer, but Elaina was exhausted and needed to rest, so we left them alone to go get some shut-eye as well. It had been a long day and a long night.

Chapter 25: Nudgin' the Knucklehead

The next few days went by with everyone getting accustomed to the new addition around the place. It really didn't change much for the four of us because we slept in the barn with the other animals anyway. Yoda hired some local guys to come out and start making plans to add on to the house. It just so happens that forty ounces of gold goes a long way toward paying for new construction and then some. Yoda gave us a curious look when we handed him four ten-ounce gold bars, but he didn't ask any questions, so we didn't offer any explanations.

Katelyn was back to tagging along with us when she wasn't helping Elaina around the house or doing chores around the farm. She seemed to have almost taken on a new purpose in life with the baby around and the girls were already referring to him as their little brother. I was hoping that it would be kind of a distraction for her so she wouldn't concentrate on the four of us so much and hopefully wouldn't dwell on the fact that we had to leave.

We talked to all of the girls a little more about their importance around here and reemphasized the need for them to concentrate on their studies and embrace this place as their new home. I knew there would be a few issues and tension from time to time as all families will endure, but they needed to know that this was where they belonged and no one would send them or take them away from that anymore.

It's still a little amazing to me to look at things from Miguel's standpoint. One day he's out here cruising around doing his own thing and the next thing he knows, he's got a full house of kids and a bunch of dudes shacked up in his barn! He was soaking up every minute of it, though, I know, after having gone so many years without his family. Life will throw an interesting curve ball at you from time to time and it's good to see that people who needed each other can accidentally come together. Or was it an accident? Something was talking to me that last night in Dangriga and I knew we needed to get back here fast, but I couldn't know why. Now I guess I know why. I also knew that we needed to be back here a lot in the near future and I wasn't ruling out the possibility of just living down here at some point. Whether I would be working for the boss or working for Miguel or even Alejandro, I didn't know, but that was going to be plan B for me if and when I needed a change.

After another conversation with Miguel, Eddy, and Elaina, and a brief email exchange with the boss, we decided it was time to head back to L.A. Elaina made a simple but delicious dinner with baked chicken, potatoes, and fresh vegetables from the garden. She was such an awesome cook and I was definitely going to miss the great food around here. This might be hard to believe, but my diet leaves a bit to be desired when I'm living in the parking lot.

We told the girls that it was time, but by now it was no surprise as they knew the time was coming. After dinner, we sat out on the porch and talked until it was late and we decided that we would leave late in the morning for the flight back.

The next morning, Elaina made a nice breakfast and had our favorite coffee brewed and waiting for us. She was still turning her nose up at it and refused to drink any herself. After breakfast, I noticed a few t-shirts were missing when I was packing my duffle bag in my room in the barn and I was fairly sure I knew who stole them. And just to show me that she wasn't ashamed of it, Katelyn was wearing my favorite Hussongs t-shirt when she walked into my room and plopped onto the bed.

"That shirt looks a little big for you," I said. She just shrugged her shoulders.

"It also looks very similar to the one that I'm missing," I added. Another shrug.

"Am I to assume that I'll have to take a trip down to Ensenada to get another one?" I asked as I continued packing.

"Where's that?" she asked.

"Little coastal town south of Tijuana, Mexico, supposedly the birthplace of the margarita," I replied.

"Will you take me there one day?" she asked.

"Sure, when you're old enough to go into a bar," I replied.

"When are you guys coming back?" she asked next.

"Not sure, kiddo. It won't be long, though. Say, less than three months," I replied.

"Three months? That's long!" she said with a shocked look on her face.

"I said less than. It could be a week if we get called back down for a job. We never know when we'll get a call. It won't be that long, I promise," I said. She just sat there and looked at me without saying anything.

"Look, you're going to be busy with helping out around here with the little crumb catcher and studying anyway. You won't even be thinking about us." I was trying to keep her from getting upset.

"Do you have any kids?" she asked next.

"Wow, that was out of the blue. Where did that come from?" I asked her in return.

"I dunno, just wondering. Do you have any kids anywhere?" she asked again.

"Nope," I said flatly

"Ever been married?" she asked next.

"Nope," I replied again.

"Why not?" she asked.

"Why do you want to know this stuff? You're a kid. Kids don't care about this stuff, right?" I asked her.

"I do and I'm a teenager, not just a little kid," she said with a stern look.

"Okay. I don't know why not. Never got that serious with a girl, I guess," I replied.

"Why not?" she asked again.

"Just how many 'why nots' am I in for right now?" I asked as I gave her a goofy face.

"Why not?" she repeated and returned the same face.

"Good question, but I really don't have a good answer," I replied.

"Well, I think you should find someone and get married and adopt me," she said with raised eyebrows.

"Ah, so that's where this is going. Got it all figured out, do ya?" I asked.

"Yep, and make it snappy, will you? I'm not getting any younger, you know," she said with an expectant look on her face.

"Yes, ma'am, I'll get right on it!" I replied.

"Ha, that'll never happen! He's lucky some of those girlfriends didn't shoot him!" Strap said as he came through the door.

"He's got a point," I said.

"Well then, we have to work on getting me back into the States so I can live with you guys!" she said next. Strap and I just looked at each other with raised eyebrows.

"Can't see that being a good idea," he said.

"Why not?" she asked.

"Well, we can work on gettin' you back into the States and all, but we gotta give you to the authorities and tell them we found you down here. Then they'll get you back to yer family," he said.

"I don't want to go back with them," she said.

"Yeah, but you're a minor, so I reckon they'll take you somewhere like a foster home or somethin'," he said.

"We'll just tell them I'm gonna live with you guys and you'll be my foster parents," she replied while looking back and forth at Strap and me. I started laughing when she said that.

"Ha ha, they'll get a kick out of that one. Can you imagine child services scoping our digs in the parking lot to see if it's suitable place to raise a kid?"

Strap was shaking his head and chuckling as well. "Yeah, they'll be lookin' at us like we're on crack or somethin'," he replied. Katelyn just stood there looking at the two of us with her arms crossed.

"Why is that so funny?" she asked.

"Uh, well, we don't exactly live in an environment that might be considered conducive to raising kids," I replied as tactfully as I could.

"You guys really live in a parking lot?" she asked.

"Yup," Strap replied. She just stood there looking at us.

"It's a long story," I said in hopes of squashing any more questions. "Look, kiddo, just chill out down here for a while and we'll see about getting you into the States down the road. But don't get antsy; you're safer here and they need you," I said.

"Okay," she said. She stepped over and hugged me and then hugged Strap. I leaned down and got face level with her.

"Are we good?" I asked.

"We're good," she replied with a smile and then hugged me again.

"Can I have some of my t-shirts back, then?" I asked next.

"Nope," she replied as she walked out of the room ahead of us. Strap looked at me as we were walking.

"So how many t-shirts have you donated to the cause down here?" he asked.

"Probably about half a dozen by now. By the way, we're ridin' to Ensenada one day soon," I replied.

"I'm good with that. You needed to update yer wardrobe anyway. You're starting to make me look bad. I have a reputation to keep up, ya know," he said.

"Really? Evidently, you and I see your reputation a little differently," I replied.

"Why's that?" he asked.

"How about I start wearing floral print Hawaiian shirts?" I asked next.

"Sure, that'd be a good start. You'll fit in with the rest of the fruit bags out in L.A," he said sarcastically. "And the flowers might even help camouflage the food stains on the front and the holes in the armpits," he replied. I pulled out the front of my t-shirt a little and looked down at it; maybe there were a couple of grease spots.

"Yeah, well, the armpit holes are supposed to be there. They're strategically engineered ventilation holes," I replied with mock seriousness.

"Uh huh," he muttered.

"Well, at least my shirts don't all have holes in the front from opening my beer bottles," I said next. He stopped and looked down at his t-shirt and stuck a finger out of a hole that was about level with his navel.

"I was wonderin' why they all had holes right there," he said with genuine puzzlement.

Katelyn was standing by the entry door to the plane and shaking her head at us and our conversation.

"Take care of that Hussongs shirt. It's got sentimental value," I told her as I climbed into the plane.

"Yeah, but not the kind of sentiment that you need to hear about," Strap said to her next as he climbed up behind me.

Tack and Sanchez were already in the plane stowing their gear as we climbed in with our duffle bags. Once everything was put away and ready to go, we climbed back out of the plane and walked with Katelyn back over to the house. Elaina and Eddy were sitting on the porch with the baby and Miguel and the other girls came out of the house as we approached. We had already talked with Eddy and Miguel about making sure things would be safe here while we were gone. We had complete confidence in Eddy's ability to handle any trouble that came along and we left them an M4 and a shotgun with plenty of ammo just for safe measure. Miguel assured us that he had not had any trouble here in many, many years.

We said our goodbyes and gave hugs and handshakes all around and then the four of us walked back over to the Green Manilishi and climbed in. Tack and Sanchez were going to do the flying today and I went to the sound system while Strap started mixing drinks in the galley. We rolled down the grass strip and lifted into the air as I dealt the cards with the Motor City Madman screaming out "Stranglehold" over the surround system.

"I'm down to you for fifty bucks still," Strap said.

"It's more like <u>two</u> fifty, you lyin' sack!" I corrected.

"Bull!" he replied, but that was all the argument he could muster.

Chapter 26: 96 Hours of Beer on the Wall

After a few rounds of cards, Strap went up front to relieve one of the guys for a bit. I kind of drifted off to thoughts about Anna now that we were over with this gig and I could go see her. I was suffering from a little self-imposed guilt for not seeing her sooner. I worry about her now that she's divorced and her real kids are grown. Even though they live close to her and she sees them regularly, I still don't like that she's alone. She got really upset with me once when I referred to her kids as her "real" kids once. I wasn't trying to be hurtful; it's just the way that I thought of them when I was a kid. Nonetheless, she got upset about it, so I have to be careful not to say that around her.

The nice thing was that now that her kids are grown, they do their best to stay in touch with me and include me in family affairs and stuff like that. It's basically because of my lifestyle as to why communication has been difficult at times.

I decided that I'd let the boss know that I was going to take off for a while and go see her after I'd been back in L.A. for a week or so. I was sure he was expecting that anyway as the other guys would probably take some time off as well. Strap's got his carnival family, wherever they are; they move around a lot, but he catches up with them from time to time. Tack has a sister that he keeps in touch with through code words in the classifieds. He sends her money to meet him in various vacation spots every so often. Sanchez has family around Texas, but I'm not sure if he really tries to stay in contact with any of them much. I don't think he does because he doesn't talk about them. It's unfortunate that he has to forfeit that to stay alive but when faced with the alternative…

The rest of the flight back was uneventful; we flew the same route back that we took going down and even stopped for fuel at the same airport on the way. I knew that I was going to have to call Janelle soon after we got back or she would give me a bunch of grief when she caught up with me. It was not that I really wanted to avoid her; it was quite the opposite actually. It's just that I'm fearful of the drama when things end badly. And it always ends badly. I've long given up on the notion that things like a relationship might actually work out in the long run because, with me, it's never like the relationship slowly starts losing its flare or anything. That would be nice because you could see things slowly start to deteriorate and prepare for it and think up some line of B.S. that you're going to give her as to why you're breaking up with her. No, with me, it's always like a bomb going off and I'm the one standing there looking around trying to figure out what happened. I guessed I'd just light the fuse and call her tomorrow.

It was late afternoon when we landed at LAX and, oddly enough, it felt kind of good to be back in sunny southern California. I have a love/hate relationship with California; I love to hate it, but for some reason, I keep coming back. We strolled through customs in the corporate terminal, which was really just a bunch of jive talkin' back and forth with ole Huggy.

"Huggy! Wus goin' on, big sexy?" I said as we came through the doors.

"Man, y'all mugs still alive? I been figurin' y'all must be worm food by now!" he replied.

"They tried, buddy, but they didn't try hard enough!" Strap said to him.

"I got that sexy lingerie that I promised for ya, Huggy. You want it?" I said jokingly.

"Don't choo be handin' none a dat stuff to me, man!" he replied while he was laughing. "For all I know, it's probly yours!"

"It is, but I know you've secretly wanted it," I said.

"Get outta here which yo crazy self! Y'all are the craziest white dudes I've ever met!"

"See ya next time, Huggy!" Strap said as we left.

When we stepped outside, the boss was leaning against a suburban waiting for us.

"What, no limo?" Tack asked jokingly as we walked up to him.

"It just so happens that they're all booked for tonight," he replied as we all shook hands. "I'm going to take you guys back to the lot to get settled in. Del and Strap, you guys can swing by to get your bikes out of my garage whenever you want. Tack and Sanchez, I took the liberty of leasing two RVs and parked them in the lot for you. We can work out the details later if you want to keep them or do something else; just let me know."

"Sounds good. Thanks, boss," Tack said.

"Yeah, thanks; we appreciate that, boss," Sanchez added.

"Don't mention it, fellas. It's the least I can do," he replied. "I want you guys to take some time off. I'm sure you were thinking about it anyway. Call me in about three weeks and we'll regroup. We'll need to discuss our new business proposition then as well. Sound good?"

"Sounds good," the four of us replied.

Back in the lot, things looked the same. I didn't really expect that anything would be different, though. It was obvious that the boss had someone looking after our RVs and pickup trucks, so it didn't look like they had been abandoned. I threw my duffle bag on the couch, grabbed a beer out of the fridge, and was just settling into a seat at the picnic table when Strap came out of his RV with a beer as well.

"Let's go check out Tack and Sanchez's RVs," he said. The boss had their RVs parked right in front of and one row over from ours so any one of us could see the other three RVs from our own. Both of theirs were the thirty-foot travel trailer types like the ones Strap and I live in with a couple of slide outs, which greatly expand the square footage of the interior. The idea of living in an RV may seem a little primitive to some, but actually, they're quite comfortable if you don't mind adjusting your lifestyle a little.

After we got the nickel tour, the four of us settled around the picnic table to discuss each other's plans. You would think that the four of us might be sick of one another by now, but it was quite the opposite. We were old enough and mature enough to respect each other's differences at times, but we relied on one another completely, and we each knew without a doubt that any one of the other three would be behind us one hundred percent. We knew that what we did for a living wasn't just a job; it was a complete lifestyle. I don't live to work, but I like to think that I work to live and despite outward appearances as far as how we live, I've never had more fun or have worked and lived with a better bunch of guys in my life. And although I might trade this for something else down the road one day, I could never replace this, ever.

I was in the mood for some serious hot wings and cold beer on tap because evidently, hot wings haven't taken off down in Central America like they have here in the good ole U.S. of A.

And whoever that dude is in Buffalo that came up with the idea, God bless him because hot wings and beer are now at the top of my personal food pyramid! Naturally, I didn't have to twist the arms of the other three as we piled in a pickup truck moments later and made a beeline straight to a place that had a sign with a picture of a buffalo with little wings on it out front.

After a few rounds of beer and our lips and tongues still sizzling from the wing sauce, we decided that we needed something more. For reasons unbeknownst to me, we decided to head down to Mexico; Ensenada, to be exact. Like I said, reasons unbeknownst to me because beer logic is different from regular logic. For example: it's like beer math in the Marine Corps; six guys times six beers apiece equals nine cases of beer. Beer logic is: "Hey, let's go find another bar for a while." "Okay, let's go to Mexico." Despite the fact that Ensenada was close to a three-and-a-half-hour drive from L.A., we didn't have anything better to do, so why not?

This scenario just happens to be very similar to what got me, Strap, and a few others in trouble in the Marine Corps once. Our unit had just arrived at LAX after a twenty-something-hour flight from Okinawa with a stop in Anchorage along the way after a year deployment overseas. Upon arrival at Camp Pendleton, we were told that we had a ninety-six, which means ninety-six hours off before we had to report back to the squadron for duty. That means a four-day weekend and evidently everything said after that fell on deaf ears. Within minutes of dumping our sea bags in the barracks, about a half a dozen of us were zipping down I-5, headed straight for Tijuana. Even though we'd been out of the country for a year, we weren't back six hours before we were leaving again.

Four days later, we arrived back at base and not so ready for work. After making a general nuisance of ourselves in Tijuana, we decided Ensenada should be our next target. No money was spent on hotel rooms and very little was spent on real food for those four days. Without allowing ourselves enough time to even get a shower and shave, we dashed into the barracks, pulled out uniforms that had been crammed in our sea bags for close to about five days, and arrived in front of the squadron barely in time for morning formation.

When the commanding officer stood in front of six bleary-eyed, unshaven, rumpled bags of camouflage, swaying with the wind in the back row of the formation, he was less than impressed. The words that fell on deaf ears after we heard the phrase "ninety-six hours off" evidently were: check into the barracks and then report to the squadron duty officer the next morning for a quick briefing. That's the thing about the military; sometimes time off isn't exactly what you might think. It's more like: you can take some time off but don't go too far and make sure that we can get in touch with you.

The formation was dismissed except for the six of us. The commanding officer departed and left us to deal with the Sergeant Major. This guy had the personality of a turnip and the demeanor of a water buffalo. His nickname was "Bitter-beer-face" because his permanent facial expression looked like his mom gave birth to him out of her anus. He just stood there staring at us with his hands on his hips with the distant sadistic gaze of a serial killer. I always wondered where the Marine Corps found some of these psychopaths. I've envisioned special farms out in the middle of nowhere where they imprison sub-humans with certain traits and attributes and force them to inbreed just for the Marines. And he didn't like our type one bit. He viewed us with contempt because we were blond-haired punks that barely kept our haircuts within regulations and cared more about motorcycles and surfing than his beloved Marine Corps. Just for extra added value, he adopted the infamous drill instructor frog-in-the-throat voice that he so sorely missed from his glory days when he started insulting our family heritages and making rude suggestions as to our sexual preferences. After his tirade, we were restricted to base for three months and got volunteered for every crap duty that he could think of. It wouldn't have been too bad if all that didn't include running the hills with fifty-pound packs every morning for those three months, though.

Fortunately, that was a distant memory as we finally rolled into Ensenada late in the evening in search of a good time. Of course, Hussongs would have to be our first stop, but we were willing to dwell wherever the dregs of debauchery should deposit us. Age and experience has caught up with us just a little, evidently, as we were not willing to go four days of nonstop drinking anymore and we found ourselves back at our RVs late in the afternoon the next day. Shaky Jake must've realized that we were back in town because he was napping in the back of my pickup truck when we arrived. I was ready for a shower and some sleep by that point and did just that. Ole Jake was going to have to wait one more day for the beer cooler to get restocked.

Chapter 27: Cerebral Rectitus

Cerebral Rectitus is a chronic medical condition that men tend to suffer from every so often, some more than others. It's when you're about to do something dumb and you know that you're about to do something dumb and you know good and well why it's dumb and exactly why you shouldn't do it, but you do it anyway.

Sometime late the next morning, I was up with a cup of goat coffee that I so lovingly made in my well-seasoned coffee press. I call it "seasoned" because I don't wash it. I threw some coffee beans in my duffle bag before we left the plane when we got in, but there was still plenty stored on the plane. When the coffee chemicals started working their magic through my system, I felt the telltale signs of a previous meal hit the ramp, telling me it was time to hole up in the ever so spacious bathroom that RVs are so renowned for. Sitting there quietly enjoying the peace and quiet of large passenger jets coming in for landing just over my head and searching for another spiritual revelation, I heard the sound of my generator sputter down to silence.

"Morning, ball-bag!" These kind words were immediately followed by the sound of plastic BBs reverberating off the side of my RV.

It's funny how easily one can go from thoughts of serenity and seeking God to murder. This was what I was thinking to myself now because this was one of those times where harassing someone really should be off limits. Besides, if my twisted little theory about taking a dump is actually proof of creation, then sitting on the toilet should be akin to saying prayers, right? You don't come up and disturb someone while they're trying to connect with God in church! So this is another time when a man should be able to enjoy the sanctity of quiet meditation while polluting the air with his own stink. But no, now I had to clean myself up so I could go out and defend myself while trying to restart my generator so I could flush the toilet.

Today, I was going to call Janelle and then go buy a plane ticket to go see Anna in a couple of days. I'd spend some time with Janelle if she wanted and then start setting Strap up for an ingenious little practical joke that I came up with several weeks ago, but I'd been putting it on the back burner until the time was right. And now the time was right. This one was going to be so good that I almost giggled out loud when I thought of it.

These are the moments that I live for; you read a lot of sappy stuff out there about what people think life is all about. People talk about family and love and God and all that, but you never hear about the absolute joy a person can obtain by dreaming up something devious and sinister in order to ruin their best friend's entire day! There's no other feeling like it. It's almost indescribable because it's the planning part that's almost more fun than the joke itself—almost. The feeling of joy comes so deep from within that I can feel my intestines jiggle with excitement as I work out the details in my head. And I was going to do it right before I got on the plane to see Anna and laugh all the way Georgia! That big knucklehead has turned off my generator for the last time, although I really doubt that because I know him and he'll keep doing it, but he'll definitely wear out that little hamster wheel in his gourd trying to think of something to get me back for this one.

When I reemerged from my RV a little later with a fresh cup of coffee and a not-so-fresh look on my face, Strap, Tack, Sanchez, and Shaky Jake were all seated in foldout chairs or at the picnic table between our RVs. I settled into a chair and adjusted my sunglasses as I let the warm southern California sun greet me in full.

"Sooo, what was all that about earlier?" Tack asked while looking back and forth at Strap and me. Obviously, he was referring to the little shootout that had just occurred. It was Shaky Jake that answered him as he emerged from my RV with a fresh cup of coffee for himself.

"Just one of the many recurring instances of childish shenanigans that myself and the other parking lot residents have become accustomed to." I nodded my head in agreement and Strap just shrugged his shoulders with a little grin.

"That's why we pay you with coffee and beer, Jake," he said. "To help ease the pain of having to put up with us." Jake toasted his coffee mug in Strap's direction before taking another sip.

"And I gladly accept the payment, gentlemen," he replied. "But the beer cooler is getting low."

"Not a problem, dude; we'll get that remedied most ricky tick," I said.

"Beer cooler?" Tack asked.

"Yep, it's kind of a community thing; everyone donates ice and beer every so often," I replied.

"I love it here already!" Tack said with a smile. After a brief discussion, we decided that a bicycle ride along the Strand toward Hermosa Beach was in order. There are a few little cafés and restaurants where you can sit outside and enjoy a nice breakfast while watching the joggers go by or the volleyball players on the beach; not a bad way to get back into the southern

California groove. Everyone out here has a bicycle because not having a bicycle in southern California is like going to a tropical island on vacation just to sit in the hotel room and watch TV; it just doesn't make sense.

Later that day, I called Janelle and asked her if she wanted to hang out that night. She knew we were back in the States and was expecting my call, so she had a place in mind already. I met her outside a restaurant in Santa Monica after I had gotten a haircut and trimmed the facial scruff a little. I figured that despite my pessimistic outlook on me and long-term relationships, I could at least make an effort by taking a swipe at some personal hygiene and a presentable t-shirt that was clean and didn't have any holes. Much to my surprise, I actually found one shirt that met those criteria, only because it had been under the seat of my truck and hadn't been worn in a really long time, but I washed it and it was good to go.

When I saw her, I was again taken aback by the way she carried herself. She was elegant and proper in that British sort of way that seemed to have lost its importance for Americans over time— Americans like me, that is. She almost looked like she should be strolling around with a dude in a pinstripe suit with an ascot and a cane. After searching the sidewalk on both sides of the street for such a dude, I walked up to her anyway. She looked at me curiously after I hugged her.

"Who were you searching for just a moment ago, William?" she asked.

"You look like the duke of something should be rolling up in a Bentley to pick you up right now," I replied.

"I'll take that as a compliment, Mr. Del Rio, but I am here to meet you, sir, and this is what I wear to work," she replied in her proper English accent.

"Well, you look pretty stylish for just getting off work," I said.

"Well, thank you," she replied.

"I washed my shirt," I said with a proud grin.

"That's good. Thank you for doing that. Would you like to go inside and get a table?" she said, shaking her head with a smirk on her face.

We ordered drinks and made small talk for a bit while we waited. I actually ordered a martini, which is rare, but I've been known to do that from time to time. This seemed like a good occasion for it.

"You look well-tanned and a little thinner than when I last saw you, William," she said.

"If you keep calling me 'William,' I'm going to start calling you 'Duchess,'" I replied.

"I'm just teasing you, Del, because anyone who goes by an abbreviated last name obviously doesn't like their first name," she said, smiling.

"So you're harassing me. I'm very hurt by that and I think that's extremely uncalled for," I managed to say, but I couldn't keep a straight face to save my life.

"I didn't realize that you're so sensitive, William. It looks like teasing you is going to be much easier than I thought," she replied and then she batted her eyelashes at me. That made me chuckle. I couldn't not like her.

"I can see that hanging out with you is going to be a problem," I said after taking a sip of my drink.

"And we both know that it won't stop you," she said while looking at me over her glass. "You can be as aloof as you want, but I really don't see the point. You can also play the tramp to the lady as much as you want if that makes you feel better also, but it would be much easier if we could just dispense with all the rubbish and get on with it." She was looking directly at me with raised eyebrows and a smile. I was really going to have to get used to how direct she could be and I think I was starting to see what made her a successful business owner.

"Okay, lady, I'll try to dispense with all the rubbish," I said, smiling back at her.

"Thank you. Now tell me about your little jungle safari. I want to hear all about it!" she asked excitedly.

"How do you know we were in the jungle?" I asked curiously.

"Your boss's girlfriend works for me, remember? Don't worry; I don't blab. But I know where you go and that you boys don't play with nice people," she replied. I did a slow scan of the room to see if anyone seemed overly interested in our conversation and lowered my voice before I spoke again.

"Not very nice people is an understatement. There's a lot more to the story than you know." I tried to keep my tone light, but I wanted to let her know that I was very serious. "Please do not talk about us to anyone. Ever. Do not even mention any of our names to other people. It could get some of us killed. I cannot stress that enough. I don't even want us to talk about it in public. And if the boss's girlfriend is talking too much, please shut her down and let me know immediately," I said quietly. Her smile slowly dissipated while I was speaking and she was quiet when I finished. She watched me like she was waiting for a second head to pop out of my neck or something and she was quiet long enough that, for a moment, I thought that she would get up and leave. She was really looking for a sign that I was joking with her, but she found none. Then she slowly leaned in across the table.

"Are you wanted by the authorities?" she asked ever so softly.

"I'm not," I said while still holding her gaze. She slowly nodded her head while she processed that for a moment.

"How do you like me now?" I asked with a half-sinister smile. She closed her eyes for a moment and then let out a sigh.

"Are you trying to scare me off?" she asked.

"Not trying to scare you, babe; just speakin' the truth," I replied. "Now you know why I said we were techy troubleshooters. It'd be easier if you played dumb about what I do. And if you want to walk away from this, no hard feelings here," I said honestly. She sat quietly for a moment and looked around the restaurant as if trying to decide what to do.

"Suddenly, I'm not the one so reluctant to jump into a relationship," I said while watching her. Her head snapped back around and she scanned my face before speaking.

"You'll have to do better than that to scare me off, William, but we should work on your fake job description. Techy nerd isn't working for you," she said as she got up from the table. "Now if you'll excuse me, I'm going to find the powder room." Then she came around to my side of the table, leaned down, and kissed me square on the lips before she walked off. Boy, she smelled good. I could feel my cerebrum entering my rectum as I watched her walk through the restaurant.

Chapter 28: You're Like the Wind between My Butt Cheeks

After spending a couple of days with Janelle, I was back in the lot with evil intent on my mind. Strap was nowhere to be seen, but his truck was there, which meant he had already picked up his Harley and was out and about somewhere in L.A., probably causing problems. This was perfect timing for me because I needed him to be away while I set him up, so I immediately went to work, not knowing how much time I had before he returned. I was underneath his RV when a pair of feet in flip-flops appeared next to mine.

"Something tells me that you're not down there repairing a leak for your friend," said a familiar voice.

"Not exactly," I replied. When the voice got closer, I looked over to see Tack peering at me under the RV.

"Do I want to know what you might be doing under there?" he asked with a big grin on his face.

"Let's just say that I'm providing a service by bringing you a little entertainment, buddy," I replied and grinned back at him. Then I slid out from under the RV, gathered my tools, and walked back to my own.

"Now all we have to do is wait," I said as I sat down and opened a beer.

"What are we waiting for?" Tack asked as he sat down with his own beer.

"Nature, dude. Just good ole fashioned nature," I said as I took a swig.

Over the next few hours, a few RV Argonauts from the lot meandered over in search of human interaction and before long a card game ensued, cigar smoke filled the air, and the raspy, growly voice of Tom Waits drifted out of the speakers. Dinger was happy that we were back, but he became immediately wary of Tack and Sanchez. When he quietly asked me about them, I told him that the government sent them here to monitor everyone. I figured that should jack up his imagination for a while. Eventually, I heard the sounds of Strap's Harley growing closer and a grin slowly crept over my face. I looked up from my cards and noticed Tack looking at me expectantly. I gave him a smile to let him know that things were going to get fun tonight.

Strap rounded the corner on the bike with what appeared to be a new friend on the back. A female by first appearances, but you couldn't be sure with him. He noticed me eyeing her closely and flipped a finger at me in response. This only made me laugh because Tack and Sanchez had turned around and they were both looking at her carefully as well. Strap came over to the table with his girl in tow to introduce her to everyone.

"What's shakin', superfly?" I said as they approached.

"I know what you're thinking," he said to me as soon as he walked up.

"What? I didn't say anything," I said in defense, but I couldn't stop smiling.

"You know what. Guys, Lisa. Lisa, the guys. Except that guy," he said while pointing at me. "Stay away from him." She greeted everyone and we made room at the table and a few foldout chairs found their way over. She sat down and someone passed a beer over to her while Strap walked back to his RV for a minute.

"What did you do to make him say that?" she asked me after a moment. I blew out cigar smoke and looked at her before answering.

"The last woman that he brought over turned out to be more man than WO-man," I said honestly and then I smiled and winked at her. "Anything you want to let us know before he gets back?" She immediately started laughing as did the rest of the table.

"Are you serious? That's so funny!" she said as she looked around the table. Strap was walking back to the table, shaking his head.

"What did you say?" he asked as he fetched a beer out of the beer cooler.

"Nothing but the truth, the whole truth, so help me God," I said. Lisa was giggling with her hand over her mouth while looking at Strap.

"What's wrong with you?" he asked me as he sat down.

"Well, don't worry, you guys. I am all female and I can prove it!" Lisa said as she started to stand up. All eyes were on her and not a word was spoken after she said that. I leaned back, crossed my arms, and watched her with everyone else, curious as to what she was about to do.

"Wait, wait, wait, you don't have to prove anything to these clowns!" Strap said quickly. A second later, I heard Dinger curse under his breath as he realized that wasn't going to get a show now.

"Do you see what you do?" Strap asked while looking at me.

"Hey, she asked, I told her the truth," I said in defense.

"Funny how you're willing to tell the truth when it suits you," he said.

"Well, yeah, I'm not going to tell it when it suits you. What fun would that be? Hey, Lisa, ask me some more questions. Now's a good time," I said, smiling.

"Don't ask him anything; just pretend he's not here," Strap said quickly. The rest of the table and the others gathered around were enjoying the exchange as we were known for.

"Okay, why do you guys call him Strap?" Lisa asked next. Strap lowered his head and clamped his hand over his eyes in defeat. There was already chuckling going on before I could answer, as everyone pretty much knew the story.

"Because it's a nicer name than what I usually call him," I said in a matter-of-fact tone.

"No, really," she insisted.

"Because he collects strap-on dildos and walks around in public wearing them on the outside of his clothes!" I said, not telling the truth at all. Lisa busted out laughing when I said that and had tears running down her face while holding her hand over mouth.

"Really? That's not true, is it?" she asked, looking at me and around the table.

"No, it's not true!" Strap said next. "Don't believe anything he says, ever. Never trust anything he tells you. As a matter of fact, you should stay away from him. He's a very bad man."

"I agree with him completely," I said. "You should never listen to me."

Later on when the card game ended and things were winding down, Strap pulled up a chair next to mine.

"What do you think of her?" he asked.

"She's fun. I like her," I replied. "Better not have any strap-ons lying around your RV, though; then she will believe me!"

"Yeah, thanks for telling her that," he said.

"You're welcome. Anything for you, buddy," I replied. "You're like the wind between my butt cheeks. The crust in the corner of my eye. The..."

"I get the picture. By the way, when are you bringing Janelle over?" he asked.

"When you're not here," I said flatly.

"That's probably a good idea. Does she know about your other woman, Gumball Sally?" he asked with a grin. I chuckled and shook my head. I'd never be able to get away from that story.

"No, I'm hoping for a threesome, so I want to wait for the right time," I replied.

"Nice. I want video," he said. "I've gotta drop Lisa off in a bit. Wanna go for a ride on the hogs?" he asked.

"Nah, can't. I've had too much to drink. I gotta crash later anyway. Catchin' a flight out to see Anna in the morning," I said.

"Awright, give her a hug for me," he said.

"Will do, boss," I said.

Chapter 29: Punkassedness

It's a good thing that he took Lisa back because things were about to get real fun and she wouldn't know what the heck to think. Strap was going to figure out real quick that there was something wrong with his plumbing if he hadn't suspected it already when he was here earlier. He was not going to want to fool with it tonight, so he'd just walk over to the port-o-john tonight and wait to look at things tomorrow when it was light out, which was exactly what I was counting on. Because we live in the LAX airport employee parking lot, there is a shuttle bus that drives through the lot that takes employees over to the terminal area to work and there are port-o-johns located at the various bus stops.

All I needed to do was wait for nature in the form of him having to go to the restroom. So I quietly dozed with the lights off in my RV to give the impression that I had retired for the night. When I heard his Harley pull up, I knew it was time to get ready because I needed to spring when he was ready to wander off to the port-o-john. About a half hour after he arrived, I heard the door to his RV open and I watched him walk off toward that direction. I quietly stepped out of my RV with zip-ties in one hand and duct tape in the other and crept over to the side of my RV where I could watch and wait for him to go inside.

As soon he closed the door, I took off in a sprint and zip-tied the door handle on the port-o-john before he could open it, when he heard me. Then, with him cussing and vowing revenge and a slow and painful death, I slowly walked around the little one-person building while unrolling my roll of duct tape. While I was doing several laps around him, I calmly explained to him that this was for all of those mornings when he turned off my generator. Then I calmly walked back to his RV, grabbed the keys to his truck, and backed it up to the door of the port-o-john. I retrieved the tie-down straps that he kept under the seat and strapped the port-o-john firmly to the back of the truck, jumped back in, and started it up. Evidently, this move caused him quite a bit of alarm because now he was screaming in order to get someone's attention in the hopes that they might come over and stop me from whatever devious plan I had concocted. His attempts did have somewhat of an effect because as I was pulling away with the port-o-john dragging behind the truck, I saw Tack, Sanchez, and Shaky Jake standing together quietly watching me, so I waved to them.

Because the little building sat on two wooden 4X4s as skids, I was confident that I could drag it for some distance without causing any harm, but I was careful not to go too fast so as not to bust the straps in case the skids caught on something in the road.

I know that I could have stopped at zip tying the door handles and that would have contained him for a little while until someone came along and let him out. And that would have been good for a little laugh, but I needed to go farther with this one because, well, I'm just twisted that way, I guess. I felt the need to make this one a bit more memorable because that's what friends do; they go the extra mile for each other.

So there I was, going the extra mile by driving down the road in the middle of the night with a port-a-potty strapped to the back of the truck on the way to Century Boulevard, which runs straight into the LAX terminal. This road is fairly busy at all hours of the day and there's a decent selection of fast food restaurants as well and that was exactly what I was looking for. I needed one where the drive-thru lane was situated in a way where I could access it the way I needed to. The risk in all of this obviously was being noticed and then subsequently pulled over by a cop, for which I would have no explanation for my actions. It was a chance I was willing to take because I was sure that I could make this happen quickly. As I turned onto Century, I could hear Strap yelling at people in their cars through the little window vents in his impromptu chariot. I, on the other hand, acted as casually as possible, driving along with the windows down, one arm draped out of the window, casually smoking a cigarette, seemingly oblivious to the screaming poophouse following close behind.

Spying what I was looking for, I flicked the cigarette and wheeled into the parking lot of a hotel that shared it with the drive-thru lane of a fast food establishment. Wasting no time, I whipped the truck around, threw it in reverse, and backed the truck right up against the wall of the restaurant, right between the two drive-thru windows, completely blocking the drive-thru lane and wedging Strap's little poophouse between his truck and the building. Then I rolled up the windows, locked the doors, stuck the keys in my pocket, and walked away.

Chapter 30: Anna

The east coast has a distinct smell from the west; not better or worse, just distinct. And the humidity is always there to remind me that I'm home. Home in the sense that Anna is here and so therefore I call it home. She lived in a quiet little suburb of Savannah where giant oaks hung over both sides of the roads in such a way that they created tunnels of shade as you drove through them. It's funny how you don't notice the moss hanging from the trees as much when you live here, but when you've been away, then you really notice it. California doesn't have moss in the trees. I'm guessing it's because they haven't figured out how to tax it or the vegetarians haven't figured out how to eat it yet.

Her house was in an older but well maintained neighborhood with huge shade trees and even a few brick roads here and there still. Her house had a covered front porch that wrapped around three sides with a porch swing and rose bushes surrounding it. The cab dropped me off in front and I stood there on the sidewalk for a minute, backpack over one shoulder, surveying the neighborhood. This place hadn't changed in a hundred years and probably still wouldn't for another hundred. She had no idea that I was coming and I didn't even know whether she was working at the hospital today or not. Even though she could retire, she still worked part time in the baby section of the hospital, of course. She couldn't ever stand to be away from them. My question was answered when I finally turned back toward the house and saw her standing on the front porch with her arms crossed.

"How long are you planning to stand out there?" she asked with a smile on her face.

"Until someone starts tossing change in my hat, I guess," I said as I walked toward the house.

"The only thing vagrants like you will get around here is a chunk of rock salt in their butt!" she said as she came up and hugged me when I reached the top of the steps.

"Hi, Mom," I said as I hugged her back. She had a little more grey in her hair and the crow's feet wrinkles by her eyes were a little deeper, but other than that, she still looked the same.

"Where've you been? I've been worried about you," she said as she pushed me through the door.

"You don't want to know," I replied.

"I'm sure I don't, but you're going to tell me anyway," she said. "And how's Harry? Are you still keeping him out of trouble?" She won't call him Strap because of what the nickname refers to.

"I thought he was supposed to keep me out of trouble," I said.

"He is," she said replied flatly. "Are you two still living in that God awful parking lot in L.A?"

"You've never seen it. How do you know it's God awful?" I asked. She started heating water to brew some iced tea for us to drink.

"Because it's a parking lot, William," she said. "You're not going to find a nice girl to settle down with while you're living in that thing."

"I don't know, I'm doing all right. Besides, I like it there," I said, shrugging my shoulders. She stopped what she was doing for a second and turned and stepped over to me.

"What's her name?" she asked, looking up at me.

"How do you do that?" I asked in amazement.

"I'm the one that tickled your feet when you were born and I know every nuance of your facial expressions, dear boy," she said, smiling as she turned back to making tea.

"Janelle," I replied.

"That's a pretty name. I hope she's not like the one that kept a crow nailed to the front door," she quipped. I had forgotten about that one, although Anna wasn't about to let me forget about her anytime soon. She liked to rib me about some of my previous relationship disasters.

"Ah no, I've moved up to dating old sea hags who like to pin albatrosses to their doors with an arrow," I said, smiling to myself. That chick was a long time ago and a wild one for sure. She was into Mother Earth and all natural healing and sort of a wannabe witch, I think. I accidentally used a bunch of her hocus pocus crap to season a pot of chili that I was making once and she about popped a spring when I told her…after she ate a bowl, of course. In my own defense, ground eye of newt looks a lot like chili powder under poor lighting conditions.

"How long have you been seeing her?" she asked when she handed me a glass and I followed her back out onto the front porch and we sat on the swing.

"I met her several weeks ago, but I've really only seen her a few days. I got busy with work for a while," I admitted. She leveled her gaze at me and smiled as she took a sip. She knows about how many of my relationships have ended in the past because she pulls information out of me like a seasoned detective. She keeps tabs on my relationship status to make sure that my mental wellbeing is in check, I guess.

"Don't be so gun-shy, William. You can't go into each relationship worrying about how the last one ended," she said softly.

"I know, but that's really not the case this time. Well, it is a little, I guess, but I really did get tied up with work. I was down in Central America for several weeks," I said next.

"Does she know where you live?" she asked knowingly with a look to go with it.

"No, but I did tell her," I said a little sheepishly.

"You told her, really?" she asked.

"Yeah, she's like you; she asks me a lot of questions," I said sarcastically.

"Good, I like her already. When do I get to meet her?" she asked. I gave her a look and she waved her hand at me, telling me she was letting it go.

"Do I want to know why you were in Central America for so long?" she asked.

"Not really," I said.

"I thought you just fixed planes," she said while looking at me hard in the face.

"We do, but it's not quite that simple," I said.

"Promise me that you're not doing anything illegal."

"Umm, well. It's a little complicated and things aren't exactly black and white in the world, Mom," I said as I scratched my neck while I looked up at the ceiling. She didn't say anything to that in response. She just gave me that expectant look that told me that I would have to elaborate a little more. I'd always been vague about exactly who we worked for and exactly what we did. Telling her that we were working as aircraft mechanics never brought on any more questions because that was what we always did no matter where we were. Mentioning the part about being in Central America probably wasn't a bright idea, but it just came out. And it wouldn't do any good to try and lie my way out of it now anyway because she could always tell when I did, which was why I gave up on that when I was a kid.

"I'll tell you the story later. Let's just talk about something else for a while," I said. She knew when the grilling got to be a little much for me and relented. I call it grilling but I know that she just wants to know about what's going on in my life. I'm not big on chatting on the phone, so this is what I get in return.

We sat on the porch with sweet tea and talked until dinnertime and then we went inside again to make some food. She put me to work making us a salad while she baked some chicken and fried some okra. I had noticed a few kids' toys here and there throughout the house and asked about the grandkids. She had five grandkids; two were her son's and three were her daughter's. Both lived within an hour's drive with their own families. Both of her real kids had gone to college, got married, and had their careers going, and seemed to be doing real well. I was glad for that because having them nearby with the grandkids seemed to keep Anna fairly occupied and kept her from being lonely, which is good because I'm certainly no help.

"How's your dad?" I asked when we sat down to eat.

"He's doing well. He asks about you often; he always liked you. We can go see him tomorrow," she replied with a smile.

Her mom died a few years before but her dad was still living in the same house. I always liked the guy and he was always cool to me. He went by Bill and that's what I've always called him. Bill had been a co-owner of a local auto parts store in town and sold his share when he retired. Whenever Anna brought me to their house when I was a kid, he would always take me into the garage and show me whatever kind of project he was working on at the time. Her mom was always indifferent to me because she never approved of Anna's attempt to adopt me, I'm assuming. That's why I think he usually made a point to spend time with me when I was there to keep me away from her. Maybe he took to me a little more because I had been named after him. I'm not sure, but I know that he didn't treat me any different from anyone else and he would save things to do on his projects that he knew I would be able to help him with.

He was a great fix-it kind of guy and he was always repairing a neighbor's mower or fixing up and old pickup truck to sell. He taught me a lot about cars and would talk about classic cars or tell me stories about working on bombers when he was in WWII when we were together. Sometimes he would have an old toaster or some small appliance that wasn't working and ask me if I could figure out what was wrong with it. After a while, I figured out that he knew exactly what was wrong with it, but he wanted me to learn how to do things myself.

During one spring break when I was in high school, while most kids were vacationing in Florida at the beach or something, he and I tore down and rebuilt a blown small block 350 that he had picked up real cheap. Besides Anna, he was the next closest thing to family to me, I guess. I know that he is the one that planted the aircraft mechanic seed in my head as a kid. Maybe he saw that I didn't mind getting my hands dirty and liked to tinker with mechanical things like him.

I remember when Anna took me to their house for a Sunday dinner once, she announced to everyone that I had enlisted in the Marine Corps and was going to be an aircraft mechanic. Bill jumped up out of the chair and came over and shook my hand and kept saying, "That's great! That's really good to hear, that's really great!" Her mom just asked for someone to pass the rolls.

After dinner, we sat in the living room and we talked about her real kids: Jack and Amy. Jack is younger than I am by about seven years and Amy by about nine, if I remember. I never spent a great deal of time with them when we were kids, mainly because I was there sporadically and the fact that there was a large age difference. Anna and her husband never kept the kids separated from me at all; there just wasn't any type of real connection, I guess. Her husband was always polite to me and never once spoke a harsh word, but I always knew where I stood. I was only a guest and that was all it would ever be.

Amy and Jack have always been overly friendly to me, especially when they got a little older. I think that, for a while, they were always unsure as to who the boy was that Mommy would show up with from time to time, but I saw a difference in their behavior when they got to be around middle-school age. I'm assuming that's when Anna explained the whole story to them, which put everything into perspective.

Amy and Jack grew up never wanting for anything because their mom was a registered nurse and their dad was a corporate bigwig at some big manufacturing company, so money wasn't that tight. I got the impression that they tried to hide or downplay that fact whenever I was around, which didn't matter to me really. I didn't hold anything against them or envy what they had. I was usually happy just to be away from the boys' home and eating great food every once in a while.

Once when I was about fourteen, I got into it with a couple of kids after school and received a nice cut on the top of my ear. It just so happened to be a day when Anna was going to pick me up to do a little shopping. I tried to hide it as best I could for a bit, but she could tell something was up and freaked when she finally saw it. Instead of shopping, she took me straight to her house and hauled me into the bathroom and whipped out this big medical kit from the cabinet and started performing surgery on me right there! I'll never forget little Amy coming over to hold my hand while her mom kept telling me to quit squirming as she tried to disinfect the cut. She just stood there and held it while she watched her mom give me three stitches as I sat on the side of the tub. Anna would joke that she used that medical kit more on me than everyone else in the household combined.

She fixed up the bed in the spare bedroom for me and I crashed for the night. Her house always smells faintly of orange blossom and the bed in the guest bedroom, where I sleep when I visit, was always the most comfortable bed I've ever slept on. For that reason, I always sleep very hard and long when I stay with her.

The next day, I woke up late in the morning and took a leisurely shower to wash the sleepy fog out of my head. Anna was out back in the garden when I stepped out onto the back porch with a cup of coffee. I watched her quietly for a while without announcing my presence. She hummed to herself while she moved through the various plants, pruning and weeding. I've always considered myself to be a very fortunate person because of her. She is proof of what a huge impact a person can have on someone else's life in a simple way and because of that I am her biggest fan and I love her dearly.

"Good morning, honey. Did you sleep well?" she asked when she saw me.

"Too well. I'm beginning to think that you must put chloroform on my pillow," I said as I sipped my coffee. She stepped up to the porch and put down her gardening gloves and pruners.

"No, I just drug your food and whisper subliminal messages to you while you're sleeping," she replied.

"I see. What do you whisper to me?" I asked.

"To settle down and live normally for a change," she said playfully.

"That's Amy and Jack's department. Besides, I'm the black sheep in the bunch; I'm supposed to walk on the wild side," I replied.

"That's just because you like to be that way," she said, smiling, and gave me a hug.

We had nice breakfast and then sat in the living room with coffee to chat some more.

"I told Dad that we would be over later this afternoon and have dinner with him tonight," she said.

"Sounds good," I said, nodding my head.

"So tell me about Central America?" she asked next. I smiled to myself because I knew she wouldn't let that go for too long. I didn't blame her. I was sure she was curious as hell. I certainly would be.

I had decided while lying in bed the night before that I could give her the straight scoop on what I'd been doing for the past few years. I had always been a little worried about telling her in the past in order to protect her, but now I've realized that I'm really just a peasant in the grand scheme of things. We need to keep a low profile absolutely, but we were far from being a secret organization. I wouldn't give her any background information on Tack, Sanchez, or the boss, but I could still give her the story without too much detail.

I laid out the whole story for her as to how Strap and I got involved, how we operate, what exactly we do but assured her that we don't transport any drugs or anything for any of these organizations. She didn't like what she heard. She admonished me for helping the drug runners, even though I pointed out that they were going to do what they were going to do whether we helped them or not. She was unmoved by my logic, as I expected, and she was alarmed at how dangerous this could be. Naturally, I didn't give her any details about some of our encounters, but she was smart enough to know that.

I recounted our most recent deployment in more detail and why the boss wanted us to stage down there for a few weeks and, for the most part, I kept the story bland up until we met

Eddy and Miguel. I wanted to lay out the story and give good background on things before I told her about the girls.

When I started telling her the about the mission where we discovered them, Anna sat mesmerized at the edge of her seat. She was leaning forward with elbows on her knees and both hands clasped together over her nose and mouth. She went through several phases of emotion, ranging from anger to heartfelt sorrow as one might expect. Tears ran down her face, but she never said a word as her whole body was completely focused on my voice and my face. She doesn't like violence in any shape or form, but she had no comment when I told her of the fate of the sex traffickers. I guess she just viewed it as a necessary evil. I continued the story in detail all the way up to me sitting on the couch in front of her. I told her about Elaina and the baby, Eddy and Miguel, and described the farm in detail. She sat there in silence staring at me when I was finished and just shook her head.

"Oh my God, I can't believe what you just told me!" she said finally. She got up and retrieved a box of tissue to wipe her eyes and came over and hugged me.

"Why didn't you guys go straight to the authorities down there?" she asked. I went into detail about how things tended to operate south of the border and that in most cases, the "authorities" were part of the problem.

"I'm sorry that I chastised you for helping the drug runners," she said as she released me from the tearful hug.

"You don't need to be sorry. You have a right to disapprove," I replied.

"I believe that things happen for a reason, William, and I think you boys did some good even though you're going about it in a dangerous way," she said as she reseated herself on the couch.

"I agree, but we don't have any plans to change what we're doing right now. We'll be on the lookout for more sex traffickers, of course, and do the best we can to interrupt them when we do," I said.

We continued talking as she asked more questions about the girls and their overall wellbeing and health. We decided to put the conversation on hold as it was getting close to when we were supposed to go see her dad.

Chapter 31: Death Watch

Bill sat at his workbench in the garage with the garage door open as we pulled in the driveway. He turned slightly at the sound of the car and looked at us for a moment as if he were pondering who had come to visit. Slowly, he reached up and turned off the light and got up from the stool on which he was sitting. The guy had aged quite a bit since I last saw him and he was moving like it. When Anna and I approached him, she gave him a hug and then he turned to me without saying anything. His expression was neutral, but his eyes were smiling as he stuck out his hand.

"Good to see you, Jarhead," he said.

"Good to see you too, sir," I said, shaking his hand. He had a strong grip and leathery hands, which told me that he wasn't using them to finger the remote control of his TV much. That and the fact that he had the guts of a weed whacker spread out on his work bench told me that he was still the handyman that I remembered.

"Still wrenching on planes?" he asked next.

"Yes, sir, I am. I don't see myself going for an office job anytime soon," I replied.

"I don't blame you. Sittin' in a chair too much will make yer pecker shrink up," he said as a matter of fact.

"Dad!" Anna blurted.

"Gravity will do its job if you stay on your feet," he said, ignoring her.

"How come I didn't get this kind of useful information when I was a kid?" I asked while looking expectantly at Anna. I got an eye roll.

"I'll be in the house until you two are through talking about your penises," Anna said as she walked into the house.

"Works every time," Bill said as he went to the refrigerator that he keeps in the garage and retrieved a couple of beers. We pulled out a couple of chairs and sat in the garage just inside the door, looking out across the drive and the road.

"You been keeping out of trouble?" he asked.

"Never did before. Why should I start now?" I replied.

"Good to hear," he replied and then took a sip.

"It's nice to have someone to sit and have a beer with from time to time," he said. "Jack's a wine drinker." From the way that he said "wine," I assumed that he didn't think much of it.

"Well, you don't want me hanging around. I'll just drink it all," I said. He snorted and nodded his head.

"Probably wouldn't be a bad way to go. Just drink yourself into oblivion," he said next. The way he said it made me slowly turn my head to look at him. He was staring off into the distance as if considering the pros and cons of it.

"Oblivion wouldn't be so bad if he didn't drag his ugly sister, hangover, along," I said. He agreed by way of a snort and seemed to snap out of the thousand-yard stare.

"I have something that I've wanted to give you," he said as he got up and motioned for me to follow. He walked over to his workbench, where an old wood machinist's chest sat, and opened a top drawer. He pulled out a very old pocket watch and turned it over in his hands while looking at it.

"This has sentimental value to me but not because it was passed down to me by my father or grandfather or anything like that. It was given to me by a complete stranger who I watched die when I was young," he said.

I looked at Bill with raised eyebrows for a moment and looked back down at the watch. Inside was an inscription that said: *Time doesn't think about you.*

"Why did he give it to you?" I asked.

"I was at a local clinic with my father when I was a boy. We went to visit a friend of his who was ill because there had been a terrible flu going around that killed many people. My dad told me to wait in the hallway while he went into the room. As I sat in the chair, I could see into the room across the hall and I saw an old man lying there. He motioned for me to come, but I was too scared at first. He kept beckoning me with his fingers and so I slowly stepped into the room. I sat in the chair next to his bed and he asked me what my name was. He told me that he didn't have any family, but he wanted to give his watch to someone. He said, 'My time is through; it's your turn now,'" he explained.

"Why is it sentimental to you?" I asked while I looked at the watch closely. It was very dull silver with some engraving on the outside that had been worn shallow over the years.

"Because of what he said and what the inscription inside says. Time doesn't think about you, to me means that it will keep passing no matter how you choose to spend it. So spend your time wisely because it's not coming back. That way, you have no regrets because when it's through with you, it's someone else's turn," he said while looking hard at me.

"I don't know what to say, Bill. Thank you. This is very nice," I said with a little embarrassment. I was never very good at accepting gifts from people. "If I may, why did you choose to give this to me?"

"You mean instead of Jack?" he asked as he turned to reach into the fridge for two more beers.

"Yeah, something like that." I replied as we sat back down in the chairs.

"Jack is a good guy, great dad, good head on his shoulders. Couldn't ask for a better grandson," he said.

"But?" I added.

"But he's straight as an arrow, black and white, by the numbers. Coaches little league, goes to church every Sunday, gets his hair trimmed every other week, never changes his hairstyle, shaves every day, even on vacation. Never gets drunk, says a foul word, farts in public, or looks at other women. The guy is a robot," he said.

"Damn, gotta love the guy," I said. "So what's wrong with that?"

"Nothing, nothing at all. But you're the complete opposite. Not only do you never follow any rules, you don't even stop to read them!" he replied with a chuckle. "That's how you came into this world and it's how you go through life!"

"Hang on now, I almost followed a rule once, I shaved last week, I haven't farted in at least four minutes, and I'm pretty sure we drove by a church on the way here," I said smugly and then drained my beer.

"That's why I want you to have the watch, because you don't think about time either. You tell it to go screw itself!" he said, laughing.

* * *

After dinner, we said our goodbyes and I shook hands with Bill. It occurred to me right then that this might be the last time that I see him alive. He was old and tired and I could tell that he had gotten very lonely since his wife had passed. The pocket watch, along with some of his actions and things he said, told me that he was ready and I could tell that he no longer had the spark that he once had. He thought his time was through now too, I guessed. It's going to be hard on Anna when that day comes. I will definitely need to be here when it does.

"You guys had a long talk in the garage," Anna said as we were driving back to her house. She said it as a statement, but it was really a question.

"Yeah, he gave me his pocket watch. He told me the story about how he got it," I replied.

"I didn't know there was a story behind it. He never told me," she said.

"That's because you're on a need-to-know basis and, apparently, you don't need to know," I said jokingly.

"Yeah? Well, you might need-to-know of another way to get home tonight, smart guy," she said.

"He never told you about the guy that gave it to him right before he died?" I asked. She looked over at me to see if I was yanking her tail.

"No, but I never asked him about it either, though, I guess," she replied. I told her the story as we were driving and we continued to talk about him for a bit. I think she knew that he was slowly checking out of life because I caught a glimpse of tears running down her face from the headlights of the oncoming cars.

The next morning, I woke up to the wonderful smell of bacon, waffles, and coffee and decided that it is not humanly possible to go back to sleep once you have awakened to such aromas. With one eye open, I trudged out into the kitchen behind my nose like a there was a fishhook in it.

"Good morning, can I get you some coffee?" Anna asked cheerfully.

"Mmph," was all that that came out as I sat down at the kitchen table where she placed a mug in front of me. Halfway through the mug, I think, is when the second eyelid fluttered open.

"What time is it?" I muttered.

"A little after six. Why?" she replied.

"Why do we need to be up so early?" I asked.

"This isn't early; this is what time I always get up. If you had a real job, you would probably get up this early as well," she replied.

"Exactly why I don't have a real job," I said sarcastically.

"I have errands to run and you're coming with me," she said as she placed a plate full of food in front of me.

"Yes, ma'am," I said as I shoved a piece of bacon in my face. As she sat down across from me at the table, she looked at me for a moment.

"What?" I asked, thinking I was in violation of some basic table manners.

"The girl that you said that was from Toledo?" she started to say.

"Katelyn," I finished for her.

"Katelyn. Do you think that she might want to go back home?" she asked.

"She wants to come back to the States, but she doesn't want to go home to her family," I replied in between chewing and slurping hot coffee. "She wanted Strap and me to adopt her and live with us, but we told her why that wouldn't work." I don't think she really meant to wear such a disturbed look on her face when she stopped eating and looked at me, but she couldn't have done a better job if she tried.

"Good Lord," she said quietly while shaking her head as she went back to her breakfast.

"Amen to that," I said.

"What about bringing her here?" she asked next.

"Can't say it didn't cross my mind," I replied.

The rest of my visit with her was relaxing and I was glad to be spending time with her. We talked more about the possibility of bringing Katelyn to see her, but I would need to talk to the guys and then Katelyn, of course, when I saw her. I fondled the old pocket watch absentmindedly in my hand as I thought about this while watching the U.S slide by thirty-five thousand feet below me on the way back to L.A.

Chapter 32: Foul Balls

Back in the parking lot, Strap, Shaky Jake, and Sanchez were lounging between the RVs with the grill going and Howlin' Wolf singing "Smokestack Lightning" on the CD player. I dropped my backpack by my door and fished a Stone Ruination out of the beer cooler and plopped down in a chair next to Strap.

"*Que paso*, righteous dudes?" I said, using my best southern California surfer dude greeting.

"Got another steak if you're hungry," Strap said as we clinked beer bottles.

"Lay it on me, bone daddy! I refuse to purchase the crap that they peddle on the airlines now," I replied.

"You have to buy the food now?" he asked.

"Yep, it's shameless too. Airlines are not the classy companies that they once were," I replied. Strap got up and threw another steak on as I told them about my visit to Savannah.

"Tack went to visit his sister somewhere. We'll all get together when he gets back," Sanchez said, meaning we'd have that meeting with the boss. Strap was being cool and relaxed and didn't say anything about his trip in the poop-house that night. This means that he'd either gotten me back already and I didn't know it yet, or he'd figured out how to get me back.

I finished the beer and decided to go change into my standard southern California uniform, which is shorts and flip-flops. I unlocked the door to my RV and was immediately smacked in the face with the most powerful, pungent odor I have ever encountered in my life! I reflexively stepped back for a moment and stood there staring inside at these little white balls all over the floor, everywhere! I looked back at Strap, who raised his beer bottle to me with one hand as he carefully maneuvered the steaks around the grill with the other.

I left the door open as I dropped the backpack back down on the ground and went over to the beer cooler again, grabbed another beer, and sat down where I was before. Sanchez and Shaky Jake were snickering as they kept looking back and forth at Strap and me. Strap came over and sat down next to me again.

"Are those moth balls?" I asked.

"Yep," he said smugly.

"There seems to be a lot of them," I said.

"I figure about fifteen hundred. Let's see, three boxes of five hundred, yep, that should be about right," he said.

"I see. Well, that should help in making sure that I find them all, I guess," I replied and took a sip of beer.

"I try to be helpful," he replied. "Speaking of being helpful, there were some very helpful police officers that helped me get out of the port-a-john that I inadvertently became stuck in last week," he said.

"Really? That's good; I was worried," I said.

"The only problem was that they cuffed me and took me to jail until they figured out whether I was telling the truth or not," he said. I started chuckling.

"I'm sure they just wanted make sure that you were safe," I suggested.

"Yeah, well, I guess they wanted to make sure that my truck was safe too because they towed it," he said next.

"Ya know, that's what I love about the police; they're here to serve AND protect," I said encouragingly. Sanchez and Jake were laughing now.

"Well, after about four hours, I finally convinced them that I had been accosted by a deranged crack-head and gave them a very good description," he said.

"And whose description did you give to them?" I asked next, thinking that I was going to have to disguise myself for a while.

"Well, let's just say that if Marty Feldman comes back to life, he should probably avoid L.A," he replied. This had all of us laughing now.

Eventually, I was able to find and dispose of all the mothballs and opened all the vents and windows in my RV. I was not sure how long it would take for that smell to go away, but I knew it would be a while, like several weeks probably. Strap had picked up my motorcycle from the boss's garage while I was gone, so I decided to ride it to meet Janelle the next day. My thinking was that the ride would air out my clothes enough by the time I got to her place that she wouldn't notice. When she opened the door and gave me a hug, she immediately stepped back from me.

"For heaven's sake, you reek of mothballs!" So much for that idea.

"Really? Must be the new starch that my dry cleaner's been using," I replied. I got an eye roll.

"I'd be surprised if you even knew where a dry cleaner was located," she said.

"Me too," I said as I stepped in the house behind her. "Wanna hop on the bike and go grab some food?"

"I'm not going anywhere with you smelling like that," she replied. "We'll have to go back to your RV and get some fresh clothes for you on the way."

"Um, well. I'm not sure that's gonna work because they all smell this way, sort of," I said sheepishly while staring down at the floor with my hands in my pockets.

"I don't want to know. Okay then, your wardrobe needs a little updating anyway, so we're going shopping. And I'm not getting on the back of a motorbike, by the way. We'll take my car," she said as she grabbed her purse and marched past me on the way out the door.

"Updating? Ah, I'm kinda good with the classic look that I'm sporting these days," I defended.

"Classic? Interesting choice of words," she said, climbing into her Beemer.

"It's a work in progress, maybe?" I pleaded.

"You stink. Now get in the car before I change my mind about letting you ride on the inside," she said forcefully.

"Yes, ma'am," I relented as I climbed in beside her. Strangely, this very scene reminded me of a time when Anna came to pick me up to go to dinner and I climbed into her car with torn and filthy clothes once when I was a kid. It seems to me that maybe this should tell me something.

After a trip to a mall and a nice dinner, Janelle decided it was time for me to show her my swanky man cave on wheels; my words not hers. Because I had promised and she wasn't about to let me slide out of it.

"I'm not sure that you really want to see it now. You know, it's kinda got the whole mothball thing going on and ..." I started to say.

"We're going because you promised me and I'm driving. Now give me some directions, please," she interrupted.

"Are you always this bossy?" I asked.

"Only when you're this stubborn," she replied.

As we were driving through the parking lot between the RVs, she noticed something odd.

"Why would someone be hanging a pair of filthy underwear from a broomstick mounted to their caravan? That is utterly disgusting," she asked curiously. Not sure if I was ready to explain that just yet, I just shrugged my shoulders and played dumb.

When we pulled up beside the RVs, about a half a dozen heads swiveled toward our direction.

"Looks your lot is having a bit of a party," Janelle commented.

"That's not a party; that's normal," I said as we climbed out of her car.

"Hey there, fancy pants. Nice clothes," Strap quipped as we walked up.

"Thanks. She didn't care for the mothball cologne, oddly enough," I replied.

"Did you tell her that it was a step up from the way you normally smell?" he said back. This brought a few chuckles from everyone else.

"No, I didn't want to bombard her with too many hygiene issues at once, ya know?" I replied.

"Good idea," he said.

"Gents, this Janelle. Janelle, that's Strap, Sanchez, Dinger, Shaky Jake, Mongo Baby, and Cooter," I said as I made introductions.

"That's an interesting assortment of names. Good evening, gentlemen. Please forgive my intrusion," Janelle said politely. And then something weird happened; as soon as she spoke, they haphazardly started getting up to shake her hand to say "hi" and brought a chair around for her. I was dumbfounded. I had no idea these guys had an ounce of manners between them. Maybe it was the British accent, or the way she dressed or carried herself, or a combination of all the above. I don't know, but they were acting real polite all of a sudden.

"Thank you, gentlemen. I recognize a couple of your faces from a previous get-together where I met Del," she said. She declined a beer, but somebody rounded up a diet Coke for her. Light conversation ensued and I showed her the RV real quick, but because it still smelled of mothballs, she didn't go in for very long.

"I'd love to know who you hired to do your decorating," she kidded.

"You might be surprised to learn that I do all of my own," I replied proudly.

"Never would have guessed that," she said.

"Another one of the hazards of living like a rock star," I said sarcastically.

"I'm sure all of your fans can appreciate that," she replied. "You still haven't explained why your caravan smells of mothballs," she said as we sat back down.

"You said you didn't want to know," I replied.

"I was doing him a favor because I didn't want his clothes to get eaten by moths while he was away. You see, we do a lot of 'favors' for each other. Why, just the other day, he went out of his way to drive me to a fast food restaurant," Strap explained. This brought a round of laughter from the rest of the group.

"How very thoughtful; perhaps you should consider using some of the mothballs for yourself, considering the assortment of holes in your own clothing," she said. This brought even more laughter as Strap evaluated his t-shirt.

"Shoot, that's probably one of his best shirts!" Cooter said with his Texas drawl.

At a glance, Janelle fit in like a debutante at a heavy metal concert, but she could definitely hold her own with her wit and charm. She seemed to be right at home with the guys and had no problem dishing out plenty of sarcasm of her own.

* * *

Another day went by before Tack came back from visiting his sister and then we all gathered at the boss's beach house for another meeting. We discussed the pros and cons of staging down in Central America and the adjustments that we felt we needed to take as far as the way we operated and provided security for ourselves. Unanimously, we decided to accept Alejandro's offer, but the boss wanted to work out a compromise with him because he had prior obligations that he couldn't ignore. That wasn't entirely untrue as he maintains close relations with old contacts and to completely ignore them could prove to be bad for business. That's the side of the operation that we leave for him to handle. We gave him the entire story and details on all of the events and told him that we felt the need to spend time and help with Miguel and company down in Costa Rica, to which he agreed. Staging down there provides increased availability for rapid deployment, which increases mission frequency. This fact along with a new deal with Alejandro just makes us all more money, which is what it's all about. With that in mind, the boss wanted us to service and restock the plane to be able to fly in two days. I threw out the idea of getting Katelyn back into the States and handing her off to Anna. All agreed that it could be a good idea and we would start working out the details immediately.

Two days later, we were fueled, restocked, and ready to roll. The four of us made a big run to a local baby store and other department stores to get stuff for the baby and the rest of the girls. It was going to be like Christmas for them.

I said my goodbye to Janelle and promised to be back soon. She told me in no uncertain terms that "we" were going to work on my living conditions when I got back. What I didn't tell her was that, unless she was talking about upgrading the dishtowels or something like that, I wasn't changing jack. I'm perfectly happy living in my little travel trailer in the parking lot at the airport.

We took off down the runway at LAX and banked south for the trip back to Costa Rica with Mick Jagger singing "Gimme Shelter" over the speakers while Strap started mixing drinks as I shuffled the cards. Tack smiled as he looked back over his shoulder at the sounds of Strap and me arguing over how much money he was actually behind on in our ongoing poker game.

We circled the farm once before we lined up for a landing late in the afternoon. We could see that some construction already been started for the additional rooms to the house as we flew over. The sound of the plane brought everyone out of the house and all the girls came sprinting across the field toward the plane as we taxied to a stop, with Katelyn at the head of the pack, of course.

Chapter 33: The Cruel, Sadistic Revenge of the Maniacal Gumball Machine!

Okay, here is the gumball machine story that I promised.

Once upon a time in a place called a mall, me, Strap, and a few other guys met up at a popular sports bar that was attached to it. It was late in the football season and there were several match ups that were going to determine where many of the teams would be watching the Super Bowl from; like from the field or their couch.

During two very grueling games and an unknown amount of nachos, onion rings, and hot wings, we were forced to drink whatever the establishment had to offer. In this case, it happened to be a nice selection of beer on tap. A few shots of tequila may have contributed to the following events; the jury is still out on that. Anyway, you get the idea; this particular NFL Sunday was chuggin' along like a running back on third and ten and the day was still young!

During a small break in the games, something horrible occurred and I am now forever scarred as a result; I decided to go shopping. I hate shopping, I really do, but I had needed a pair of jeans for some time but was avoiding it because I also avoid malls. Since the next game that I wanted to watch hadn't started yet and I was already at the mall, I thought it would be a good time to dash in and get a pair real quick. The obscure look that

I got from Strap when I announced my intentions should have been a warning to me.

Walking through the mall, I noticed a series of gumball machines in the middle, especially the one that had the real big, multicolored gumballs. I always loved those things and I needed something to help with the stale beer breath anyway. I inserted a quarter, twisted the knob, and nothing came out. I twisted the knob back and forth a few times and then smacked the side of the machine to let it know that I was not to be trifled with. Still, nothing came out. That having been my only quarter combined with ignorant drunk guy mentality, I decided that shaking the piss out of the machine should convince it to give up my gumball.

The method by which I chose to molest the machine required me to squat down slightly and kind of bear hug it while I shook it real hard. After a couple of vigorous attempts, I finally gave up on the machine and decided it wasn't worth it. When I turned to walk away from it, I realized that the twist handle had inadvertently hooked itself through one of my belt loops on the front of my pants while I was shaking it!

I paused there for a moment once I realized this and attempted to act casually while trying to think of something to do. The height of the machine along with its close attachment to my crotch could easily give a passerby the impression that I was trying to engage in some sort of perverted sexual activity with the machine. Realizing this, I began to make several attempts to dislodge it by unhooking the handle from my belt loop. Because it was so tight up against me, it was difficult to see exactly what I needed to do to unhook it. As a result, I started performing an interesting assortment of funky gyrations by rising up and down and swinging and twisting my hips back and forth, all to no avail. Picture this if you will while keeping in mind that there are shoppers walking around the mall.

By this point, I was in a near panic because people had begun to take notice of my apparent intimacy with the gumball machine. I decided enough was enough and so I just needed to bust the belt loop and leave the area quickly before I drew a crowd. I tried gripping the machine real tight in front of me while pulling my hips away to bust the belt loop. Not having any luck, I repositioned my feet and pulled away again, and again without any luck. I couldn't believe how well this belt loop was sewn on! Now, out of sheer panic, I gripped both sides of the round case at crotch level in front of me while pulling and thrusting my hips back and forth and trying to break free like I was humpin' this thing like a dog in heat! This would have been a great time for me to have been carrying a pocketknife or, if you were a shopper, a video camera.

Mall security announced their arrival by coming up behind me and asking:

"Sir, can I ask what you're doing?" Obviously, the common sense Del had already left the building by this point, so I didn't have a lot of ammo left in the brain bucket that would have enabled me to talk myself out of this. I am truly my own worst enemy because the right thing to do would be to politely explain what had happened. The wrong thing to do would be to tell him where to go until I was finished with his girlfriend. Remember what type of alcohol was deadening what few little brain cells I still had at this point, so you know which path I took—the one that went straight south.

Oddly enough, mall-cop didn't appreciate me referring to the gumball machine as his girlfriend, because then he radioed his mall-cop buddies and told them that he had a drunk and disorderly situation and that this would require police assistance. During all of this, I was still trying to dislodge Gumball Sally from my pants, which prompted the mall-cop flunky to say something intelligent like:

"Sir, I'm going to have to ask you to refrain from damaging the machine." I think this was where I made cracks about his job status by questioning his educational abilities, etc.

To be fair, I'm sure the mall-cop was a nice guy and all, but I was thoroughly pissed at that point because I had been captured by a gumball machine that was obviously just getting revenge at me for abusing it in the first place. That and the fact that he wouldn't even attempt to help me by producing a pocketknife or something to cut me loose. Maybe he would have if I hadn't insulted him.

The cops came and cuffed me while I was still stuck to the machine and stood there asking me stupid questions as to what I was attempting to do, all while a crowd of shoppers had been steadily growing. When they finally cut me loose and turned me around to escort me away, I could see at the front of the crowd behind me, Strap with the biggest grin on his face along with the rest of the guys that I had left at the bar. What led them to leave the bar and go into the mall themselves, I've never asked, but what would it matter?

I hung my head in defeat not because of how embarrassed I was, but because I knew that I will never, ever be able to live this down and that there will always be somebody around that won't hesitate to remind me of that fateful day whenever an opportunity presents itself.

The End

About the Author

M.T. Baird spent four years in the Marines in the mid-eighties followed by a continuing career as an aircraft mechanic with a major U.S air carrier. Baird currently lives with his wife and faithful Boxer companion in their home in Indiana, constantly invaded by their grown and not so grown children and grandchildren.

Baird has spent the better part of his life conducting extensive research and testing of the human body's ability to chemically separate liquids. Primarily, this testing has been focused on formulas derived from the fermentation of starches such as cereal grains, the most common being malted barley. The separation process results in the extraction of water and nitrogen as well as dissolved phosphates and potassium. The purpose of these experiments is to help establish the necessity of the human element in relation to the need for recycling fluids naturally.

Quite remarkably, these experiments are conducted simultaneously with another area of advanced research. This includes significant observation and testing of constant uninterrupted gravitational pull as it relates to inanimate objects. For testing purposes, this focuses primarily on barstools and lounge chairs. Invariably these experiments also seem to identify or elicit random areas or periods where gravity will cause an undesirable effect on the person conducting the experiment, causing them to rapidly and significantly decrease their distance in relation to the floor.

62814446R00158